Created with Vellum

PRAISE FOR OVERKILL

"I finished reading in three sittings and was almost late for work one day because I couldn't tear myself away. It gave all the feels of watching Buffy for the first time, but now with characters like me!"

    - **V.S. Holmes**, Author of *Blood of Titans*

"Overkill has everything from vampire hunting to mystery, romance, twists and turns, and pristine descriptions. There are even some pop culture references sure to give the reader a chuckle or a smile."

    - **Cynthia Brubaker**, Author of *Gomada Academy*

"Buffy who? Eric and Tony are the vampire hunters you want to be reading about! Wilham has a way with words that completely immerses you in a fictional world. The characters are so relatable, diverse, and *real*, that it makes it so easy to fall into the storyline."

    - **Whitney L. Spradling**, Author of *These Dangerous Fates*

Hunters of Ironport: Book Two

FRESH HILL

Lou Wilham

Midnight Tide

PUBLISHING

This book is for all those who think it's too late to change.
It's never too late.

CHAPTER 1

INACTION BUZZED along Tony's nerves, making his skin feel too tight. It manifested in the jittering of his right leg, the heel bouncing up and down just above the floor hard enough to make the water in their glasses vibrate on the table. If he bounced it a little harder, they might spill over. The water. His nerves. All of it. Rise to a boiling point that would make him look like a complete dumbass.

Why had he even come to this fucking dinner? It wasn't like he had anything to offer to the conversation. And he certainly wasn't making Dash look good by acting like a child who couldn't sit still.

His collar was too tight, and the polished shoes Dash had picked out for him pinched his toes. Trapped in his own skin, that's what Tony was. A vice had formed around his lungs tighter than any binder he had ever worn. He couldn't breathe, and he was starting to grow dizzy.

Dash reached down beneath the tablecloth to squeeze Tony's knee. His hand was dry and cool, like he didn't have a care in the world. Like he did meetings like these every day.

Well. He was the mayor's brother, so he probably did. But that didn't make Tony any less stressed out. Because fuck, he was the *mayor's* brother. And so far out of Tony's league, he wasn't even sure how he'd gotten Dash to agree to that first date a couple months back.

Trauma bonding, probably. Shit like that happened to people who had been in life-or-death situations together. It didn't change the fact that Tony wasn't worthy of Dash's notice.

He kind of missed the easiness of spending time with Marcelino. How they'd been able to just hang out and shoot the shit—even if missing someone who'd left him to fucking die left a bitter taste in his mouth. Things weren't like that with Dash. Everything with Dash felt . . . loaded.

"You need to calm down," Dash murmured, his grip tightening on Tony's knee enough that Tony could feel his nails through his immaculately pressed slacks. They were Dash's slacks, actually. Tony didn't own slacks. He'd never had a need for them.

"It's dark out." It had been dark out for a solid hour at that point. It was early spring, the days were still short, and that meant Tony shouldn't be sitting at a table-clothed table wondering which fucking fork was the salad fork. He should be out in the cool night air, following his nose to the nearest undead thing. He had a fucking job to do.

Dash's gaze flicked over to the couple on the other side of the table. Tony hadn't caught their names, but he had caught their professions. A doctor, and a lawyer. Fucking power couples. How did that even work? They both had to work really long hours, right? When did they see each other? Second thought. Maybe *that* was how it worked. They just never saw each other, except at dinners with the mayor's brother where they put their best face forward.

"Charlie, Jake, would you please excuse us?" Dash didn't wait for their agreement. He rose and held his hand out to Tony, a silent command that Tony was helpless not to heed.

There was no ignoring Dashfield B.M. Chadwick when he looked at Tony like that, all glittering eyes and mouth turned up in a slight smile. So, Tony went willingly. Let Dash lead him away from the table toward the bathrooms at the back of the restaurant, then into a little alcove tucked away where no one could see or hear them. Tony was hemmed in, his back to the corner, goosebumps rising along his skin. He wasn't sure if he liked it or not—the feeling of Dash looming over him like a predator. On one hand, it was kind of sexy. On the other, Tony was very much unused to being prey.

"What's this all about?" Dash pressed, straightening himself up further as if he needed to emphasize the few scant inches he was taller than Tony. The feeling of being smaller didn't make Tony feel safer in this circumstance, the way it had with Marcelino. Why was Tony still comparing the two? "Is this about Eric?"

That might be why he couldn't stop thinking about Marcelino. Because Dash kept fucking bringing him up, like some jealous asshole. Which was stupid. Tony had hardly spoken to Marcelino in the months since Britt's funeral, not even via text. They'd found a way to avoid each other while out on patrol, each sticking to their own side of Ironport. A feat achieved only through Lu and Finn's interference.

"No." *At least, not entirely,* Tony didn't add. Having a fight in the middle of a fancy restaurant that required collared shirts was probably not the best thing for his relationship, or Dash's image, so Tony decided to keep that last bit to himself. "I just feel like I should be doing something."

"Doing *what*, exactly?" Dash asked. He brushed a strand of Tony's long strawberry-blond hair back behind one pierced ear, his fingers lingering, cool and shiver-inducing, along Tony's skin.

"Hunting." It came out breathier than Tony intended it to, and he realized how close they were all of the sudden. Dash leaned in, bracing his weight on one hand behind Tony's head, and Tony shifted backward, his neck craned to give Dash the best possible view of his throat. Fuck. He was hard up for it, wasn't he? He needed to get fucking laid. "I should be out on patrol."

Dash tilted his head, more birdlike than confused puppy,

and not half as cute as it should be. His blue eyes narrowed, tongue poking out to lick his lips. Definitely not cute. Sexy, maybe. Interest zinged along Tony's nerves, heading south.

"You worry too much," Dash said, his voice soft, just this side of chiding. "Let Eric take care of things for a bit. You're allowed to have a night out."

It sounded true, when he said it that way. Tony found himself relaxing back against the wall, his muscles loosening as Dash's voice washed over him like a siren's call.

"Besides, there haven't been any attacks in months. Not since Eric took out that nest." Dash hummed, his fingers lifting to trace along the length of Tony's neck, nails scraping light enough to not leave marks, but hard enough for Tony to feel the pressure of them right down to his toes. "Eric doesn't need your help."

Tony flinched, the words stinging. But . . . Dash was right. Marcelino *didn't* need him. He'd been doing fine before Tony showed up to Ironport, and since Marcelino and his team had taken out that nest, things had been quiet. Tony couldn't really blame Marcelino for not wanting to go out on patrol with him, not after what happened. He was a liability. Likely to drag Marcelino down and get someone hurt. Couple that with the fact that Tony couldn't fucking trust Marcelino to have his back, and it didn't make sense for them to work together as a team. Not when the threat levels were low and Marcelino was so clearly capable of dealing with the leeches on his own.

"Let's just go back to dinner," Tony said, trying to hide the way his eyes burned a little with unshed tears. Why was he crying? He didn't need *Eric Marcelino* or his friendship or anything else. He didn't need anyone. Least of all some stuck-up pretty boy Venator who had left him for the vampires to feast on for what felt like weeks.

Dash sighed, the air blowing too cold against Tony's neck where Dash's mouth had gotten impossibly close. When had he closed that distance? Tony's head was swimming a little with the darkness of the alcove and the smell of Dash's expensive cologne. He wondered if Dash would be okay with making out in the bathrooms for a bit. Just to take the edge off. Probably not. He never seemed up for PDA, at least not to the degree that Tony was.

"You're allowed to have time for *you*," Dash murmured against the skin of Tony's neck, brushing first cool lips, then his tongue along the spot at the hinge of Tony's jaw. He shivered. Leaned into the contact. He needed more. He'd *been* needing more for months now. But every time they got close to that, Dash pulled back. Strung him along a little more.

"I know that." He did. Sort of. Tony knew that Dash kept saying it, giving him what felt like explicit permission to take time off, to focus on himself. *Especially after the attack*, he would say, and every time he did Tony was back in that room, the dark closing in on him, reminded of how helpless he was. It made the words hit harder. But still, in the back of his mind lingered a voice that said he wasn't good for anything other than slaying. It sounded oddly like his *father*. He gave himself a mental shake, hoping to clear it the way one might an Etch A Sketch.

"Well, even if you don't seem to believe me"—Dash's lips twitched up into a smile that should have been kind but showed a little too much teeth—"I'll keep saying it until you do."

Tony grumbled but let Dash reach down, take his hand, and lift it to his mouth where he pressed a lingering kiss to the inside of Tony's wrist. A gentle nip at the tender skin made Tony's toes curl and his head go fuzzy. His body relaxed entirely, all thoughts of patrol and Eric slipping away as Dash sucked a bruise into the spot. A strangled sound left Tony, his body all but slumping against the wall and nearly sliding down it.

"There, that's better, isn't it?" Dash's voice floated through Tony's brain, warm and syrupy sweet. "Good boy."

The soft words startled a moan out of Tony, and he turned to putty in Dash's hands. Dash said something else, another instruction probably, then he pulled Tony away from the wall and back into the main dining room.

"Are you high right now?" Lu asked, her green eyes narrowed on him where he leaned against the frame of her bedroom door.

He'd only meant to check on her and tell her to shut her fucking light off. It was past ten and she had school in the morning. But after a night with Dash, he felt slow and languid. So he pressed his weight into the door to watch his little sister where she was on her bed, head bent over a textbook. She looked peaceful.

"No," he answered after perhaps a moment too long of staring at her, trying to catch up with what she'd asked him.

Lu snorted.

"Why?"

Lu ducked her head back to her textbook as if by avoiding eye contact she could avoid the fight brewing between them. Fat chance. It had been brewing for weeks now. Not that Tony knew why. Maybe they were both on edge with the lack of activity? Or maybe it was the fact that he was pent up, needing to get laid? Maybe Tony's discontent and anxiety were rubbing off on Lu? There was no way to really tell.

"You always seem to come back high when you go out with *him*," she said to her textbook, not even attempting to hide how she felt about Dash. Not that he didn't already know. Lu was never the type to hide her feelings, and when she'd learned that Tony and Marcelino were officially over, she'd been nothing if not vocal about how absolutely stupid she thought Tony was about this whole thing. She'd also wanted answers he didn't have. It all played out oddly like a divorce might on TV. Which was just fucking weird. He'd only been sleeping with Marcelino for a couple of weeks, and they hadn't been anything more than that. At least not officially.

"Maybe I'm just happy." Was he though? He couldn't really tell.

"You were never like this with Eric."

"Maybe I wasn't happy with Marcelino." But that didn't feel right, and he couldn't explain why. His time with Marcelino was blurry, hazed over by the immediacy of the threat looming over them, and the trauma that came after it. Tony wasn't sure what had been real and what he was making up anymore. Maybe all of it.

"Bullshit." Lu cut him a hard look, her lips pursed. "I've never seen you—"

"Well it doesn't fucking matter now, does it, Lu? It's over."

"Yeah but—"

"Go the fuck to bed. It's late." He turned on his heel and headed for his own room. The need to get out, to beat the shit out of something, taking hold of his muscles again. Dash said Marcelino didn't need him out on patrol. Dash told him to take a night off. And maybe Dash was right, but what Dash didn't know wasn't going to hurt him.

CHAPTER 2

THE BLOOD WAS tacky under Hunter's shoes, making his feet stick to the ground.

Gluing him in place.

No escape.

No way out.

The metallic scent of it got caught in his nose. Burned his eyes.

His vision turned blurry, watery, but *somehow*, he could still see Britt lying in the middle of the floor, floating in a pool of something so deep red in color it almost looked black. She was clear as day. Sharp, and crisp. While everything else around her blurred and muddled together like a rainy window.

But her face—pale and pained—her *face* was so fucking clear.

A scream clawed up his throat. Dug its talons into his gums.

Something dropped, ripping Hunter out of that world, out of that place, and back to where he'd been double checking the bag Eric used for hunting. His hands shook, tight around the zipper, sweaty and slick enough that he almost lost his grip. And a streak of hot tears slid down his cheek, spattering his glasses in droplets. With the back of his hand, he hastily rubbed them away and focused again on the contents of the duffle.

Stakes.

Silver garrote.

Baseball bat.

Emergency medical supplies.

It looked like Eric's pack for the night had just about everything. Why did Hunter feel like something was missing? Had he charged the earbuds Eric would need to stay in contact with home base? Damn it. He couldn't remember. Not that Eric had really needed the backup over the last couple of months. But the night he didn't have easy access to it would be the night he needed it. That was Murphy's Law.

"Hun, where are my keys?" Eric asked, coming into the study from the kitchen, a Pop Tart dangling from his fingers.

"Next to the door. Did you eat dinner?"

Eric waggled the Pop Tart through the air in answer.

"That's not dinner." Hunter sighed, his head hanging over the duffle bag he was currently digging through, long black hair falling into his eyes. "Did you at least feed the kids?"

"Of course, I fed the kids! What sort of dorm parent do you think I am?" The affronted set to Eric's mouth was particularly kissable. Hunter shook himself, forcing his gaze back to the bag. What the fuck was wrong with him? Britt wasn't even cold in the ground—in a manner of speaking—and he shouldn't be looking at other people. He should be mourning. He *was* mourning. Still aching all over when he thought of Britt. He didn't think that feeling would ever go away. It would settle in his joints and stay there until the day he died, like arthritis or rheumatism. But it was easier to ignore, to think past, when Hunter was faced with Eric and his bright smiles, and his too-big honey-brown eyes.

Goddess, he was fucked up, wasn't he? Using his best friend to forget his dead wife. Yeah. *Definitely* fucked up. He was going to be struck down for this, sent to the worst parts of the After when he died. And he'd deserve it too. He was the *absolute* fucking worst.

"Eric! Eric! Eric!" Bert's voice broke through Hunter's self-flagellation and drew his attention to where Bert stood in the door holding his tablet, his round face bright. Out of the corner of his eye, Hunter saw Eric's head jerk away from where he'd been watching Hunter to focus on Bert as well.

"What's up, buddy?" Eric turned to face Bert more, brushing the crumbs from his Pop Tart on his thighs before his hands settled on his hips, the movement stretching his sweatshirt tight across his chest.

"Are we interrupting something?" Lu frowned, her red head coming into view behind Bert, arms crossed over her chest, her tone unreadable. She'd been around more often these days, and Hunter kind of wanted to ask why. Wanted to ask if it was because Tony was dating Dash Chadwick? Or if there was something else going on? But every time he geared up to check in with her—which wasn't his job, he knew that, it was Eric's, Hunter just couldn't keep himself from seeing the kids as his own the way Eric did sometimes, and wanting to make sure they were okay—she'd quickly distract him with something else. She'd bring up some project she was working on, or excuse herself to head to the library and work on homework. It was unsettling. He half thought about calling Tony and asking, but that didn't seem a good idea.

"Nothing. Eric was just looking for his keys." Hunter zipped up the duffle bag, ignoring the heat of Lu's stare on the side of his face. She was too observant by half, had probably learned that shit from Tony. Damn Venator. Thankfully, Eric was fucking oblivious—at least where people who were attracted to him were concerned—or Hunter would probably be in real trouble.

"They're by the door, where they always are," Lu said, her green eyes narrowing further on them, flicking between Hunter and Eric like she could see the weird tension that had slowly built between them over the last few weeks. Hunter shifted—his bare toes curling in the rug beneath him, catching on the thick fibers to keep himself grounded—and prayed nothing showed on his face. Lu would say something if it did. She was like that.

"Right. Silly me." Eric laughed, the sound too high, a little forced, but when Hunter looked to try to figure out what the fuck that was about, Eric had turned his back entirely on Hunter. "So what was it you guys needed?"

"Lu and I were just going over the latest vampire migratory data, and what we've been able to get off the Ghost Tracer." Bert bounced on his toes, his short dark curls bouncing with him. He looked for all the world like a puppy who wanted a treat for a job well done. It was kind of adorable. "We know the negative energy readings won't necessarily correlate to vamp activity, but we were thinking maybe you should . . ."

Bert's voice faded to the background of Hunter's awareness as he went back to digging through the pockets along the sides of the bag, pulling out the earbuds and checking the charge.

Not that they really needed the kids to go over the Ghost Tracer data—Hunter had already spent a couple of hours doing it himself. He had planned out Eric's patrol route for the evening down to the minute, because he was neurotic that way, and if he couldn't go with Eric to protect him, this was the least he *could* do. It helped him to feel slightly less powerless. Only slightly. Maybe if he joined a coven, he'd have enough power to really act as an asset to Eric and his team of baby Venator . . .

But he couldn't join the coven in Ironport; he refused to be beholden to fucking Connor. That left him very few options. Maybe he should look into the covens in Moondale again? He hadn't been desperate enough for all that when he'd come of age a decade ago. He thought he could do it all on his own, arrogant little sod that he'd been. But the power imbalance between him and Eric was becoming more obvious every night Hunter helped Eric pack up his gear and sent him off with not more than a prayer to the Goddess that he'd make it back to campus in one piece.

He still had nightmares about the night a vampire had gotten onto campus and stabbed Eric in the stomach. About holding Britt while she slipped away in his arms. About a vampire grabbing him through dry wall and ripping him into a floor littered in bodies and covered in blood.

Yeah, he'd definitely have to do some digging.

And maybe see about going to therapy too, fuck.

"Great, this lines up perfectly with the route Hunter picked for me," Eric was saying when Hunter tuned back in to the conversation. A note of pride colored his tone, but Hunter wasn't sure if that was for the kids or for his research. Probably for the kids. Why would Eric be proud of *him*? Wishful thinking, that's what that was. Being starved for affection.

Hunter needed to get the fuck out of this house before he did something intolerably stupid. But where would he go? Back to the apartment he'd shared with Britt? No. That didn't . . . No. He didn't want to do that. The halls rang too loudly with memories. He hadn't been back except to pick up his things since the night *it* happened. Since the night he lost her. Eric had suggested he stay, and fuck him, Hunter had stayed. It was easier to distance himself from that place. And besides, it wasn't like he was sharing a place with *just* Eric. There were the kids too.

"Hun." Eric had leaned into his space a little more, bent over so he could force Hunter to meet his eyes where he was staring listlessly at the duffle bag under his hands. "You good?"

Not really.

I don't want you to go out tonight.

I've got this horrible feeling that you won't come back.

The nightmares were worse last night. Blood coating my hands. People dying. You *dying. What will I do if I lose you too?*

"All good," Hunter lied. "I'm just gonna pop this in your trunk."

Eric tilted his head, his lips lifting upward in a little smile. "I could make a dirty joke about that."

"Probably better if you don't." The duffle scraped across the table as Hunter lifted it by the strap onto his shoulder. It was heavier than he'd been expecting, and he tilted slightly under the weight. Which was, unfortunately, not enough to completely distract him from the way Eric's face fell at his comment. He turned, putting distance between himself and the disappointment that settled in the air between them. "You should eat something before you go out."

Eric wrinkled his nose. "I don't like doing a heavy meal before patrol. Makes me feel weighed down."

"You don't like eating a heavy meal right before bed either. But if you don't eat a real dinner, you'll wind up with a migraine tomorrow, and then you'll be fucking unbearable." Hunter would know, he'd been the one to treat Eric's most recent bout of migraines. Which seemed more frequent without Britt there to remind Eric to take his fucking meds and fill his prescriptions when they ran out. Goddess, he missed her. "Eat something."

"I'm not *that* bad." Eric huffed, following Hunter through the house and out into the cool spring air. He didn't even flinch at the section of concrete Hunter and Ava hadn't been able to get clean yet, Eric's blood still staining the sidewalk where the vampire had stabbed him.

Hunter wasn't so strong, his stride going purposefully long to step over the spot, like he could get blood on the sneakers he'd slipped on at the door. He couldn't. It was entirely dry. Had been dry for *weeks*. But it was still there, and the memory of that night would probably stay fresh in

Hunter's mind at least until it was gone. The dreams weren't helping.

"I'm not," Eric insisted when Hunter didn't respond.

Hunter snorted. "You definitely are. You get all whiny, and needy."

The trunk to Eric's beamer popped open on its own, and Hunter brushed past the mostly repaired back passenger-side panel. The bend from where Eric had been slammed against it was popped out, but the paint job to protect it from rust didn't match with the rest of the forest green. It was two shades too light. Hunter had already drawn attention to it once, and it'd bitten him in the ass.

"You like it," Eric teased, leaning his hip against the passenger-side rear quarter panel, his eyes sparkling in the fading spring light.

Swallowing around a dry throat, Hunter hid his face behind the trunk lid, hoping to hell Eric didn't see how flushed it was becoming. He *did* like it when Eric was like that. He liked taking care of people. He liked taking care of *Eric* in particular. "I have better shit to do than babying a grown man."

Eric hummed softly but didn't argue. Definitely better if he didn't. There was a certain amount of flirting that happened when they argued, and Hunter just . . . he just wasn't ready for that. Or maybe he was *too* ready for it. What the fuck was wrong with him?

"I think I'm gonna go to Spin a Yarn. Do you need anything?" Maybe Ava could talk some sense into him. Or at least listen to him bitch about how Eric strutted around in those ridiculously soft pajama pants that made Hunter want to rub his face on them. He slammed the trunk and stepped back, reaching up to tug at the ends of his hair.

"Do you need a ride?"

Yeah, because being trapped in a car with you right now is a great idea.

"No. I'm okay."

"I'm gonna need you to stop being so fucking gone on Eric for about two-and-a-half seconds so I can count these stitches," Ava said, her russet-brown fingers tight around the sleeve she was adding a scalloped border to. It was for a cute little top, perfect for the incoming summer season. Cropped, with long flowing sleeves that almost looked gauzy thanks to the loose stitch she'd chosen, and in a pale yellow that would complement her complexion nicely.

"Rude." Hunter sniffed. He gave the yarn she was using a threatening tug, and Ava glared at him. "But okay."

He was quiet for about ten seconds—she'd said two-and-a-half and he'd lasted that long, hadn't he?—before he started in on it again. "It's just, you know, I've never really been attracted to anyone else."

Ava huffed, dropping her hands—and the crocheted sleeve with them—to her lap. "Do we really have to do this now?"

"Yes." He refused to look away from the hard look she cast his way, even when she rolled her eyes at him. "I'm in crisis mode here, Ava. Halp."

With a groan, Ava leaned forward to stuff her project into the basket at her feet so she could give him her full attention. She really was the best friend either Hunter or Eric could ask for. And Hunter was grateful she was as good at keeping secrets as she was at giving advice. "Is all this angst because you feel guilty about pursuing him after Britt passed?"

"Obviously. It's only been a few months."

"You're right, that's too soon." Ava nodded. "But Britt told you to move on. And she knew, didn't she? That you held a torch for Eric?"

"I wouldn't call it a torch," Hunter protested.

A look of raised brows and wide eyes from Ava made Hunter sink down further into his chair. Guilt crept in, prickling along his spine. He knew that wasn't Ava's goal, but . . .

"Of course, she knew." Because Britt was good like that. She'd known since the very beginning, and she'd never once been jealous over it, or angry. It helped, of course, that she also knew she wasn't second to Eric. She wasn't someone Hunter had ended up with just because he couldn't get Eric. If he had wanted to, he was sure he could have made the thing with Eric work, at least at the time. But he knew Eric wasn't ready for something serious then, and he'd taken one look at Britt, and everything had just . . . *clicked*. Hunter had fallen hard and fast for her.

"Are you looking for my permission to date your best friend—"

"*Our* best friend."

"I'm not claiming him today, he pissed me off earlier. Or are you asking me what the proper mourning period is for your wife? Because three months isn't really long enough."

"No. I know that. And this could get—"

"Messy. I'm aware." Ava rubbed at the bridge of her nose for a moment, then sighed. "I don't know the right answer here, Hunter, honestly. I wish I could give you a clear-cut timeline for when it's okay to move on like that, but I can't. Everyone grieves in their own way, and maybe your own way is to find solace in someone else."

Hunter shifted, his fingers picking at the ends of his hair. "That is so . . ."

"Not helpful." She kicked his ankle lightly until he looked up at her, meeting her blue eyes with his own. "I'm sorry."

"I wish people would stop saying that to me."

"Not about Britt, about not having a good answer for you.

Despite what you and Eric seem to think, I'm not an *all-knowing lesbian*." She said the last three words in a tone of superiority, her wrist flapping around like some kind of old-timey lord.

"You're not?" But he was smiling a little now, the mood lifted by her theatrics. "I could have sworn . . ."

She kicked him again, her sneaker tugging at the hair on his legs even through his leggings, and he hissed. "Stop whining." Rolling her eyes, Ava grabbed her project again, pulling it into her lap. "All I can tell you is that if it doesn't feel right yet, don't do it. And make sure you're doing it because you want to be with Eric, not because you need a distraction from the pain of losing Britt."

"But Aaaava, when will I know if it *feels* right?"

Ava snorted. "How the fuck am I supposed to know? I assume you'll just feel it!"

"Uuuugh. Fiiiine." Hunter groaned, his head falling back against the chair. After a minute of quiet wallowing, he lifted his head to look at her again, a smile tugging at the corner of his lips. "So tell me about this mystery date you're going on."

"Absolutely not." Ava threw a skein of yarn at him, and the heavy mood was gone.

"Fine then, show me again how to do the single crochet. I want to make a scarf."

Ava released a long, exaggerated groan, and scooted her chair closer. "Pay attention this time. I'm not showing you again."

CHAPTER 3

THE QUIET SHOULD HAVE BEEN refreshing. Eric Marcelino had spent his entire adult life—and most of his formative years—on the knife's edge, going out every night to put his life on the line with no thanks, and certainly no recognition. He couldn't have thanks or recognition when a good ninety-five percent of the population didn't even know that vampires existed. Fucking normies.

One would think that a couple months with low vamp activity, a few weeks where he didn't come home bleeding every night, would be a nice reprieve. A staycation, as it were.

One would be wrong.

Without the constant uptick in adrenaline, without the fighting every day, all Eric felt was . . . useless.

What purpose did an active Venator serve if not to protect their people from vampires? What good had all those years of training, and almost dying nightly, been if the vampires just went away one day? What was he *for* if not to fight tooth and nail to keep a tide that just kept coming at bay? What purpose did he serve?

Even his teaching status didn't amount to much of anything if vampires stopped showing up to Ironport in droves as they had been all his life. If there stopped being a need for Venator in Ironport, then there was no need for someone to train the next generation either. What—what would he *do* if all of that went away?

He didn't have a degree. He wasn't *good* at anything outside of slaying vampires. And there was no retirement plan for Venator. Just the assumption that they'd die before they hit thirty. Which he hadn't. By some miracle, he hadn't. He kind of wished he had now. It would have been easier if he had. Then this all would have fallen to someone else who would have been more prepared to move on from it. Someone who wouldn't be *stuck*, like he was.

Bert, maybe. He would have been a solid choice. Without vampires to combat, Bert could have melded into the research department of Moondale University. Turn that giant brain of his into something useful to society.

Nik would have been another solid choice. Athletic, and caring. He could have gone on to be a coach or something. Or maybe work in physical therapy. He was certainly smart enough for that.

Kate could have left vampires behind and joined her sister on the force. Or maybe not. Maybe she'd have chosen something else for herself without the threat of vampires looming over her all the time.

Chase had his art.

Lu was whip smart, she'd bounce back without vampires to fight, and Tony wouldn't let her fall on her ass.

Finn might be trickier. But she was still so young. Young enough that turning on a dime and finding a new life wouldn't be that difficult for her. They all were. That was the beauty of not having hit proper adulthood yet: there was still time to *change*.

Eric didn't have time to change. He'd made his choices. He was what he was now. He couldn't go back to school. He couldn't choose a different path. Slaying vampires was his life; without it, he'd have nothing.

Add all that unrest to the fact that there was something about this lull that just didn't feel right. It was too easy. Too sudden. They had gone from multiple attacks a week to nothing. Maybe if it had only been the local vamps that had gone away—which would have been weird enough because he hadn't known about them until a few months back then they just up and disappeared again?—he wouldn't have thought too much about it. But it wasn't only the local vamps, it was the transient ones too. Vamp activity had never been so low, not in over a century.

Hunter thought this was cause for celebration.

Eric thought it was cause for panic. He had a gut feeling that this whole thing was the calm before the storm, or the eye, or whatever. That it was a precursor to something worse, more deadly.

No one seemed to believe him.

And yeah, sure, maybe it was partly that he was terrified of change, of becoming obsolete, but that wasn't the *only* reason his skin prickled with anxiety. There were other reasons. So many. And Eric trusted his instincts, first and foremost.

Which is how he wound up outside the hospital instead of following the patrol route Hunter and the kids had set for him. It was a good route, he'd give them that—logical, especially given the data they used to create it. But there was one thing that a computer could never account for: instincts. And Eric was curious. He needed to see if he was right about something.

"Come on, fuckers, you can't go without blood bags," he murmured to himself where he leaned against the building beneath an awning and a light that had long gone without a bulb replacement. It's where he typically hung out when he staked out the hospital. He'd have thought they would replace the light, especially since he hadn't been by in a few weeks, but no, the corner stayed dark as pitch. It probably had more to do with the cigarette butts littering the area than someone being lazy, but who was he to judge?

Besides, it provided him the perfect sight line to the back door where they unloaded the blood supply into the hospital. So he wasn't going to complain.

The truck backed up to the loading bay, diesel fuel hanging in heavy clouds in the still-cool air of early spring. And Eric took a step closer, his eyes narrowed to peer through the dark. There wasn't any movement apart from the hospital staff doing their thing. And his hair didn't rise, his skin didn't break out in goosebumps. No vamps in the vicinity.

Well, none that were setting off his Venator radar, anyway. But he hadn't been able to smell the local vamps before. Who was to say they didn't have some kind of cloaking spell that would hide them from his other Venator senses as well? They had to be working with a witch, that was the only explanation. Connor maybe? Or someone from Moondale?

Eric shook himself and focused back on the task at hand. It wouldn't help anyone to get distracted like this. Then he might never get his answers as to what the fuck was *really* going on in Ironport. But a moment later, the truck drove away from the loading bay, and the door was pulled shut with a decisive whoosh of air.

"Nothing." So either the vamps were really gone, or they were getting their blood somewhere else.

"Don't make something from nothing," Kalla had said a couple weeks back when he expressed this worry to her. And he hated to admit it—because admitting that one's ex and the town sheriff was right always felt kind of like losing—but maybe she *was* right. Maybe this was all over. Maybe he was—

Something caught his eye, a figure moving in the dark, their shadow just a touch darker than the surrounding night. He might have missed it if he wasn't looking for it. And even if he was, he couldn't be sure he'd seen what he thought he'd seen. It would be easy for his mind to make up something that wasn't there with how stressed he was.

He followed the writhing shadow anyway, because fuck it.

It changed speeds once it was away from the pavement of the hospital parking lot, taking off in a run. Almost like it knew he was following it. Eric sprinted after it.

Water soaked into the hem of his jeans as they ran through the wet grass that surrounded the hospital. It was just beginning to turn green after a short winter. His tennis shoes squelched in the mud, but he didn't slow down.

Once they reached the streets of Ironport, it got harder for the figure to remain hidden, but they managed somehow, sticking to shadows and back alleys. Exhilaration hummed through Eric's burning muscles. It was nice to run again. To chase. It felt like it'd been so very long.

The figure turned down an alley, disappearing from view for a couple seconds, but by the time Eric reached it, he found the alley empty. Or at least, it *looked* empty.

"I know you're in there," Eric bluffed. He couldn't smell the person above the stink of day-old garbage and car fumes, but there was no exit off this alley. They had to still be down there. Unless they'd scaled the side of the building, which despite what movies liked to depict, was absolutely outside the realm of possibility even for vampires.

He reached into his pocket, clenching his fist around a stake there, letting the rough grain of the wood steady his nerves. It had been so long since he'd slayed a vampire; the need of it sat heavy in his stomach, making every muscle of his body prickle on pins and needles like they'd been asleep for the months that spanned the interim. He took a step into the dark.

It was hard to see without the lights of the street, but he managed, his eyes adjusting quickly, one of the few benefits of being a Venator. Something moved down the end of the alley, so swiftly it was hard to track. Silent, missing the trash cans and clutter. Almost like it was flying. But that was equally impossible. Vampires couldn't fly. They couldn't shape-shift. They couldn't do half the shit they were able to do in movies. Eric wasn't sure where that lore had gotten its start, but he wouldn't be surprised if vampires themselves had been behind it, using it to trick humans into not being able to identify them in real life.

He moved toward the shape, careful to keep his body blocking the exit, his fingers tight on the pendant around his neck—the image of Diana, his Cross—and lunged.

The figure lurched forward at the exact same time, arms extended, fingers curled like claws, and grabbed Eric by his clothes, his neck, his hair, anything they could get their hands on, even while they hissed away from the power of the Cross. He heard the seams of his jacket groan in protest as they tumbled to the ground, rolling in the leftover food wrappers and other debris that littered the pavement as both tried to gain purchase, get the upper hand. Eric lost his grip on the pendant around his neck.

Goddess, he was going to smell like absolute ass when he got home.

Well. At least that meant Hunter probably wouldn't fuss over him. Which would be a bonus, because honestly there were too many mixed signals going on there for Eric. He was just a poor, confused, guilt-ridden college professor. Hunter and his Diana-damned dimples should have some fucking mercy on him.

Eric got the upper hand, his knee pressed into the figure's abdomen, and he finally got a whiff of them. There was the smell of blood, of death, of *vampire*, clinging to their skin, but it was covered up by layers and layers of something floral. Not perfume, because perfume this strong would follow a person, and there had been no scent lingering behind them.

Something else. A charm. A spell. A potion. Something *magical.*

Whatever it was, it hit Eric's nostrils and burned all the way up his sinuses, going right to his head. He sneezed then winced, pain blossoming behind his eyes, making them water almost immediately. "Fuck, fuck, fuck."

He jerked back, his ass hitting the ground hard enough to jolt his spine, but it was difficult to focus on that with what felt like a fucking ice pick going in through his right eye. Goddess. It had been so long since something had triggered a headache that bad and that quickly. He was usually more careful than this, avoiding scents that might cause them, and taking his meds at least semi-regularly—smoking when he didn't. But Britt was *gone.* And his 'script hadn't been filled in at least a couple of weeks.

Scrambling away until his back hit the wall, Eric pressed the heel of his hand into his eye, trying to relieve some of the pressure. It didn't help. Nothing was going to help. *Fuck.* And he'd left his earbud back in his car. How was he going to get home like this?

The vampire had stopped moving, their eyes trained on him as he tried to curl in on himself to get away from the smell. But it seemed like it was in his fucking nose now. Every inhale jamming the ice pick further and further into his fucking brain.

They chuckled, the sound raspy and delighted as they crawled closer. "Poor little Venator. What is it? Do you have a headache?"

"Fuck you." Eric spat, kicking out to try to get them away from him, but they kept advancing, the smell growing thicker. Cloying at his throat.

Fuck. Fuck. Fuck.

"You know, I've never had Venator before. I wonder what you'll taste like." The vampire leaned in closer, their breath ghosting over his skin. "I know Chadwick said the Ironport

Venator were off limits but . . . I can't be blamed when one serves themselves up for me on a platter, can I?"

Eric grabbed the stake from his pocket, swinging it wildly as he squeezed his eyes shut to hide his suddenly sensitive retinas from what little light was coming into the alley. It wasn't helping. Nothing was helping. And then he felt the saliva dripping on his neck, soaking through his collar.

Why hadn't he brought his earbud? Why had he come out alone? He *knew* better now. He knew he could rely on his team if he needed them. Goddess, he was going to throw up if he had to take in one more deep lungful of that scent. The ground spun under him, his fingers going cold and clammy from the pain. Stars danced across his vision, which was strange because his eyes were closed.

The vampire loomed closer.

"Hey!" someone shouted from the mouth of the alley, their voice making Eric's eardrums cringe and feel like they might burst, his heart pounding so loudly he didn't hear what came next.

CHAPTER 4

SHIT. Shit. Shit.

There he was.

There he was.

There he was.

For the first time since the funeral. For the first time since the breakup. For the first time since—

Tony could have an existential crisis later. After he got the leech the fuck off Marcelino. Goddess, he was just as pretty as Tony remembered. How was that even possible? He'd thought he was making that shit up.

Another pained gasp ripped Tony from his thoughts. His feet moved before he even told them too, breaking into a steady jog, dodging overturned trash bins and old boxes. "Hey!"

The vampire paused, lifting its head to look at Tony with gleaming blood-red eyes. It licked its lips. "*Two* Venator for the price of one? How does a guy get so lucky?"

A snarl ripped through Tony, and he slammed his body into it, taking it to the ground with him. There was a part of his mind—the part not focused on grabbing the bloodsucker by its neck to keep it away from his throat—that recognized how this scene was a strange mirror of the night he and Marcelino met, but he'd have time to think of that later.

"Where's the stake?" Tony asked, reaching out blindly for

the piece of wood he'd heard bounce across the pavement. It couldn't have gotten far. Unless it had rolled under one of the dumpsters. Fuck.

Marcelino didn't answer, and a quick look over Tony's shoulder told him that he was still curled in on himself. His hands looked as if they were pressed so hard to his eyes that it was a miracle he hadn't shoved them back into his skull. There was another pained gasp, almost a whimper, or a sob, but Tony didn't have time to focus on that and what it meant. He'd have to check Marcelino over for injuries after he'd dispatched the fucker that was still snapping its teeth trying to get to his neck.

The vampire's fingers clawed at his face, digging deep scratches into his cheek and making Tony wince. He pulled a hand away from its throat to land a punch to its jaw, enough to stun it so he could reach for one of the hair pins tangled in his long curls. But—they weren't there. He hadn't put them in his hair before he'd slipped out of the house a half hour ago. Too busy trying to keep Lu and Dash from noticing where he was going to bother with anything more than a hair tie. Fuck. He'd come out here completely unprepared. That was so fucking stupid.

Teeth bit into his hand. Slicing through skin, and nerves, and muscle.

"Motherfucker!" He lurched back and tried to rip his hand away, causing the vampire's teeth to rip and tear through his skin, making the injury worse. That was going to scar. "Marcelino! I need the fucking stake!"

With Tony's grip loose, the vampire scrambled out from under him, rolling into a squat. Blood dripped from its mouth, glistening in the dark.

"What?" Marcelino groaned, but Tony could hear him moving, finally. Soft pats that were likely the sound of his hands searching the ground for the missing weapon.

"Fuck it," Tony muttered. He didn't have fucking time for

this. He reached over to rip Marcelino's pendant from his neck.

"Hey!" Marcelino protested. But Tony was already scrambling to his feet, the necklace strung between his hands like a garrote. He'd have to be careful so he didn't lose the pendant; Marcelino would fucking gut him if he lost his Cross.

"Here vampire vampire," Tony cooed, clicking his tongue. There was blood in the air, enough of it to send the vampire into a frenzy. Tony wondered if it was half-starved; that seemed the only explanation for the red of its eyes, for the way it had tried to corner a Venator in an alley.

The vampire hissed, saliva dripping from its mouth.

There was a beat, a tiny reprieve, where Tony was able to slow his breathing, focus on his heartbeat, and get himself in check enough that when the vampire lunged, he was ready for it. He side-stepped, getting his body out of the way— careful to keep himself between the vampire and Marcelino— his arms outstretched enough to loop the silver chain around the vampire's neck. He *hoped* it was silver. Honestly, it was a gamble without checking with Marcelino, but they didn't exactly have time for all that shit. And besides, he couldn't imagine Marcelino wearing something like that without it also doubling as a weapon. He was too good, had been at this too long, for that.

The moment the chain hit the vampire's skin, it started to sizzle. *Real silver then. Good.* The vampire struggled, tried to back away, but by then Tony had looped around to the side of it, pulling the chain with him, burning through the brittle skin of its neck.

It screeched, flailed, but the harder it tried to get away, the further the chain dug into its skin until its head hung half off its neck. Another sharp tug, another hard yank, and Tony had pulled the silver all the way through what was left of the vampire's throat.

Its head bounced once on the ground, hissing, then it

crumbled away into dust, leaving behind only the fangs, which he heard land softly against the ground. Tony coughed, choking on the ashes, trying to wipe his face on his sleeve.

Marcelino was still huddled on the ground, his body curled in on itself, but he was looking at Tony now. Well. More like squinting.

"My, my, my," Tony said, licking his teeth and holding the necklace out to Marcelino. Blood and viscera covered it where it had cut through skin, bone, and muscle on its way to beheading the vampire, but he was sure Marcelino had some fancy jewelry cleaner at home that would take care of that. "How the tables have turned."

"Fuck off." But the words sounded strained, like Marcelino was saying them through a throat stripped raw by screaming.

"What the fuck is wrong with you?" Tony nudged Marcelino with his foot, frowning when he curled in on himself a little more. "Let me see it."

"See what?" Marcelino scrubbed at his face, his eyes squeezed closed.

"Wherever that fucker got you."

"They didn't get me. I'm fine."

"You're not fine. You're curled up in the fucking fetal position, sitting in an overturned dumpster like a stray kitten. Let me see it." Why did he care? He shouldn't care. They were broken up. And that had been Tony's decision. He shouldn't give a flying fuck if Marcelino got hurt while on a hunt. But he did. Something inside of him reached out for Marcelino, wanting to huddle him in close and hide him way from the world, wanting to protect him. Which was absolutely batshit because one, Marcelino didn't fucking need protecting, and two, Tony sure as shit wasn't the protect-anyone-outside-of-family type.

"I said I'm *fine*," Marcelino snarled, kicking Tony lightly in the shin. "Just fuck off."

Tony glanced at the end of the alley, at the light beyond, gave some serious thought to leaving Marcelino there to bleed out, then grumbled a little. He couldn't do that. Couldn't see the legend that was Eric Marcelino snuffed out in a back alley like a common normie. So instead, he squatted down in front of Marcelino and bullied him to his feet. There was some wincing and cursing, but eventually Tony had Marcelino's weight slung over his shoulders and was half-dragging the other man to the street.

By the time they made it to Tony's car—parked a couple blocks down, in front of the dispensary where he'd told himself he was just going to go in and get some weed and instead had been distracted by the sounds of a struggle—Tony was almost carrying Marcelino. Marcelino's feet skidded across the cement, his head hanging heavily forward.

It was a balancing act to not drop him and get the passenger-side door open, but Tony managed somehow, aided by years of practice doing the same with Lu. Then he deposited Marcelino into the seat and leaned over to buckle him in as he leaned back into the headrest, his breathing shallow. Tony slammed the door on his way over to his own seat, and saw Marcelino visibly wince through the windscreen.

"Okay," he said once he was situated, keys not even in the ignition yet. He wasn't pulling away from this curb until he got some fucking answers. "Talk."

"There's nothing to talk about, just take me back to my car. It's at the hospital."

"You can go fuck yourself if you think I'm letting you drive the twenty minutes back to campus when you can't even open your eyes." Tony was an asshole, but he wasn't enough of an asshole to let Marcelino go when it looked like he'd probably drive straight into a fucking ditch. That was the last thing he needed. Imagine how pissed Lu would be if she found out Tony had let her favorite teacher die like that.

Marcelino opened his eyes just a crack, peering at Tony

through the slit in between lashes, but it looked like it pained him to do so, his brows drawn together, his mouth twisted. "They're open. See?"

Tony barked a laugh, and Marcelino winced again. "Just barely."

A groan, and Marcelino closed them again before covering them with his hand like the streetlights shining in through the windshield were killing him. "I have a migraine."

Chewing on the inside of his cheek, Tony watched Marcelino for a moment, debating how bad it was, then nodded to himself. "I'm driving you home. You and one of your Scoobies can come get your car in the morning when you've slept whatever this is off."

Marcelino didn't argue further. He let Tony put his keys in the ignition, start the car, and pull away from the curb to head toward the mountains, toward the safety of Moondale U.

They were quiet for a long while, the only sounds Marcelino's soft but shallow breathing, the rumble of the car beneath them, and Tony's grumbled curses as he tried to steer with his injured hand so he could operate the clutch, until Marcelino said, "They stunk."

"Who stunk?" Tony's eyes flicked from the road to look over at Marcelino where he was now covering his eyes with his arms, doing everything in his power to keep out the light. He'd probably be covering his ears too if Tony had turned on his music, but he hadn't. Migraines were nothing to fuck around with.

"The vampire. They had something on them to cloak their scent, and it made them smell all . . . strong, and floral." He sniffed, dropping an arm so he could scrub at his nose with his wrist. "Like grave flowers."

Tony hummed thoughtfully but didn't say anything. He didn't know what that meant. He didn't know shit about magic; he didn't have any witches in his life. Marcelino would have to figure that out on his own, call up his witches and ask them. Besides, Dash had made it clear that Tony should stay out of this as much as he could. Marcelino didn't need him. It would be better if Tony didn't insinuate himself into anything else.

Something curdled in Tony's stomach at the thought. He ignored it in favor of parking outside the dorm. "Well, there you go, pretty boy, home safe and sound."

Lowering his arms, Marcelino squinted at the house through the glass. "Yeah. Uh. Thanks."

"Do you need me to carry you over the threshold like a damsel or some shit? Or you got it?"

"I think I'm good." But he still hadn't moved. It looked like he was gearing himself up to do it, like he needed to talk himself into rolling out of the car. He leaned forward, eyes squeezing shut again like the motion made him dizzy.

"Goddess damn it, I'm gonna have to fucking carry you, aren't I?"

"No. I uh—I can do it."

"The fuck you can. Look at you, Bambi, you can't even find the door handle."

"I said I got it."

Tony grunted, opened his own door, and rolled out of the car, already halfway to retrieving Marcelino when the door to the house opened and Hunter spilled out. He was dressed in baggy sweatpants and a T-shirt that looked like it might be Marcelino's, his hair tied over his shoulder in a loose braid, glasses discarded somewhere.

"Eric?" Hunter asked. His bare feet slapped against the sidewalk, ignorant, or maybe just uncaring, of the cold. The passenger-side door had somehow been opened, like Marcelino in his irritation had finally found the energy to find the handle. "Hon, what the fuck happened?"

"He's got a migraine. Said something about the vamp smelling all floral and shit." Tony backed away from where he'd been ready to haul Marcelino from the car and carry him up the walk himself, giving Hunter room to work as he leaned against the hood of his car.

"And you didn't have your earbud with you, did you?" Hunter scolded, mostly ignoring Tony as he pulled Marcelino into his arms.

There was an easy closeness there, and Tony was forced to wonder if maybe Hunter had finally gotten what he wanted. Which he recognized as a fucked-up thought. Hunter hadn't wanted Britt to die. He hadn't wanted to lose his wife. But . . . but he got Marcelino in the exchange, didn't he? A churning jealousy gurgled in Tony's stomach that he decided it best to ignore.

"Left it in the car. Didn't think I'd need it." Marcelino leaned heavily against Hunter, not fighting him as he hustled him onto the sidewalk.

"You're a fucking idiot," Hunter chided, shaking his head until dark curls fell loose from his braid into his eyes.

"I know. I know."

They were halfway up the walk when Tony realized neither of them had even acknowledged him, and the jealous thing in his stomach gave another sickening lurch.

"You're fucking *welcome*," he mumbled.

Neither of them noticed, too caught up in their own shit.

CHAPTER 5

DRIVING to Dash's house wasn't Tony's *best* idea, and he recognized that, but just because it was a bad idea didn't mean he could stop himself. He was furious with Hunter and Marcelino for ignoring him. Hurt by the way they'd both cut him out of their lives so neatly. Even if it had been his own doing. Even if he had been the one to tell Marcelino they were over, and then go radio silent on literally everyone else for weeks. Even if none of them had really been his friends.

He gripped the steering wheel tightly, staring up at Dash's house, the rain starting up, cold and aching in his joints. He shouldn't do this. He knew that. He shouldn't go up there and seduce Dash. Revenge sex wouldn't be good for their relationship, he knew that from past experience. But again, he couldn't seem to stop himself. All rational thought was out the window at the first sign of hurt.

The engine kicked off without him even realizing he'd turned the key, then he was up the walk, ringing Dash's doorbell several times in quick succession, making himself as annoying as possible. He should walk away. He should trot his little ass right back down the sidewalk and to his car. He should go home to Lu and sleep in his own bed.

Dash wanted to take things slow. He said he didn't want to rush into sex, not after how Tony and Marcelino had gone down in flames. And Tony had said he'd respect that. Had said that he understood. Yet. . . here he was.

When Dash opened the door, Tony was standing there, his hands stuffed into his pockets, rain dripping from his curly hair into his eyes.

"Tony," Dash said, a frown curling one corner of his mouth. "What are you doing here? And why do you look like —Did you go out hunting tonight?"

Shame zinged down Tony's spine, making him curl his shoulders in around his chest, trying to hide, to make himself smaller. There was disappointment in Dash's tone, and he deserved that, every bit of it. But he didn't really know why. He was a Venator, damn it. Hunting vampires was in his very DNA. Why couldn't Dash see that? Why couldn't he accept it? But—but Tony didn't want to lose him either.

"Not really," he lied, his toe scuffing on the brick stoop as rainwater crawled down his spine, making him shiver. "I just went out to get some stuff and stumbled upon a vampire attacking Marcelino. I couldn't just . . . *not* step in." Certainty fled him, the realization that he'd let upset and anger put him in a situation he didn't want to be in hitting him like a slap. He noticed Dash hadn't moved out of the door yet. That he hadn't invited Tony in. What did that mean? "Right?"

Dash watched him for a moment, blue eyes flitting about his face, his clothes, never seeming to settle. Then after a long moment he sighed, his own posture slumping, and he stepped back away from the door as he muttered a soft, "Come in, let's get you dried up."

Tony didn't have to be told twice. He stepped in to the warm light of Dash's home, let the heat seep into his skin, and shut the door behind him while Dash went off presumably to retrieve towels. It was a nice little place. Decorated like Dash had hired someone to do it. The hardwood floors shone in the small foyer's lights. Music, soft and soothing, came from one of the rooms farther in. But Tony didn't leave the front rug, afraid to drag his grime into Dash's space. It was just so fucking *clean*. Almost unlived in.

"I should probably shower too," Tony called, hoping Dash was still in earshot. He lifted the collar of his jacket up to sniff himself and blanched. Fighting in dirty alleys among the refuse could do that to a guy.

"Yeah, probably," Dash agreed. He'd reappeared with two big fluffy towels in his hands, his footsteps oddly silent for someone who'd never been trained as a Huntsman. Tony shook the thought aside and reached for one, stripping off his jacket to start drying his hair.

"You could join me, if you wanted." Tony peeked up at Dash through his lashes, offering him a little smirk and a raised brow.

Dash huffed a laugh, shaking his head, but that wasn't a no. And Tony sure as shit wasn't going to take it as one. A soft hum left Dash, his gaze warm on Tony's skin as he bent over to untie his boots and leave them on the rug. It felt like forever that he left Tony hanging out on the ledge, made him wait for an answer. Tony wasn't sure anymore if that's just how Dash was, or if it was some weird kind of foreplay to him. It wasn't really his bag, the whole waiting, edging thing, but he could get behind it if that's what Dash was into.

Once his socks were also discarded and the towel hung around his neck, Tony took a step toward Dash, reaching for his belt loops—because he was still dressed at fucking midnight, like a weirdo—to pull him in close. Dash let himself be pulled, pressed his hips into Tony, then frowned as the wet from Tony's jeans presumably seeped into his slacks.

"Pants off too," Dash said, nipping at Tony's jaw and spinning out of his hold. "Then you can follow me."

It wasn't a yes. But fuck off if Tony was going to let the chance pass him by. He struggled out of his wet jeans, the too-tight fabric clinging to his thighs, and almost fell into the wall for his troubles, but then he was righted again and following

Dash like a fucking duckling. His hungry gaze landing on Dash's hips as they wiggled on the way up the steps.

"I don't have everything we'd need," Tony mumbled, self-consciousness creeping in around the edges. He'd done this before, hadn't he? Danced around the subject with Marcelino. But Dash knew he was trans, knew what he'd need to make it work between them.

"That's fine. I have you covered, my darling," Dash cooed softly, and Tony felt himself sink a little deeper under the waves that were Dash Chadwick's affections. Goddess, who needed to breathe when one could let the tide take them out to sea and drown them in the soft rumble of Dashfield B.M. Chadwick's voice. "You let me take care of everything."

"Yeah." Tony gasped, rubbing his thighs together slightly to relieve some of the pressure. It did next to nothing to settle the heat there. "Yeah. Okay."

"What a dick," Ava hissed into the phone, her voice harsh enough to make Eric almost cringe away from it. He wished he'd put her on speakerphone, then at least she wouldn't be right beside his ear. But he'd also kind of wanted to keep this conversation private while Hunter piddled around, gathering supplies to patch Eric up.

"Not so loud," Eric mumbled. He leaned further back into the recliner in the library. It was the only place in the whole house without any windows aside from the bathrooms, and right then any light from the outside burned his eyes. Even through the cool cloth Hunter had placed across his face, his fingers gentle and oddly reverent. It was nice, but it wasn't really helping with the throbbing pain in his neck, or the feeling of a fucking ice pick going in through his eyeball.

Nothing was likely to help that, not really. Aside from meds, and sleep. Maybe pot. But he really wasn't in the mood for the smell.

"Sorry," Ava grumbled, and it sounded like she was shifting around wherever she sat. Probably her bed. It was rather late. He was honestly surprised she'd answered at all. "But honestly, Eric, what the fuck?"

"I don't know, Ava. I don't know what the fuck." He kind of wished he did. It might make this whole thing easier if he knew what the fuck was going on in Tony's head. If he could explain that hurt look, and the gruff but gentle way Tony had handled him. It had felt like—Well, it had kind of reminded him of before. Before Tony had decided Eric didn't mean anything to him. Before Britt died. Before Eric added more scars to his patchwork of human skin. Before . . . everything.

And that was doubly confusing, making Eric's head hurt worse. Because he couldn't still like Tony. Not after the shitty way he'd dumped Eric and then gone completely no contact. He couldn't. Or rather, he shouldn't. Just like he shouldn't be feeling anything but friendliness toward Hunter. Fucking hell. Eric needed to just . . . disappear or some shit. To go away until all of this resolved itself. He didn't have the emotional maturity needed to deal with this shit.

"It's fucked up, is what it is." Ava, always the one to hit the nail right on the head, bludgeoned said nail so hard, it practically came out the other end. That metaphor didn't work. Did it? Fuck it. He didn't know. He was too bloody tired for this. This and everything else.

"Yeah. It is." Eric could still picture Tony's face when he looked back at the mumbled words that sounded vaguely like 'you're welcome.' He'd looked . . . he'd looked upset. Heart-broken, almost. Like he was on the outside looking in. But that had been his choice, hadn't it? That had been what he'd *wanted*. Eric was just doing what Tony had asked him. Moving on. Except—except not *really* moving on, though, was he? Because there he was, not dating anyone, not sleeping with anyone, living with fucking Hunter, who he knew damn well he shouldn't even be *looking* at as anything other than a friend. And yet, he was. Because Eric Marcelino was a fucking moron. Always had been.

Never count on King Ricky to make good decisions. That one always thinks with his dick. Or so people used to say. Maybe they still did. Eric didn't know, he didn't talk to people anymore.

"What're you going to do about him?" Ava asked, ripping Eric from his thoughts.

"Nothing." There was nothing he could do about Tony. He couldn't chase him out of town, even if he wanted to, which he didn't. Because Lu was still here, and Eric would never in his fucking life be able to turn his back on a baby Venator who needed him. But there was no way he and Tony could go back to being friends, not in Eric's mind anyway, because they had never been friends to begin with. They had been fuck buddies. Then it had felt like a little more. Like some-thing maybe Eric could get used to. Like something he could maybe allow himself to have. He was so fucking stupid some-times. He really should know better by now. Venator weren't built for long-term relationships; they weren't allowed to have things like that. They were meant for blood and war.

"Eric," Ava said, voice soft but a little pressing, like maybe she'd said his name a couple of times. "You still alive over there?"

"Only barely." Which felt true. He felt like he was barely clinging to life these days. "I didn't call you to bitch about Tony."

"You didn't?"

"No. I didn't." Eric peeked an eye open to watch Hunter where he was creeping back into the room, trying to be as quiet as possible lest he make Eric's migraine worse.

"Then why *did* you call me?" Ava sounded amused now,

her voice going up with a smile. He wished he could keep that amusement there all the time. He wished he didn't have to bring her back down to earth, ever. She was his best friend. His platonic soulmate. His twin separated at birth. He loved her with everything he had. And he was going to have to take that amusement from her.

"Because I wanted to ask you about the centennial. You have family over in Moondale, right?"

"One batty aunt." Ava sounded like she was rolling her eyes. "That doesn't mean I know anything about their centennial. And why are you curious anyway?"

Eric pulled the cloth from his eyes and set it across the arm of the chair where it would no doubt fuck up the leather, but it was hard to care about shit like that. He took the pain meds from Hunter, setting them on his tongue, then the glass of water to down them in one gulp. Hunter took the cloth and went to run it under cool water, leaving Eric and Ava alone once more. Eric pulled the phone away and put it on speaker, if just to give his now-burning ear a break.

"It hasn't happened yet, has it?" He really should put shit like that on his calendar. He needed to know things about Moondale and their fluctuating magics. But it had never seemed important before. Not until Janet—the mayor, and his ex-best friend, Goddess Ironport was home to too many of his ex-somethings—pointed out that maybe the influx in vampires they were seeing was due to the centennial in Moondale.

"No, not till fall. Which means—which means either Janet was full of shit, or we should be seeing more vamps than we are."

"Well, we already knew Janet was full of shit." Hunter leaned over Eric, nudging him gently back till his head rested against the recliner again, and replacing the cool cloth across his eyes. "How's that feel?"

"It's still up my fucking nose, Hun," Eric grumbled.

"I'll get you some coffee beans in a minute." Hunter tutted softly, pressing his cool fingers to Eric's cheek then his forehead, likely checking for a fever.

"Regardless," Ava continued, unfazed by what she heard on their end of the line. She knew what it was to treat one of Eric's migraines. "I'll ask my aunt, see what she can tell me about the centennial."

"Great. And I'll uh . . ." Another wave was hitting him. It had faded a bit thanks to Hunter's gentle care, but it was coming back and would likely double if the pain at the base of his skull told him anything. "I'll think of something for me to do in the morning."

"Right. Hunter"—Ava's tone went all business—"get this dumbass to bed."

"Aye aye, captain." Hunter gave a lazy salute, even though Ava couldn't see him, and retrieved the phone from where it was sitting on Eric's thigh. He hung up, not even saying goodbye, then started to manhandle Eric from the chair.

"Noooooo," Eric whined. "Just leave me here to die."

"Wish I could, hon, but captain's orders."

"Goddess, you two are the worst."

"Yup. Totally." Hunter sounded like he was smiling, but Eric refused to open his eyes to see, instead trusting Hunter to guide him through the library and up the stairs.

"I hate you both."

"If that makes you feel better, go ahead."

"Ugh, why are you so fucking agreeable right now?"

Hunter didn't respond, he just hummed softly, his voice low and a little scratchy as he dropped Eric onto his bed and began fighting him out of his soiled jeans.

"I should shower. I smell like garbage." He really did. That might have been part of why his headache was coming back. Well, that and Hunter seemed to have forgotten that he needed coffee beans to clear his fucking sinuses of the smell from the vampire. But he wasn't going to complain about that now. He was too tired.

"Do you think you can stand up long enough to do that?" Hunter sounded doubtful.

"No. Probably not." The urge to invite Hunter to help him in the shower sat heavy on Eric's tongue, but he swallowed it down, thick and scratchy, because he knew better. He really did.

"Then there's your answer." Hunter didn't wait for any more complaining, he just grabbed Eric's ankles and pulled Eric into lying correctly on the bed, then tucked the blanket up to his neck. "I'll be next door if you need anything. Just bang on the wall."

Eric grumbled, burrowing down further into his blankets, the cloth across his eyes making his pillow wet. He didn't care. It was nice to lie down. It was nice to have someone else take care of him for once. "Thanks, Hunter," he mumbled, only half awake now. "Love you."

He thought he maybe heard Hunter trip over something in his floor—probably a discarded pair of pants—but Hunter didn't say anything back. He just left the way he'd come and shut the door quietly behind him.

CHAPTER 6

ERIC WAS STILL SLEEPING off his migraine when Hunter crept down the hall, the floorboards silent under his steps, to peek into his room the following morning. He lay on his back, his chin dropped so his mouth hung open, snoring softly. Drool slid down the side of his face. But he'd never looked more peaceful, and Hunter found himself unable to move from his spot.

He leaned against the doorframe, watching Eric's chest rise and fall with each deep breath, and felt . . . Well. *He* felt at peace. Which was strange, but for as long as Hunter had known Eric—which was over a decade at this point—he'd always been running.

Running.

Running.

Running.

Running from danger.

Running toward danger.

Running into a fight that never seemed to end.

Venator didn't usually live past their midtwenties. Tony and Eric were anomalies. Eric especially. And it showed on nights like last night where everything in his body seemed to hurt, and his face was lined with anxiety. But with the watery light of early spring coming in through the window to settle on his face, Eric looked impossibly soft. It was a jarring reminder, to Hunter at least, how young Eric had been when all of this started. How he'd been just a kid—younger even than the baby Venator in his class—when he was thrust into a war he didn't seem to be able to win.

A soft grunt drew Hunter back to the moment, where Eric was grumbling in his sleep, likely at the light coming in through the curtains. Sighing, Hunter twitched a finger, and the blackout curtains drew closed the rest of the way, bathing the room in darkness. Then he stepped back from the door and shut it softly behind him. He traced a silencing charm into the wood that would hopefully muffle the sounds from the kids as they got up and started getting ready for school.

Slipping his phone from his pocket on the way down the stairs, Hunter dialed Ava.

"You didn't tell him," he said when the line opened, skipping the preamble of a hello entirely.

Ava groaned. "No. I didn't tell him. I was under the impression that *you* were going to tell him."

Hunter shuffled into the kitchen, jabbing at the coffee pot until it beeped back at him, starting the process of getting his first dose of caffeine ready. Not that it'd do much at all. Caffeine didn't work for him the way it ought to, but he still liked the taste of coffee, and decaf didn't taste the same— even if people said it did.

"Hunter," Ava said, her tone a warning. "You do plan to tell him that you're keeping an eye on the Ghost Tracer, don't you?"

Biting at his bottom lip, Hunter scratched his cheek. "Not as such."

"What does that mean?" Oh good, she'd skipped from warning to accusing, going right over annoyed. Delightful. That was definitely not a bad sign at all.

"That means I wasn't going to tell him until I had solid evidence that something was going on. He's got enough on his plate right now, Ava. We don't need to be adding to it with the weirdness that is the negative quagmire of Ironport."

Ava grunted, disapproving. "Except it's not a negative quagmire right now, is it?"

"No. It's not." He shifted away from the coffee maker, cutting it a glare when it did nothing but gurgle, and headed to the library to pull his tablet from the messenger bag he'd left there the night before.

It was better to keep himself busy when Eric was out on patrol, otherwise he'd wind up hovering over whatever baby Venator was on duty in the control room, and he'd already been told off for doing that enough times in the last couple of months. Eric and the kids didn't want him, or need him, watching over them like that. They needed him to get fucking answers on what the fuck was going on. Besides that fact, sitting still just watching a screen for that long? He'd definitely pass out, then where would he be? Not awake and waiting for Eric when he got home, ready to patch him up.

"From the readings I've got over the last week . . ." he murmured, shifting the phone so it was perched in between his shoulder and ear, freeing his hands to tap on the screen and pull up a chart. Low. Everything was so low. Which didn't make sense. Even if he didn't have historical data to compare it against, it was all so low. "The negativity in Ironport is like, super low. It'd be better if I had something to compare these readings to."

"Right. There's no telling if it's a time of year thing, or what," Ava agreed, and he was grateful for her all over again. To have a witch who understood how his mind worked and wanted to protect Eric just as much as he did was probably the only thing keeping him sane at this point. Well, that and the fact that if he wasn't sane then who would look out for Eric? No one. "And we don't exactly know how much the energy correlates to vamp activity."

"Not really. I mean yeah, when we found that nest there was a huge spike, but that was obviously a trap."

"So it could have been them sending up a flare on purpose."

"Right. Add into that all the pain Tony and Dash were in? There's no doubt that they contributed to it. And the way it went away right after?"

Ava hummed. He could hear her fingers tapping against something in the background, likely in her own kitchen as she got ready for the day. She was a notoriously early riser, had probably been up for at least an hour by the time Hunter called. "What about the fangs from last night? Local or transient?"

"I don't know yet. He was so fucked up when he got back, I didn't have time to run them under a microscope. I'll know in about an hour though, after I make it to the lab." He didn't even know if Eric had gotten the fangs from last night's vampire; he hadn't asked. Maybe Tony had them. Or maybe they'd left them in the alley to be swept up with the rest of the trash. Goddess, he hoped not. Vampire fangs in the wrong hands could be real trouble for Ironport. "But either way, there was no sign of a spike from that vampire."

"I don't like this, Hunter."

"I don't like it either," Hunter agreed, pinching at the bridge of his nose, smudging his glasses very likely. "It makes sense that vampires wouldn't turn up on the negative energy spectrum, since they're not exactly human. But I can't help but feel that we're missing something, and I don't know what."

"I'd venture to say we're missing a lot of things."

"Real fucking helpful, Ava." Noise from the kitchen caught his attention, and he tilted back to see Bert shuffling in, scrubbing at his face as he made his way to the fridge. "I've got to go, the kids are up, and someone's got to make them breakfast."

"Mm-kay. In the meantime, I'm going to do a little research on negative energy. There's not a lot in the history texts, but I think I might be able to find some forums online about it."

"Search the witch who made the Ghost Tracer. What was her name?"

"Icarus Ashthorne."

"Yeah. She made this thing, and I wouldn't be surprised if she had an online presence."

"Right, I'll get back to you." Ava hung up without another word, and Hunter stuffed his phone into his pocket before heading back to the kitchen to feed the gremlins.

The lab was quiet. Too quiet, really, after how used to working at the dorm Hunter had gotten. He didn't know when he decided to do most of his work there. It was definitely after the funeral, after he just never left. But he couldn't quite pinpoint what had caused him to make the change. Maybe there was no specific thing. Maybe it was simply a series of events, a series of small choices that slowly changed how he worked over time. Like when a person stopped wearing their retainer after their braces, and slowly their teeth went back to the way they were.

It was probably that. Probably something that had snuck up on him.

Either way, he was grateful that he was in the fucking subbasement of one of the buildings and thus could have his music on blast while he worked. It made it feel less like the walls were closing in, or like something was lurking in the corners, watching him. It still didn't dull the loneliness that had crept into his chest after losing Britt—not the way being at the dorm when it was packed to the gills with Eric and his kids seemed to dull it—but it was something, at least.

That being said, the heavy metal music screaming in Hunter's ears blocked out the sounds of the door banging open and closed behind someone as they made their way down the stairs into his *lair*. The kids had taken to calling it that at some point, mostly because it had no fucking windows and probably a bit because of the way Hunter hunched over the old-school black lab tables—like out of a high school science class—looking more creature than man.

"Dean Cochburn told me to bring you this," Ava's voice shouted over the sound of the music, and she slapped a manilla folder down in front of him, startling Hunter enough that he reared back and nearly fell off his stool. Would have, if not for Ava grabbing him by the arm and righting him. Goddess, her reflexes were fucking quick.

"When did you see Dean Cochburn?" He scooted the folder closer, not opening it in favor of eyeing his friend, who was staring back at him as if daring him to say something foolish. Jokes on her, they both knew that was just a matter of time. "Are you *dating* Dean Cochburn?"

Ava rolled her eyes, pulling out a stool and flopping down beside him. "Why do you and Eric do that? Why do you always jump right to the dating thing? Can't I just have friends and acquaintances who happen to be women?"

"You coooould," Hunter said as he leaned over to press his shoulder into hers, forcing her to take some of his weight lest he send them both to the floor, "but that's not what this is."

"Maybe it is."

"Maybe it's not."

"Hunter."

"Ava."

"Even if it were more," Ava hedged, looking away from his face to glance down at the folder, her fingers picking at a corner, which had somehow been folded back and now looked a little ragged, "I'm not ready to put words to it yet."

Hunter hummed thoughtfully. He tore his eyes away from her and forced himself to look into the microscope again. "All right."

"All right?" Ava squeaked.

"Yeah. All right." He shrugged, not looking up from the fangs on the slide. "You'll tell me when you're ready though, yeah?"

"I will." She sounded grateful, nudging back against him in careful companionship. Then she cleared her throat and opened the folder, drawing his attention back to it. "Anyway, this is what Vanessa—"

"Vanessa," Hunter repeated, bemused. When had Ava and the dean gotten on first name basis?

"—could give me on Icarus Ashthorne," Ava continued, speaking over him and ignoring the questioning raise of his eyebrow. "She was able to pull some strings with the Moondale Board of Magic and get some information. Said it was because she was looking to bring Icarus on as a guest lecturer at Moondale U. I figured we could start with this."

"Is she thinking of doing that?" Pushing his glasses further up his nose, Hunter peered down at the sheet on the top of the stack.

> Name: Icarus Ashthorne
> Gift: Medium
> Specialty: Necromancy
> Distinction: Crow Witch
> Age: 34
> Coven: Coven of the Forgotten

"So our girl likes to play with the dead, that makes sense." Hunter narrowed his gaze on some of the offenses listed under that information. A series of minor things when she was a child, from conjuring a spirit in the middle of class when someone was bullying her, to making the sheriff go bald for a little while with a potion. He flipped the page, still reading, and whistled when he got to the record of her dealing with not one but *two* soul eaters in the last few months. "Goddess, she's got some power on her, doesn't she?"

"Definitely," Ava agreed. "From what I've gathered, the board isn't too happy to have her in their borders, but there isn't much they can do about her when she's proven herself so useful."

"Neat." Hunter chuckled to himself, shaking his head as he flipped to the next page. "She's also created a digital grimoire, it looks like, and some other bits and pieces. Oh, says she's got a forum."

"Yeah. I did some digging through it this morning. She doesn't have anything really to say about vampires, unfortunately. But there's lots of good information there. Ashthorne really knows her stuff."

"I can see that." It was impressive. For a witch her age to be this powerful, to have this much to her name. And this was just the stuff written down. Just the stuff the Moondale Board of Magic was willing to share with Dean Cochburn. Just what they knew about. How much else could Icarus do that they *hadn't* learned of? "Bummer that she doesn't have anything about vampires."

Ava shrugged. "She's got plenty of theories on negative energy though, and how it affects an area. From what I gathered based on her online presence, she's made the rounds, did a lot of traveling over the last decade, has seen some shit."

"Okay, well, maybe we'll check in with her later. If we can't sort this out on our own. I don't want to bring in someone outside of the circle if we don't have to. Not yet." But Goddess, did he want to pick Icarus Ashthorne's brain. Like maybe more than he'd ever wanted to pick anyone else's. "For all we know, she's the witch the vampires have on their payroll."

"You think so?"

"Not really, but the less the vampires think we know, the better." Plus, he didn't want to have to explain a trip in to Moondale to Eric right now.

Hunter knew keeping things from Eric wasn't a good idea, necessarily, but he really didn't want to add to Eric's current worries. Confirmation that something weird was indeed going on in Ironport would kick Eric's anxiety up to an eleven, and that wouldn't get them anywhere, not yet. Not until they had some kind of plan. Which was why Eric didn't get direct access to the Ghost Tracer, and neither did the kids. They saw the data, and only the data Hunter *wanted* them to see. It was definitely a bad idea to keep shit from Eric. But Hunter had always had shit impulse control and a protective streak a mile wide.

"So the vamp from last night," Ava said, cleanly changing the subject, likely noticing how Hunter had dove into his own head and might not be coming out anytime soon.

"The vamp from last night," Hunter agreed, switching gears. "I don't know if Eric got the fangs. He was too out of it. So I'm just gonna have to check in with him, and if he didn't get them . . ." Hunter shifted, frowning to himself. "I guess I'll have to ask Tony."

"Oof," Ava huffed. "I don't envy you *that* conversation."

Hunter shrugged again, turning back to his work. "Somebody's got to do it."

Chapter 7

IT WAS quiet when Eric finally rose from the hellscape that was another migraine. Too quiet. For a house full of young adults, it should never be silent as the grave like it was. Especially not a house full of young adults that also happened to have one Hunter Delacroix in it. But when Eric closed his eyes again and listened to the space around him, there wasn't even a single solitary creak of a floorboard, nor a whisper of a book page.

"Fucking hell, what time is it?" He rolled over in search of his phone, smacking one hand in the bedding, hoping to find the little box made of circuitry and glass. No go. "Fuck."

Lifting the covers meant letting in the cool air, but there didn't seem to be much of a choice as he assumed the damn thing had somehow gotten up beneath the comforter or fallen to the floor. It wouldn't be the first time he kicked it out from under the blanket to land on the carpet below. Eric grumbled, peeking down at his toes, his legs still clad in yesterday's boxers—the ones with the little vampire bats on them that Ava had gotten him as a gag gift last Christmas. But even as he peered into the dark, he found nothing.

"Damn it." The room spun a little when Eric struggled to slide up into a seat against the headboard. Traces of the migraine from last night still lingered around the edges, making stars dance in front of his vision. *I really need to get my meds refilled. Fuck.* His calloused hands scraped irritatingly against the stubble on his jawline as Eric scrubbed at his face, then looked toward the nightstand in search of his glasses.

The objects on the surface were a blur, but he recognized them well enough even if they were mostly just shapes. A glass of water, a bottle of medication of some kind—probably pain killers, likely from Hunter because he was a fucking saint—his glasses, a mug containing pens, two mugs containing the dregs of coffee long since expired, and one over-bright coaster made by none other than Bert himself. No phone.

Fuck me.

Then the ringing started. Somewhere in his haze the night before, he must have un-silenced his phone—like a fucking psychopath. And now it was somewhere in his room, making the most Goddess-awful noise known to man. Because he'd let Hunter pick his ringtone when he was high about eight years ago, and Hunter had of course chosen something from Looney Tunes. He thought it was Porky Pig, but it had been so long since Eric had watched anything vaguely Looney Tunes-related that it was honestly kind of hard to remember.

And it just kept fucking going. Stuttering along. Telling him he had a phone call. It would have been less annoying if he'd let Hunter record one himself, like he wanted to.

Or if I'd just left my fucking phone on silent, like a normal person.

Once he was finally able to focus on the sound through his aggravation, Eric thought it might be coming from the direction of the pants he had worn the night before. The ones that either he or Hunter had stripped him out of and left in the middle of the floor.

He wondered if he just sat in bed and glared at his pants, maybe the person would hang up. Hopefully they wouldn't even leave a message, because then he'd feel obligated to call them back, and no one wanted that. There was a heartbeat during which the ringer stopped, and Eric breathed a sigh of relief thinking maybe they'd finally given up, but it started up again soon after.

"I'm coming. I'm coming. Fucking fucker," Eric grumbled, struggling out from under the comforter when his legs got tangled up in it. Finally, he made it to the floor—on his hands and knees, but he was there damn it—and scurried over to his pants. When he pulled the phone from his pocket, Hunter's bright smile stared back at him from the glare of the screen.

With a groan, Eric hit the answer button, turned the phone on speaker, and grunted a "What" out into the quiet room.

"Well good morning to you too, sunshine." Hunter chuckled from the other end of the line. Because he was now, and would always be, a morning person. Asshole. Eric wasn't exactly sure how he did it, because Hunter was also a night person. It didn't make any fucking sense. And honestly, Eric didn't want to think too hard about it; he had too much else on his plate currently. Hunter's insomnia was something best left for Hunter to deal with.

"My ringer was on," Eric said, as if that explained everything from the grumpiness in his tone, to how long it took him to get to the phone.

Hunter hummed, like he understood completely. He probably did. The whole vendetta against ringing phones seemed to be a millennial thing. "Gross," Hunter said, confirming Eric's thoughts. "Well, I was just calling to check on you. How's your head?"

"Feels marginally less like someone tried to shish kebab my brain while it was still in my skull, thanks for asking." That was no doubt thanks to Hunter's care last night. But Eric was too fucking tired and strung out to get sappy about that right now. Plus . . . mixed signals. He didn't—He couldn't think clearly enough to wade through them at that particular moment. Best to leave the mushy stuff alone for another day when he was slightly more coherent.

"Take some more pain killers. You're passed the six-hour window, you can have another dose."

"Or I could go dig through your stash and smoke out on the porch. The kids aren't here, no one would have to know." Eric knuckled the sleep from his eyes, letting out a sigh as he turned to lean his back against the bed.

"You have to teach classes this evening." Fuck Hunter and his being reasonable and responsible. That rat bastard.

"My kids wouldn't even notice."

"Bullshit they wouldn't."

"Fine. I'll take the pills." His phone hit the floor with a dull thunk, and Eric crawled the couple of paces to his night-stand to pull the bottle of pain killers down and shake two into his hand before gulping them down. "Happy?"

"Exceedingly." But Eric could imagine him rolling his eyes, even if the tone was cheerful. Which was adorable, ridiculous, and annoying all rolled into one package, like the rest of Hunter. "There was another thing I needed . . . What was it?"

"I don't know." Eric ran his fingers through his hair, snagging on tangles and scrunching up his face when he felt how greasy it was. He'd probably been sweating while he slept. Gross. The sheets and comforter would have to be washed, there was no way around it.

Eric heard Hunter snap his fingers on the other end of the line. "Oh. Right. Where did you put the fangs from last night?"

"I didn't get them." And although he knew Hunter wouldn't begrudge him that, knew that it wasn't his fault, Eric couldn't seem to help the shame that settled into the base of his spine. It dragged him into a further slump, his hips sinking lower into the carpet, his back curving painfully against the bed frame. Failure never felt good, even when he knew no one would blame him for it. "I can text Tony—"

"No. No need. It's all right." Frustration lay heavy under

the words. Like Hunter was a little upset, but not by Eric being unable to get him the teeth, probably. If Eric knew anything about him, it was the lack of information, the missed opportunity for further study, that bothered him. Which was fair. They needed all the information they could get if they were going to stop what was coming. The eye of the storm could only last so long. "Did the vamp say anything to give any hint if they were local or transient?"

"They didn't. But they did say—"

I know Chadwick said the Ironport Venator were off limits but . . .

What did that mean? Was Janet in league with the vampires? Was she on their payroll? Maybe that's how they'd gotten a witch to do magic for them. Maybe the whole Council of Creatures was in on it. Is that why the vampires were lying low now? Were they just biding their time until something bigger happened? Until Janet said the word?

Or . . . was it Janet at all? Was the vampire just spouting bullshit?

He needed to talk to someone else who was there that night. But there had been many times over the last few weeks where he'd tried to talk to Tony and gotten nothing but silence in response. Tony either didn't pick up his phone, or he left Eric on read. Neither of which got Eric the answers he needed.

Dash. Dash was the next source of information.

"Yoohooo . . . King Ricky," Hunter called, a forced laugh at the end. Like he was worried but was trying to cover it. "Did I lose you over there, big guy?"

"No. I'm still here." Sorta. Because already his mind was working on who he'd need to call to get in touch with Dash Chadwick. He'd never been friends with Dash, even when they'd gone to the same school, which hadn't been for long seeing as how Dash was three years younger than him. So he'd been a freshman when Eric was a senior.

"What's going through that pretty head of yours?" Hunter pressed.

"Nothing."

"You said the vampire said something to you. Was it about where they were from?"

"No. It wasn't about that." He wasn't sure why he was keeping this from Hunter. Hunter had the head for these things. He'd be helpful in what Eric was planning. But Eric just . . . He just didn't want to drag Hunter into this any deeper than he already had. It was bad enough Hunter was living in a house full of Venator. Bad enough he was one of Eric's best friends. Bad enough he'd lost his wife because of a mission with Eric. There was already a target painted on his back, and enough loss filling his eyes to drown all of Ironport. No sense in making matters worse. "It was just something about wanting to see what a Venator tasted like. You know how vamps are."

Hunter hummed like he didn't believe Eric, like he was hearing all the things Eric hadn't said, but he didn't press anymore for answers and their conversation continued on to other things.

"Look what the cat dragged in," Janet said, leaning back from the paperwork she had been hunched over when Eric slid through the door to her office. She looked much too pleased with herself, her lips twitching up in one of those closed-mouth smiles Eric had always hated. "What brings the illustrious Eric Marcelino to my humble workspace?"

Eric fought down the urge to snort. If there was one word to describe Janet's office, it was not humble. *Lavish* would be more like it. With mahogany furnishings and leather-bound books lining the wall of bookshelves, it smelled of leather and old paper, like an ancient library. If Janet wasn't sitting in the middle of it all, looking like some kind of queen surveying her lowliest subject, Eric might have been tempted to make himself comfortable on the Chesterfield and grab one of the old books, just to look at and sniff—because the old typeface was usually even worse with his dyslexia than the modern fonts. But she was, and he wasn't.

"I need to speak to your brother. And the easiest way to chat with Dash is to go through you." Leather creaked under him where he sat on one of the tufted chairs before her desk. He crossed one leg over the other, forcing a posture of nonchalance. Because he couldn't show his hand to Janet. Not if she might be in on this.

"You could have just asked McMahon, you know. He and Dash are practically joined at the hip these days." Janet leaned further back in her chair, raising one perfectly plucked blond brow. What a bitch.

"Tony isn't taking my calls at the moment," Eric said bitterly. It still stung. He wasn't going to pretend it didn't. Besides, if Janet thought she had the upper hand, she'd be more likely to help him set up a meeting with her brother.

"You could go to his house. You know where he lives." She stared at him now, pale-blue eyes fixed on his face like she was looking for any twitch of discomfort, any tell. Looking for a weakness, a chink in his armor that she could exploit for her own amusement. Not gain, because she didn't need to gain anything from him. She already had everything. The life he was supposed to live. The house he was supposed to live in. The car he was supposed to drive. The position he was supposed to hold. All according to his parents. Meanwhile, he had a class of six baby Venator, a crooked dorm, and a car that was probably on its last leg.

Yeah. No reason to prove your superiority, Jan, we all get it.

Eric chewed on the inside of his cheek thoughtfully. How

to convince her to help him without putting her on the defensive? How to keep her from asking too many questions? He'd have to appear to swallow his pride, he supposed.

"I don't particularly want to run into Tony there." He shifted in the chair slightly, showing his upset at the very idea, making it clear to her how uncomfortable he was. "I'm a little jealous, so sue me." He shrugged, sniffing and scrubbing at his nose.

Janet watched him a moment longer, seeming to relish in what she saw. Bitch. Then she nodded. "All right, Marcelino. But I'm doing this as a friend, you understand? Don't piss Dash off and have this come back on me."

"Of course not. I'll be the perfect gentleman."

She slid a business card to him, a phone number scribbled on the back. "What do you need to talk to my darling baby brother for anyway?"

Downplay it, Eric. Cover it up. Lie. He shrugged. "I just have a couple of questions I still need to ask about the raid. Stuff for the database, you know."

"Ah yes. We Huntsmen love our paperwork." She chuckled, and Eric felt his shoulders relax a bit.

"We do indeed." That was an understatement if there'd ever been one. Eric swore that every mission he went on came accompanied by no less than ten pages of paperwork. All of that information fed into the database to help them better understand their prey. He'd leaned on it heavily growing up. With no Venator to teach him, and none of the Huntsmen in Ironport willing to take the time, Eric had to rely on reading. On learning all he could about vampires from the Huntsmen historical accountants. And why shouldn't he use that resource? He was a member of the Huntsmen community—technically—after all. His knees cracked as he stood and stuffed the business card into his back pocket. "I'll just see myself out. Thanks for this, Jan."

CHAPTER 8

LU WAS STARING AT TONY, her gaze loaded heavy with questions and disapproval, and Tony wasn't clear as to why. Not the disapproval bit—he got that. Love bites from Dash littered his scarred chest and shoulders; there was even one just beneath his ear that had stung when he'd washed his hair this morning. Like the soap bubbles were going right into his blood stream. But it wasn't like hickeys and teeth-shaped bruises were a new thing for him. He'd always enjoyed being marked up by the guys he slept with. And it was far from the first time that Lu had seen them either. So what was with the look?

"Can I help you with something?" he asked finally, when it got to be too much, when he swore the heat of her gaze was scalding his skin. Tony swiped at the sweat trickling down his brow, the towel he left down in the basement for this exact purpose rougher than he remembered. Why was he so sensitive all the sudden? Why did everything feel like it was suddenly too much? Too bright. Too loud. Too smelly. What the fuck was wrong with him?

A soft grunt came from the corner where Lu was curled up in the old bamboo swivel lounger they'd bought at a yard sale back in Miami. When he glanced over, he found her knees curled up to her chest so she could peer at him over the top of her book, the obnoxiously green cushion sliding down from her weight. She didn't respond right away, just squinted harder like she was trying to see something better. Which was silly, because of the two of them, she had perfect vision where Tony had to wear fucking contacts.

"Spit it out, shitbird," he grumbled, draping the towel around his neck and pulling the hair tie from his hair so that he could slick the strands that had fallen loose back up into the band. "I don't got all day."

"Why do you have a vampire bite on your neck?" She rose from the chair, setting her book down into it, and paced slowly across the basement floor to get to him. Almost like she was afraid of scaring him off, or maybe afraid he'd lash out. Fucking ridiculous. There was no world in which he'd be afraid of his kid sister, or in which he'd lash out at her the way his father might have. Sure, sometimes he was an asshole to her. But that was just in his nature. He was kind of an asshole to everyone.

"This?" He tilted his head, running his fingers over the mark Dash had left behind. Callouses caught on the skin, drawing a wince. "It's just a love bite from Dash."

"He broke skin," Lu said like a question. Disbelieving. "And has fangs?"

"What? No. Of course not." Frowning, Tony ran his fingers over it again. He hadn't noticed before, but it was scabbed like Dash had in fact broken skin. Not that Tony would have minded, but why hadn't he noticed it before? Why had he thought it was just bruised? That didn't—that didn't make sense. "Shut up, Lu. What do you know?"

"I know there's a bite on your fucking neck that looks like a vampire bit you."

Maybe it wasn't from Dash at all? Maybe it was from the fight with the vamp the night before?

"Maybe one got in a little too close." He shrugged, hoping to cover his own confusion. "It happens, you know."

"You said it was from Dash." Lu wrinkled her freckled nose, disgust lining the words. "Which is it?"

"I don't know." Tony pulled his hair down again, some part of him trying to hide the mark from her scrutinizing gaze. When had she learned to be so observant? He swore that the last time he had a boyfriend, she hadn't noticed fuck all about their relationship. And she hadn't had anything to say about Marcelino either. Other than *don't fuck this up for me, Tony, I like him being my teacher*. Which was fair. His horniness shouldn't get in the way of her education. Ever.

"You don't know?" She stepped in closer, moving on her toes so she could peer at the mark through green eyes squinted so narrow, he wasn't entirely sure how she was seeing through her lashes at all. "Or you don't want to tell me."

"I don't know! Okay?" He lashed out, giving her a gentle shove out of his personal space. Not hard enough to make her stumble, but enough to make her take a step back. Give him room to breathe. "Jesus, Lu, what's with the fucking third degree? These things fucking happen, you *know* they do!"

"They don't happen to you." Lu's jaw ticked, her face going a little blotchy with anger. "They've never happened to you."

"Well apparently there's a first time for everything, Lu!"

"You don't have to yell at me!"

"You don't have to be such a nosey little bitch!"

"Fuck you!"

"Fuck you!"

She spun on her heel, stomping back over to her chair to grab the book she'd been reading, then headed for the stairs without a backward glance. "You know, Tony, sometimes you're a real asshole."

Tony tsked, rolling his eyes. "Don't you have somewhere to be?"

A huff, then she was stomping up the stairs and slamming

the door behind her. Leaving him alone with the punching bag hanging from the ceiling and the marks on his skin. He frowned to himself, fingers brushing over the one she'd been scrutinizing again. It couldn't be a vampire bite, right? There was no way. Dash's canines were kind of pointy. Some people's teeth were like that. He went to the mirror that leaned against the wall to check his form, pressing in close to try to see what she saw. But it just looked like a normal bite to him. Sure, yeah, Dash had broken the skin, but it didn't look like a *vampire* bite.

"Fucking dramatic little brat." He scoffed to himself.

No one was home when Hunter got back from the lab. All the kids in classes, and Eric out doing whatever Eric did before he had to teach and slay for the rest of the day. Maybe grocery shopping? There had been a list tacked to the fridge that morning, and it was gone now. So yeah, very likely grocery shopping.

It continued to amaze Hunter how well Eric took care of the baby Venator. How he put his whole life on hold for them, for *this*—making sure they stayed alive, and protecting all of Ironport without so much as a nod of thanks from anyone. But Hunter supposed Eric didn't really have much choice in the matter. Fate had dealt Eric Marcelino a fucked-up hand, and he was just making the best of it. At least Fate had also kind of made him unkillable. Or so it seemed anyway.

Kicking his shoes off at the door—they always made it onto the little shelf where they belonged *somehow*—Hunter slid his feet into a pair of house slippers. They were fluffy and had little witches riding brooms on them. Eric had probably found them at the Halloween store last year and thought they were funny. That was his entire sense of humor boiled down to a pair of fleece-lined slippers. Most of his personality really, because it was a gift, a just because, that he'd bought because he saw them and they made him think of Hunter.

It was endearing.

Hunter was endeared.

Who wouldn't be? Jerks, that's who.

There was no way to deny the happiness that had lit up Eric's face when he'd presented them to Hunter. No way to quell Hunter's desire to keep that smile there all the time. He couldn't, he knew he couldn't, but that didn't mean he wasn't going to fucking try. Even if the slippers were cheesy as fuck. Which they were. They had fucking glitter on them. That didn't change the facts.

And the facts were that Hunter had it bad.

He had it bad, and guilt gnawed at him. Made the food in his stomach sour. Made it hard to focus through the intrusive thoughts of *This is what Britt would want. Is this really what she would want? I know she said when she was dying that I should move on, but . . . But is this too soon? This is almost definitely too soon. And she probably only said that because she was dying. Shouldn't I be dressing in all black and hiding my face under a veil or something?*

He shook himself, blinking away the tears that burned and made his vision go blurry. His next breath shook on the inhale.

"You can't break down in the fucking foyer, Hunter. You're right by the fucking door. Get away from the fucking door. Go upstairs. Hide in your room. You can have a breakdown there." But even as he said the words, his feet remained unmoving, glued to the floor. It had been a long couple of months. Too long. They dragged oily, and slow. And for so much of them he'd been good, he'd been strong. He'd kept his head up, and not let anyone see how much his chest ached sometimes.

But sometimes . . . sometimes it got to be too much.

Sometimes, on the monthly anniversary—which was today, fuck, why had he even bothered getting out of bed?—pretending to be normal cost him dearly. Sometimes he didn't know who he was fooling, because Eric would look at him like he knew—he knew!—and Hunter would understand that he wasn't fooling *anyone*.

The wall loomed closer. Hunter didn't realize he was leaning forward, crumpling into a ball, until his forehead was pressed into the rough paint. Goddess, what the fuck was wrong with him? One minute he wanted to jump Eric's fucking bones, and the next he could hardly breathe, the air catching in his lungs.

He slid down, irritating the skin on his forehead until he was curled over the ridiculously kitschy slippers, his knees pressing hard into his chest. It shouldn't make breathing any easier, but it did somehow. What it didn't do was stop the tears.

"Goddess above and below, couldn't you just have a breakdown in the shower like a *normal* person? Who the fuck cries over slippers?" The words sounded choked, even to his own ears, even though they were garbled up by the feeling of being underwater.

A breeze kicked up, rustling the long curls hanging against his neck, then someone was beside him. A pale, freckled hand reached out for him, carefully telegraphing the movements so as not to scare him. "Hunter. Hunter, are you all right?"

He sniffed hard even though it hurt like shit, lifted the collar of his shirt to wipe his face, and turned to see the bright green eyes of one Lu McMahon trained on him with concern. "How did you get in here?"

"Finn told me where Eric stores the spare key." Lu shrugged, her gaze flicking over his face, searching for something. Maybe looking for an injury to explain the way he was crouching in front of the shoe shelf like a weirdo.

"I'm all right, Lu. Just had like a—" He flapped his hand around, not even really sure what he was trying to say. Telling her that he was going into a grief and guilt spiral probably wouldn't make her feel any better. And Hunter didn't exactly want anyone worrying about him. Least of all the baby Venator. They had enough to worry about.

She eyed him for a minute more before she nodded. "Okay."

"Okay." He nodded too and used his hands to leverage himself back to his feet, hoping it looked smoother than it felt with his head starting to spin from the lack of air. Fuck. He was a mess. He was such a mess. No one should have to live with the fucking mess that was Hunter Delacroix. "So what's up? Shouldn't you be in class?"

"Yeah, but I was kind of hoping to talk to Eric." Lu brushed strands of bright red hair back from her freckled face, her nose crinkled a little. "Is he here? I didn't see his car out front."

"No. It's just me. But maybe I can help. Come tell me what's going on."

"I could just come back," she murmured, her lower lip between her teeth.

"Nonsense." Hunter smiled at her, his dimples popping a little, but she still seemed unsure. "If it's not something I can help you with, I promise we'll go find Eric. All right?"

With a glance back at the door, she lingered a moment longer.

"I'll make you some hot chocolate."

"With marshmallows?"

"Is there any other kind?" he called over his shoulder as he headed for the kitchen, fully expecting her to follow. When he turned to grab the milk from the fridge, he was pleased to see that he was right.

Asking right away would probably have made her defensive, or nervous. So Hunter turned on some music, and they were both silent as he worked around the kitchen, gathering ingredients and heating the milk on the stove. It took a little while, but that was all right. The methodical motions of making something with his hands—almost like potion making—dragged him out of his own head while still letting him think. It was peaceful.

When the cocoa was finished, he poured some into a mug shaped like a unicorn—because kitschy was kind of Eric's brand, and he'd been the one to buy all the dishes for the dorm—slid it across to her, and said, "Now spill."

It took a moment. Lu sipped her hot chocolate carefully, staring down at the counter in front of where her mug had been sitting. But Hunter saw it the moment she decided to open up.

"It's Tony," she said softly, like she was afraid if she spoke too loudly her brother might hear her. "There's something off about him lately. Ever since the raid, really."

"Off how?" He needed to tread carefully on this. Hunter didn't want Tony thinking that he was sticking his nose in where it didn't belong. No one had any business criticizing how Tony raised his sister, and Hunter didn't want Tony thinking that's what he was doing.

"He's bitchier than normal." Her fingers tapped against the ceramic, her nails making a soft *tink, tink, tink* noise. "And when he comes back from seeing his boyfriend, he's all . . . loopy. Like he's high. But he hasn't been smoking lately, so that's not it."

"Ah, I see." Hunter leaned back against the counter, nodding slowly. He thought maybe he was beginning to understand the problem. "Are you sure this isn't—"

"Before you say it, this has nothing to do with Dashfield fucking Chadwick."

Hunter tilted his head, dark brows raised high enough he

felt his glasses move with the rest of his skin, as if to ask, *Are you sure?*

"Do I like Dashfield Chadwick? No. But I haven't liked half the assholes Tony's dated. He has a tendency to pick guys who just *look* nice, but usually they're dicks. That's his whole MO. I think it's because—" She stopped, pursing her lips, and shook her head. "It doesn't matter why. The point is, I don't usually like Tony's boyfriends. So that has nothing to do with this."

"Mm-hmm." Hunter was willing to give her the benefit of the doubt, willing to listen. Which might have been more than most adults would do for a kid her age. Seventeen. Fresh out of high school. Fuck, it was more than any adult had ever done for him.

"But he's got these bites, Hunter. They look like vamp bites. But he says they're from Dash." She wrinkled her nose, disgusted at the thought, then repeated, "But they *look* like vamp bites."

Scrubbing at his face, his rings almost catching on the eyebrow piercing over his right eye, Hunter let out a long sigh. The kind of sigh that made a person's shoulders hunch a little. It sounded like Lu was getting worked up because she didn't like Tony's new boyfriend. And maybe that's all it was. She wouldn't be the first kid her age who didn't like their guardian's significant other. Hell, Hunter had hated half the people his stepmom dated after his dad died. But that didn't mean he should brush it off. That didn't mean he shouldn't check in.

"What are you expecting Eric to do about this?" Hunter had a feeling he knew, and he was one-hundred percent positive that whatever Eric did in this situation would just make it fucking worse. If Dash was abusing Tony, then Eric running in there trying to pull his white knight act would just entrench Tony further. And if Dash wasn't abusive, then Eric would look like a jealous asshole who couldn't get over his ex.

"Go stake him," she said, deadly serious. Which should have been hilarious because she had marshmallow stuck to her upper lip, but Hunter couldn't quite find the humor in it.

"Well, we're not doing *that*."

Lu huffed, annoyed, her green eyes narrowing on him like he'd disappointed her. Like she'd expected more from him. Which was kind of silly, really, because she had to know that Hunter wasn't going to tell Eric to run off and stake the mayor's brother. No matter how much of a piece of shit he was.

"But I'll do some digging, and I'll check in with your brother. If there's something to worry about, we'll take this to Eric, and I'll carve the stake myself. Deal?" He held out a hand, his many silver rings glittering in the yellow kitchen lights.

She glared at it, tongue sticking out of the corner of her mouth, then nodded once and grabbed his hand.

CHAPTER 9

"FOR THE RECORD," Bert said, his tone anxious and crackling where it came through the earbud in Eric's ear, "I think this is a stupid fucking idea."

"I'll make a note." Eric tapped his fingers nervously on the steering wheel. He didn't need Bert to *tell* him this was a stupid idea. He knew it already. He knew damn well he could be heading into an ambush situation. Especially if Janet was as tied up in this thing as he was beginning to suspect she was. But just because it was a stupid idea didn't mean Eric wasn't going to go through with it. He may have learned something about teamwork and relying on his people over the last few months, but it hadn't broken his reckless streak. Besides, he was still the only line of defense between the vampires and Ironport—he couldn't walk away from that. Even if it meant putting his neck on the line, both figuratively and literally.

"You should have taken someone with you," Bert huffed. He was sitting in the squeaky chair, and it screeched loudly in the background as he spun it round and round, because Bert was just that kind of person. Always looking for the thing that would annoy the people around him the absolute most.

"Like who?" The place where Dash had set up the meeting was decidedly fishy. Well, *fishy* was probably a nice way of putting it. Generally speaking, people didn't have business meetings at a marina. Unless of course the person you were meeting was some TV mobster or a used-boat salesman. But Eric hadn't been to a business meeting in probably close to a decade, so maybe etiquette had changed? Either way, he didn't like it.

"Hunter. Kalla. Ava." Bert sounded like he was listing them off on his fingers, and Eric could imagine him doing just that. Ticking off names like someone else might grocery items. Goddess, he was such a little shithead. "Literally *anyone*."

"And risk making it obvious that I'm suspicious of this fucker? Yeah, no thanks." His kit—a big black duffel bag—sat splayed open on the passenger seat, and Eric stared down into it, wishing not for the first time that he had a way to hide weapons on him less conspicuously. Tony's hair pins were fucking awesome; Eric would be lying if he said he wasn't jealous of having a weapon that also acted as an accessory. It definitely put people more at ease around Tony, although everything else about Tony McMahon seemed designed to keep people on edge. Either way, it would have been helpful. Instead, Eric was forced to stuff a stake into the pocket of his windbreaker and hope to Diana no one noticed it.

Is that a stake in your pocket or are you just happy to see me?

"And besides," Eric added, sliding the holster for a dagger into the back of his pants, "how do you think that would go down? Me bringing one of my exes, or my bestie, to meet with a different ex's current boyfriend."

"Dude, I tell you this because I love you. You need to learn to keep it in your fucking pants."

Eric scoffed. It wouldn't be so laughable if Tony hadn't been the first serious sexual partner Eric had in like five years. Goddess, he was a mess. "Are you trying to slut shame me right now, Humbert?"

"No. But seriously. If you'd just stop sleeping around, then maybe your social life wouldn't be such a mess."

"Counterpoint. If I stopped staying friends with my exes,

then my social life wouldn't be such a mess." Not that he was going to do that. Eric had never been able to walk away from someone like that. Usually people had to be done with him before he was done with them. Kalla and Hunter were prime examples, Tony was another. Because if Tony hadn't severed all ties, cauterized the wound, Eric would have let it bleed him dry until he was completely exsanguinated. Because he was a fucking idiot.

"Counter-counterpoint. Maybe just get back with Hunter."

Leaning forward to press his forehead to the steering wheel, Eric groaned. This was an old argument, one he and Bert had rehashed over and over the last couple of months. Because Bert was a persistent little fuck, and somehow he'd begun to think of Hunter as his other surrogate parent. Had imprinted on him like a duckling during game nights and not let go.

"Oh look, Dash is here, better go." He wasn't. The dock was still painfully empty, no sound but the lap of water on the hulls of boats. But Eric needed to get the fuck away from this conversation before he screamed.

"Doesn't mean we can't keep talking about this." Bert sounded prim. Like he was sitting up straighter in his chair.

"Yes, it does," Eric said seriously, leaving no room for any more of Bert's nonsense. "I need to focus, and you're supposed to have my back. If you can't do that, then go get me someone who can."

"Fine. Fine. I'll wait till after you're done." Bert huffed, the chair creaking beneath him again. Eric imagined him hunching over the keyboard, his neck craned up to see the many screens.

With one last bang of his forehead against the steering wheel, Eric cut the engine and got out of the car. It was still cold enough that he needed a jacket, but warm enough that he'd ditched the thick coat he wore during the winter months.

His breath fogged in the night air as he paced careful steps down the dock.

It was lit by short lights, the kind someone might line their walk in, but it didn't do much good on a dock. Thankfully, the moon was full, meaning Eric wasn't likely to walk off the end of the dock on accident. Not that it would be the first time he'd gone in the water involuntarily; he'd just rather not do so before at least mid-June. He wasn't the polar-bear-plunge type.

The night was still, apart from the soft creaking of the lines holding what few boats hadn't gone south for the winter or been pulled out of the water, into their slips. Early spring left the marina more empty than full, but that was par for the course in a coastal town this far north. And the ones that were full were mostly boats that didn't look as if they'd seen inhab-itants since fall. Likely locals who had packed away their perishables and left their home away from home with a bubbler and the hope that they wouldn't get flooded out come hurricane season as had happened once or twice before.

A single boat down the end of the dock had its interior lights on, but none of the back ones in the cockpit were lit. Could be someone living on their boat—people did that sometimes. Not as frequently in Ironport, which was a little further up the river, as in Moondale, but still regularly enough that it could be nothing.

"Where the fuck is he?" Eric muttered to himself, doing another sweep. The dock Dash had pointed him to wasn't overly large. It could house fifteen, maybe twenty boats? Half the slips were empty. Most of which were dark. And Dash hadn't given him a slip number or a boat name to go by. Just said, *meet me on pier F*. Which should have been enough to make Eric antsy. And had been, hence Bert muttering to himself in his ear. "Will you shut up? I'm trying to listen!"

"Listen to what? There's nothing there, dude. I'm telling you. No energy spikes. No signs of life at all that I can tell."

Okay, so Bert was grumpy now that Eric wouldn't talk to him about Hunter. Super mature of him. "Dash stood you up."

"It's too quiet." He stepped carefully over a plank that looked like it was in sore need of repair. He was exposed, out in the open, and he hated it. But there was nowhere for anyone else to hide either. If this was an ambush, he'd see them coming. Which he supposed was a bonus to this location, but it didn't make the hairs on the back of his head lie back down. "Someone is watching me."

Bert hummed softly, his fingers flying over the keyboard on the other end of the phone, the *click-clack* coming through over-loud in the silence of the water and the night.

A shape moved on one of the boats, catching Eric's attention from the corner of his eye, but when he looked that way he didn't see anything. Still, he made his way across the pier to get a better look. He reached the edge of the dock and stepped onto the finger pier that rested between the boat where he'd seen the shape and an empty slip.

His hand tightened around the stake in his pocket, muscles on high alert, ready to spring into action, but—but he was facing the wrong fucking direction! *Apparently.*

There was a loud splash, the sound of something large breaching the water, then it latched onto his ankles and pulled him in.

Fuck, there goes the earbud, he thought right before he hit the surface and the cold river water seeped into his clothes, weighing him down. He was never going to be able to get the smell out of his shoes. More hands latched on to him—how many, he couldn't be sure as he thrashed around to get free— dragging him down toward the muddy bottom, clawing at him, trying to press the air from his lungs.

He kicked out. Knocked something or someone hard in the face. A soft grunt followed the impact of rubber shoe sole meeting bone. So, likely not a river spirit then. Something closer to human. Something nastier.

It was too dark to see in the murky water. Too heavy. Every movement a struggle. His lungs burned. His jacket caught around his arms. His jeans grew steadily more weighted down. Every flailing motion was a futile attempt to not sink. He stripped off his jacket, let it float away on the tide. And with a hard kick to something that must have been sensitive if the yelp from the person was anything to go by, he broke loose from the seeking hands and pushed back to the surface to suck down air. Splinters embedded themselves in his fingertips—stabbing and burning—where he grabbed the side of the pier and tried to haul himself up onto it in spite of the good foot-or-so gap between the tide and the planks. Why the fuck hadn't this one been replaced with a floating dock like so many of the others in this marina?

A grip, cold and firm as iron, wrapped around his ankle again and yanked hard enough to dislodge his precarious grasp. He had just enough time to gulp down another breath before he was dragged under. A blow to his stomach left him choking, coughing, almost sucking in water. Fuck. *Fuck!*

He closed his mouth, pressing his lips together so hard it felt like his teeth might clack right through them, and if they didn't, there would still be a bruise come morning.

Now that he wasn't panicking anymore—well, not quite as much, he wasn't expecting to be fucking drowned tonight, all right?—Eric remembered the dagger in the back of his pants. His hands were going numb from the cold, but thank the Goddess he could still feel the pressure of the metal against his fingers. The blade bit into him as he struggled to get it free, cutting through the thin skin at the small of his back, adding blood to the murky depths. Eric hissed at the burn of the river water settling into the wound in a way that would no doubt cause infection. But he would have time to worry about that later.

He lashed out wildly with the dagger, catching something, stabbing in, but he lost his hold on the slick handle. There was a muffled gasp of pain, and whatever had been attacking him lurched back, away, leaving him enough space to get to the surface again. He coughed up water. Choked on it. Then turned to watch the face of Noah M. floating beside him. His eyes were red as scarlet, fangs poking into his lower lip.

Eric heaved another breath and shoved off from the dock, kicking away from Noah. It sent him out of the slip, toward the main part of the river. If he could put some distance between himself and Noah, he might be able to escape. He'd need to. He couldn't fight like this. He was soaked through, and while it wasn't quite cold enough for hypothermia, that didn't mean his numb fingertips and jittering muscles would be capable of fighting Noah, not right now. Especially in a place where Noah had the upper hand because he didn't need to fucking *breathe*. Sometimes it was better to run than fight. Or swim, rather.

Noah might have been a vampire. Stronger. Faster. But Eric had one thing on his side: he knew for a fact Noah was afraid of open water, especially at night. Which was good common sense, really, but Eric had never *had* good common sense. So he swam out to the middle of the creek, turning back over his shoulder for a moment to see if Noah would follow. But Noah had pulled himself up onto the dock and was shifting from one foot to the other like he wasn't sure what to do. There was a hole in his black T-shirt, pale, gleaming skin visible through it in the moonlight. Likely where Eric had stabbed him, and his vampire healing had done its thing. *Fucking vampires.*

That was fine. That was completely fine. Eric just had to get far enough away that hopefully Noah's vamp eyes wouldn't be able to see him moving through the water. There was some danger of a boat coming upon him, but he thought it was late enough in the evening, and early enough in the season, that he'd be safe.

The urge to goad Noah sat on his tongue, but he ignored

it. There would be time to hunt that motherfucker down and get answers later. For now, he needed to find a safe place to swim to shore and get himself home.

Home.

All the way in the mountains of Moondale U.

Without his fucking car.

This was gonna suck.

CHAPTER 10

IT WAS a nice night out with Dash. A night without anyone else to interfere. Usually, Dash wanted to show Tony off, like some prize he'd won. *Look at the guy I'm dating. He's the second-highest-ranked Venator in the world.* It was kind of nice for someone to look at Tony's slay average and be proud of him for once. Not to scoff at him and say, "Second highest? Well, what 'bout the first?" like his father had years ago when Tony had reached that rank. You know, before the vampires had torn him to itty bitty, bite-sized pieces. Tony should maybe feel bad about that, but it was hard when he knew his father had one-hundred percent gotten what he deserved.

But even if it was nice that Dash was proud of him, proud to be seen with him, Tony liked it better when they were alone. When there were none of Dash's high-class friends to impress. Of course, they were still at a fancy restaurant with at least three too many forks, none of which Tony knew the function of, but that was all right. Because it was just them. Just them and some dish Tony was pretty sure he could make better if he made it at home.

Dash leaned into him, let Tony run his hand up his thigh under the table so it could rest over his cock in his slacks. He'd even glared down the maitre d' when the man tried to tell Tony he couldn't come in without a tie. It was kind of romantic, and definitely hot.

Tony remained sober enough to drive Dash home, and when they stopped at his house, he idled for a moment out front.

"I could come up," he said, licking his lips, his eyes flicking purposefully from Dash's face down to his crotch. "Finish what I started at the restaurant."

"You need to get home to check on your sister," Dash reminded him, responsible as ever. Why? Why did he always have to be so responsible, so reasonable?

"You could come home with me then. Lu wouldn't mind." She would mind. She'd be fucking pissed if she found out Tony had brought Dash into their house for a sleepover. Tony had been careful about when Dash and Lu spent time together, and he'd made sure that so far Dash wasn't invading Lu's space. But she'd have to get the fuck over that eventually. She was nearly eighteen, a fucking adult. He should be allowed to have his boyfriend over.

"She would mind. You know she would." Dash rolled his eyes, but his smile didn't fall at all, like it was plastered onto his face, painted there, mysterious and dark, like the fucking Mona Lisa. Goddess, how did one man get to be so good looking? It didn't seem fair. Tony would bet if he took a cleaver and split Dash's face in half, it would be perfectly symmetrical. How?

"She'd get over it." Eventually.

Dash sighed heavily, leaning back in his seat and taking the hand that Tony had been squeezing his thigh with, threading their fingers together. "How about I come by tomorrow for breakfast instead? You go into work late, right? And Lu doesn't have classes until the afternoon?"

"Yeah." Had they gotten to the point in their relationship where breakfast dates were a thing? Did that mean they were going backward or forward? Tony wasn't really sure, and there wasn't someone he could ask about these things. Most of the friends he'd had back in Miami had promptly fucked off when they found out he was moving up the coast. Not that he could blame them really. They were the sort to go out clubbing, and one couldn't exactly do that when there were four fucking states between them. It wasn't like any of them could afford to fly up to Maryland just to go out for drinks. And Tony didn't exactly have the time or funds to go back to Miami.

"You don't sound super confident." Dash laughed a little, stroking his fingers over Tony's knuckles. It was a slow, hypnotizing motion. Hard to think through.

Tony shrugged. He sometimes hated how Dash could see down to his uncertainties. Could read him like a fucking book. It didn't seem fair at all when everything about Dash was locked up tight, Fort Knox compared to Tony's public library.

"Come on, my darling, don't let tonight end this way. I'll see you in the morning." Dash leaned across the gear shift to run his nose along Tony's neck, murmuring softly. "Trust me, we'll figure this out. Yeah?"

It was hard to tell him no then. Hard to force the issue further. And Tony was too fucking tired to bother, really. "Yeah. I'll see you in the morning. Let's say eight?"

"Eight is good," Dash murmured against his skin, the heat of his breath raising goosebumps along Tony's neck. "See you then."

He was out of the car and to his door before Tony could even think to protest or chase after him. He turned once with his hand on the knob to shoot Tony a wink before he headed inside, and Tony let out a long, gusty sigh. Fucking hell.

Tony sat there for a moment, willing his heart to stop racing and his blood to stop pounding. Reciting all the cookie recipes he knew by heart in his head—ingredients included—until the burn of his belly cooled and he was finally able to lift his hands to the steering wheel without them shaking. Then he yanked down on the gear shift, throwing the car into reverse, and sped away from Dash's house.

The drive back to his place wasn't that long, even though he and Lu lived in a vastly different neighborhood than Dash. Dash's place screamed old money. With houses that were probably built around the turn of the century and kept up so that they looked nice, and clean, while still having each home be unique unto itself. Whereas the townhouse Tony had found for himself and Lu was just another in a row of houses just like it. All with the same front door color. All with the same shutters. All with the same little stoop.

Except . . . except the stoop of 201 Crescent Lane—*his* stoop—had a dark shape on it. Something large and shivering curled onto the front mat—which didn't say "welcome" because Tony wasn't a fucking idiot, he knew what kind of trouble those things could cause. When his headlights flashed over whatever it was, it moved just enough that Tony could catch the gleam of an eye before it curled more tightly in on itself. It looked like a person. It had to be a person, right?

Tony reached into the glove box and pulled out one of the stakes he left there in case of emergencies. He wasn't exactly in the mood to be some leech's late-night snack. It would really ruin his night.

Yeah sure, leeches didn't usually cower on the doorstep to Venator homes, but there was a first time for everything. And if he'd learned anything from the events of a few months back, Ironport was a fucking anomaly when it came to vampire activity.

He slunk closer, the roughhewn wood of the stake biting into his hand. It would have been better to use one of his silver hairpins, but he'd foregone those in favor of a hair tie that would actually keep his curls out of his face the entire time he was with Dash. Dash liked to have his neck bare, for what reason, Tony didn't know. But who was he to shame someone else's kinks?

At this new angle, he could almost make out the face of the creature hunched on his stoop like some kind of gargoyle. Almost see the long slope of a nose, the bow of—

"Marcelino?" Tony stopped, the stake falling to rest at his side, fingers going lax. "What the fuck are you doing here?"

Marcelino lifted his head, his dark hair hanging in his eyes like it was wet, lips blue in the cold. He didn't have a jacket on, and the thin long-sleeved shirt he was wearing clung to him, showing off every shivering muscle. "Got—got into—" he stuttered, stumbling over his words, or maybe struggling to get them out past teeth that seemed intent on chattering. "Into trouble."

"Fucking hell." The seams on Eric's jacket groaned as he stuffed the stake back into his pocket and took two quick strides to Marcelino, lifting him easily in his arms. His clothes were damp from whatever he'd gotten himself into, and freezing to the touch. Cold enough that goosebumps rose on Tony's skin. "Come on, let's get you inside before you catch hypothermia."

"Not—not cold—e-enough for that." But upon closer inspection it wasn't just his lips that had a blue tinge to them —his fingertips did too, and the tip of his nose looked red and raw. He shivered where Tony had him in a bridal carry, hard enough that Tony nearly dropped him. He probably would have if it weren't for how Marcelino clung to his shirt, to the lapels of his jacket.

"Bullshit it's not." Tony huffed. It was a struggle to unlock the door with a shivering man in his arms, but Tony wasn't willing to put Marcelino down now that he had him wrapped up against his chest. Although he couldn't really pinpoint why. This definitely seemed like something he shouldn't be doing after a date with his boyfriend, but somehow Tony couldn't get his hands to let go.

Eventually, he managed to kick the door open. It swung hard, bouncing off the wall beside it with a noise loud enough that it should have brought Lu running. "Lu! Lu!" he called, nudging the door shut behind him with his foot, not even bothering to lock it as he made his way into the living room. "Lu, get down here, you brat!"

"She's not—not home. Knocked on—on the door. Rang th-the bell. No answer." Marcelino pressed his face in closer to Tony's neck, his cold cheeks making shivers race down Tony's spine, and refused to let go of where he'd fisted his hands in the lapels of Tony's leather jacket. Either that, or he couldn't. It was entirely possible that his extremities had fucking locked up on him. "Didn't—didn't know where else to go."

"All right. All right. Just relax. Calm down," Tony hushed, his hands moving to rub warmth into Marcelino's chilled skin none too gently. "We need to get you out of these clothes and into a warm bath, or your fucking fingers are gonna fall off."

"I'm not going to get fr-frost bite. I told you!" Marcelino growled, showing teeth, and wasn't that just fucking adorable?

"Fine! You won't get frost bite." Tony rolled his eyes and grabbed the blanket from the back of the couch. It was sherpa lined, would probably hold the water more than get Marcelino warm, but Tony needed a fucking barrier between them if he was going to carry him all the way upstairs. Marcelino grumbled at him, but ultimately let Tony practically smother him with the blanket while wrapping him up like a burrito then scoop him up again.

"You're nice," Marcelino slurred against Tony's shoulder on their way up the stairs.

"And you're fucking out of it. Did they bite you?"

"No. No bites. But—" He swallowed roughly, shifting a little like he was suddenly uncomfortable where Tony was holding him. "But I cut my back with my dagger."

"Add it to the list," Tony muttered. The bathroom light clicked on when he nudged it with his elbow, and Tony had Marcelino in the bathtub in short order. "We need to get you out of your clothes. Do you think you can stand to get out of those jeans?"

"I can do it. I just need—I just need a minute." Marcelino's breaths were coming in hard pants now, his chest juddering with each one. He was going to lose consciousness, and soon, if Tony didn't bring his fucking temperature back up. Fuck.

"No minute." Tony didn't wait for him to say anything else. He ignored Marcelino when he swatted him away, and started to work on stripping off the thin long-sleeved shirt. Marcelino was pale underneath, from a combination of blood loss and cold. There was a mottled bruise on his stomach and a red gash up his back, gaping a little. It would scar, no matter what Tony did to try to stop it. "Fuck, Marcelino, you got yourself good, didn't you?"

"Accident," Marcelino said through clenched teeth, his arms curling around himself to try to keep him warm, nipples and skin pebbled. He was more toned than Tony remembered. There was a bit of weight gathered around his midsection, but it did nothing to detract from the wiry muscles that lined his chest and arms.

"Right. You said. Let's stand you up to get you out of these jeans, then I'll start the water."

Between the two of them, they managed to manhandle Marcelino to standing, his hands braced on Tony's shoulders, fingers digging in as he balanced precariously and Tony worked to undo the buttons after Marcelino spent too long fumbling with them himself. That done, he sat Marcelino gingerly back down in the tub and got the water started.

Now that Tony got a better look at the cut on Marcelino's back, he saw that it had mostly stopped bleeding, healed over by his Venator abilities. It probably just needed to be cleaned out and have some butterfly bandages applied. All of that would have to be done post-bath.

"You think you can manage to sit here and not drown yourself while I go fix you some tea?" Tony asked from where he knelt by the tub, unable to keep the annoyed edge from his tone. But he wasn't annoyed at Marcelino; he was annoyed with himself. Because the urge to get in there, to see if they could both fit and make the water lap over the ceramic edge, sat strong in his bones, made him twitch. But he couldn't really explain where it came from, or why. He and Marcelino were over. Had been over for months now. And even before they were, they hadn't been cuddle-in-the-bathtub kind of people. They had been more fuck, and . . . and what? Had that been it? Had there been something else? He didn't think so. Then why did Tony's body itch to reach out for Marcelino like it was fucking muscle memory.

"Mm-hmm." Marcelino's legs were stretched out in front of him, his bare feet braced on the tub beneath the spout, keeping his head and shoulders above water. Chances were, he *probably* wouldn't drown if he passed out. Tony was willing to take those odds so long as it meant putting some space between himself and Marcelino. So he left, hoping Diana would watch out for the idiot in his tub.

Damn it. He needed to get his fucking head on straight. The counter dug in to his hips where his weight was heavy against it, and he leaned over to bang his forehead on the cabinet above. "What the fuck is wrong with you, man?"

He waited there, eyes closed, breath evening out, but he couldn't wipe away the image of Marcelino wet and shaking on his stoop not but twenty minutes ago. It had seared itself into the back of his eyelids like a Goddess-damned daguerreotype. When the only answer to his question was the sound of the kettle screeching, Tony poured them each a mug of steaming water, dropped a teabag in each, and headed up the steps.

Marcelino was still in the tub. The color had returned to his skin in a rush, leaving him rosy cheeked. His head was tilted back, brown hair brushed away from his face, his chin tilted toward the ceiling. He looked like he might be asleep, but when he heard Tony enter the room, he peeked one eye open.

"You gonna tell me what the fuck happened tonight?" Tony asked, setting one of the mugs on the lip of the tub where Marcelino could take it between fingers red with recirculating blood, and sigh.

"I don't know that that's a good idea."

"Why not?"

"Because you're gonna be pissed." Marcelino sipped from his mug, not even wincing as the liquid no doubt scalded his tongue. Maybe he was still a little fucked-up from the cold and the blood loss. Tony had looked him over thoroughly, and there weren't bites on him, so it couldn't be vamp venom.

"Try me."

Marcelino shrugged, muttered, "It's my funeral" under his breath and finished his tea in a single gulp that sounded like it fucking hurt. Then he set the mug on the lip of the tub with a hollow *clunk* and leaned back again against the wall, not looking at Tony. "I was supposed to meet Dash Chadwick at the marina tonight. We were going to talk about some of the weird shit going on in Ironport."

"Weird shit?"

"Yeah. The vampire that attacked me the other night? The one you saved me from?" Marcelino flapped his hands around, clearly getting himself worked up about this. He did that sometimes, talked with his hands, but Tony couldn't remember how he knew that. "They said something about Chadwick telling them to leave the Venator alone."

"It *what*?" That didn't make sense. None at all. Except . . . except something niggled at the back of Tony's mind. Something told him maybe it did make sense. Maybe it made more sense than anything else that had happened recently. "So you think my boyfriend is in league with the vampires?"

"No. Well, sorta?" Marcelino huffed, tilting his head to look at Tony through where his dark hair had flopped into his face, fixing Tony with those big Bambi eyes. Pinning him down. Tony felt like squirming, but he remained perfectly still. Then he said, "Whatever I might have thought, it's weird that I was attacked by a vamp who seemed to be waiting for me in the exact spot your boyfriend told me to meet him, isn't it?"

Tony's blood ran cold.

"Yeah. Well." Tony took another sip from his mug, forcing his movements to remain slow, unhurried, to hide how rattled he was by what he'd just heard. "There's about a dozen explanations for that."

Marcelino's wide eyes narrowed, and he huffed out a disbelieving laugh before slumping down in the tub again. "Yeah, sure there is."

Tony scowled at him and rose to his feet, heading for the door. He needed to get Marcelino the fuck out of his house. It made things too confusing. Just as he reached the door, he thought he heard Marcelino murmur, "I've missed you," but it was probably just his imagination.

CHAPTER 11

ERIC WAS MISSING—A thirty-four-year-old man was fucking *missing*, like a kitten, or a toddler on the beach—and Hunter was frantic about it. His heart thudded so hard against his rib cage, it was painful. He hadn't taken a full breath since Bert called him to tell him what was going on.

"There was this like . . . *yelp*, and the line just went dead," Bert had said. Which was worrying. So fucking worrying. A yelp. Eric didn't fucking yelp. And he sure as shit wouldn't have let the line go dead like that, not when he knew Bert was on the other end. Not if he had a choice. Eric wouldn't want them to worry. That's just who he was. He didn't want to inconvenience anyone. Didn't matter how many times they all told him that wasn't possible.

"I found his car," Hunter sighed into the phone at his ear. Ava and Kalla were on the other end, a three-way call. Kalla had agreed to take the hospitals; since she had a flashy badge she could wave around to demand answers. Ava had gone to the cemeteries, but she wasn't alone.

There was another voice in the background. A murmured "There was no one in the crypt."

"Did you bring a *date* to search for our missing friend?" Hunter practically snarled. He didn't know what made him angrier: the fact that Eric was missing, or the fact that Ava thought it appropriate to bring a date on their search party.

Kalla clicked her tongue derisively but didn't chime in, so he couldn't tell who she was being judgmental toward: him or Ava.

"Look," Ava said, and he heard her shift the phone closer, her voice getting louder, a little distorted by its proximity to the mic, "I was with Nessy when I got the call. I couldn't just—"

"Nessy." When had Ava and Dean Vanessa Cochburn—Eric and Hunter's *boss*—gotten to nickname basis? Was it when Hunter was too wrapped up in his grief and Eric to notice what was going on with his friend? Not that he would have been allowed to notice; Ava was the secretive type. He may not have even known she was dating the dean of Moondale U until they were fucking moving in together if Eric hadn't disappeared that night.

Kalla snorted but stayed quiet.

"Fuck off, Hunter." He could imagine the roll of Ava's eyes that accompanied the scoff. "Like I was saying, I couldn't just leave her behind. She wasn't going to let me when she saw how freaked out I was."

"I wasn't going to let her drive either," Vanessa called from farther away.

"You're not helping, Ness."

"Didn't claim to be." Hunter liked her already. She sounded like she wasn't taking any of Ava's shit, which is exactly the kind of woman Ava needed in her life.

"Well, isn't that sweet," Kalla muttered to herself.

The casual way they spoke to each other made something dull and aching throb in Hunter's chest, but the feeling was quickly drowned out by panic again. "All right, stop being adorable for about two fucking seconds and tell me what you've found."

"Nothing," Ava said.

"Nothing," Kalla agreed. "Dispatch says no one called in a report matching Eric's description. And I'm at the hospital now. They have no record of anyone being brought in tonight."

"I even tried scrying for him, but he's not turning up. It's weird." Ava sounded disturbed by that fact, and honestly, so was Hunter. Scrying in Ironport, like most other things in Ironport, was shoddy at the best of times, completely useless at the worst. Something about the proximity to a nexus without actual access to its magic making the not-quite-city to the west of Moondale a magical quagmire. But they'd never had trouble finding *Eric* via it before. The magic in his blood from the Venator gene was usually enough to send out a pretty strong signal.

"What if he fell in the water?" Vanessa asked. She sounded like she was closer now. Maybe pressing her side up against Ava's, sharing warmth and comfort. Goddess, Hunter missed that feeling. Missed knowing someone had his back like that.

"You think he drowned?" Kalla's tone went up an octave, panic making it quiver. Hunter's own heart began to race again, rocketing up toward his throat, threatening to spill his meager dinner onto the gravel of the marina parking lot.

He heard Ava make a noise—half whimper, half question.

"No. Not that," Vanessa was quick to say, but it sounded like maybe she wasn't completely ruling that possibility out, which didn't help matters.

Hunter forced himself to take a deep breath in through his nose. One. Two. And out through his mouth. Forced his shoulders to drop down away from his shoulders. He asked, "Then what are you saying?"

"Well, sometimes crossing a lake or a river or whatever messes with scrying. It's not uncommon for natural waterways to muddy a person's magical signature." It was true, and it was reasonable, and it made Hunter feel a little calmer. But only a little.

"But he didn't cross the river," Ava said, a frown in her voice.

"No. But he might have crossed the creek." Hunter leaned forward on his toes, squinting through the dark at the other side of the water. The marina where Eric left his car was on one of the smaller creeks connecting to the river that ran from Moondale up to Ironport or down toward the island of Eventide if one followed it far enough. It was wide, sure. Enough for the docks to stick out a ways on both sides and not impede traffic, but not wide enough for an experienced swimmer like Eric to not be able to cross it. Especially not with his adrenaline high and his Venator strength kicked into full gear. "What's on the other side?"

"Ummm . . ." Ava shifted, her clothes crinkling against the mic. "I think that's that neighborhood, you know, the real fancy one?"

"Chadwick lives there," Kalla supplied.

"Okay, well what's on the other side of that?" Hunter pulled his phone down away from his ear, putting it on speaker so he could pull up a map and look for himself. After a moment of searching, he found his answer. "Those little row houses. The old-school ones that were built way back, when Ironport first got started. Before it sprawled."

"Oh right." Ava agreed. There was a *click* on the other end of the line, like she'd snapped her fingers. "I dropped Lu McMahon off there the other day. That must be where she and her brother live."

"Great." Hunter huffed, his rings catching on his nose when he scrubbed at his face. *Just fucking great.* He pushed his glasses up into his hair so he could rub his gunky eyes. There was no doubt—at fucking all—that he looked like shit. He'd been crying and frantic for what felt like hours now. And he was going to face down Eric's ex.

"You don't really think he went there, do you?" Kalla sounded wary and disapproving. Which wasn't productive at the current moment, but neither would be Hunter getting into a fight with her on the phone when they should be finding Eric. So he opted to ignore it.

"You said he wasn't picked up by the cops, and there is no record of him at the hospital. So either he's wandering the streets freezing to death . . ." The wind whipped up at that exact moment as if to emphasize Hunter's point, clawing at the gunmetal scarf Eric had crocheted for his last birthday and threatening to rip it away. Hunter curled his shoulders, wishing he'd worn his coat instead of the thin jean jacket and flannel combo he'd thrown on hours ago before he left the house. But there hadn't been time to change when he'd gotten the call from Bert that Eric was missing.

"Or he washed up on the shore somewhere," Kalla said.

"Not helping, Kalla," Ava snapped.

"Just trying to be realistic here. Someone has to be."

"No, you're just being a bitch. As usual. We'd know if Eric were dead. *I'd* know. We're connected. We're—"

"If you say platonic soulmates one more fucking time, I'm gonna come through this phone and—"

"Enough!" Hunter hissed, silencing their bickering. "There will be time for you two catty bitches to go at it after we find Eric. For now, Ava, get me Tony's address."

"Already typing."

"Kalla, I want you to run by the house and pick up Eric's spare keys. You and Ava can come get his car when you're done."

Kalla grunted her acceptance, which likely meant she'd wanted to argue but sensed the steel in his tone, and hung up. His phone dinged a second later and when he pulled up the text from Ava, he found the address to Lu and Tony's house.

"All right, you two head back too. I don't want more of us out than needs to be. Not if someone is hunting us." And someone *was* hunting them. Hunter was sure of it now. There was no way someone would have gotten the jump on Eric if someone weren't targeting them. The question was, how long had it been going on? And who was the hunter?

"Right." Ava's tone was all business now. The crispness of it smoothed over the worry and the anxiety, and it made Hunter feel a little better. There was a plan in place, a plan they could all follow. He'd show up at Tony's door, check to see if Eric was there. If he wasn't, they'd deal with that then. "I'm going to try scrying for him again. It might be easier from the house, since we'll be away from Ironport."

"Probably," Hunter agreed. He turned to grab the door to his truck and clamber inside. It wasn't warm anymore, hadn't been for several minutes, likely. He'd been poking around the marina long enough that the chill from outside seeped into the metal and fabric. Goddess, he couldn't wait for spring. Not summer. Spring. Where the world got a bit warmer, but not sticky hot yet. "And umm . . . make sure the kids are all right."

Ava sighed. "Yeah, I will."

"Bert was really shaken up."

"I know."

"Okay."

They sat in silence for a few minutes as Hunter's truck rumbled to life, the heater blasted as high as it would go, and his leg bounced against the floorboard. He probably shouldn't wait too long. If he did, Tony might be sleeping by the time he got there and he wouldn't get any answers. But he was—well, he was kind of procrastinating on seeing Tony again. Shit had been really fucked up between Tony and the rest of them lately, what with the breakup and Tony not talking to them. Hunter didn't feel equipped to deal with that, not after the night he'd had.

"Hunter?" Ava called when the quiet stretched too damn long.

"Yeah?"

"You're gonna find him." She said it with all the confidence a person could have. Like putting the thought out into the universe would make it so. Maybe it would. Hunter hoped it would.

"I am," Hunter agreed, and took the truck out of park.

The phone rang while Hunter was driving over the creek toward the more populated areas of Ironport. He didn't recognize the number, but with Eric's phone out of commission, he wasn't about to not answer it.

"Hello?"

"This is Hunter, right?" the person asked. They sounded vaguely familiar, but Hunter had never been good at placing voices. That was an Ava skill. She had a knack for it. Could hear an actor in a commercial and know exactly who it was without even having to see their face. She'd recognized Crowley from *Supernatural* in a *Doctor Who* commercial once, and Hunter hadn't believed her. He'd lost fifty dollars that way.

"Yeah. What's up?" His fingers tightened around the wheel as he pressed the phone into his shoulder to free his other hand and turn on his signal.

"You need to come pick up Marcelino. He's here."

Relief washed through Hunter so quickly, it nearly made him dizzy. He had to inhale deeply to keep himself from curling up into a fucking ball in the driver's seat. Eric was all right. He was all right and he was somewhere Hunter could pick him up from. He wasn't being held hostage by vampires. He wasn't washed up on the shore of the creek. He was with someone.

"Here where?" Hunter asked, praying to the Goddess that Eric wasn't too badly hurt.

The person clicked their tongue, and *that* was a sound Hunter recognized without having to see a face. Tony McMahon had made that exact fucking sound to Eric's face at Britt's funeral. Like he was disgusted by the very sight of him. "It's Tony."

"Yeah, I got that. But where are you?" Hunter wasn't going to admit that he hadn't known who it was on the phone at first. Because that would be admitting weakness. And one did not admit weakness to one's best friend's ex. That was in the code, or whatever.

"At my place. 201 Crescent Lane. On the corner of Crescent and Wolf." He hung up without another word. It felt like some kind of power move, enough so that it had Hunter gnashing his teeth the rest of the way to the house.

The lights were still on upstairs when Hunter parked, but not in the lower level. He wasn't going to think about what that could mean though, because Eric was all right. Eric was all right, and Hunter was going to take him home.

Tony answered the door and motioned him inside shortly after he knocked.

"Where is he?" Hunter poked his head into what he presumed was the living room and found no one on the couch or in any of the chairs.

"Upstairs." Tony didn't wait for Hunter to follow, just headed up the stairs set between the kitchen and the living room. The landing at the top of the steps was dark too. Like Tony wasn't home long enough to bother turning on any lights. Lu must not have come back home after she left Hunter, which reminded him—

No. He'd save that for another time. Shit was too high strung as it was right now. He didn't need to add anything to it by opening his mouth. He just needed to get Eric home, and look him over, then he could worry about—

"Eric?" Hunter choked when his eyes finally landed on where Eric was sprawled out on Tony's bed, clearly wearing

Tony's clothes. The shirt was too broad across the shoulders for him, and the legs on the sweatpants were about an inch too short. It was a weird dichotomy, and it made Hunter . . .

It made Hunter . . .

All right, so it made him a little jealous. Because what the fuck had Eric been doing here with Tony this whole time while they were looking for him? While Hunter was losing his fucking mind, certain that Eric was lying on the side of the creek somewhere, Eric was here. Getting naked with his ex.

And that's when Hunter Delacroix opened his big fucking mouth.

CHAPTER 12

"I DON'T GIVE A FLYING fuck what Lu told you!" was the first thing Eric heard when he eventually began to surface from the hazy place he'd been since jumping in the creek.

It was hard to focus on things when he was so cold. Hard to latch on to anything that was real. All he could remember was dragging his trembling body down the street of a neighborhood. The houses growing smaller and smaller the farther he got from the water. Cars drove past him. One of them might have even honked their horn. But he kept going. Kept dragging his feet, the toes of his still-squelching shoes scuffing along the sidewalk as he headed toward . . . something. He couldn't explain it. It was probably muscle memory. His body giving him directions while his brain was offline. But eventually he wound up on Tony's doorstep and knocked, and knocked, and rang the bell, and prayed to the Goddess that someone would find him before the cold sank any deeper into his bones. When no one answered, he collapsed on the stoop, shivers racking his body.

And now he was here. And Tony and Hunter were shouting at each other.

"Then show me the bites," Hunter challenged, stepping into Tony's space. His eyes were wide and wild behind his glasses. Eric didn't think he'd ever seen his friend so angry before. *Livid* would be the term he'd use, actually. Hunter was always mild, sweet even, happy-go-lucky. But now he was a raging storm. Eric didn't even know Hunter had this kind of rage inside of him. It made him wonder what it took to bring that rage out. It also sent a shudder down Eric's spine that he told himself had everything to do with the lingering chill from the creek.

"I don't have to show you shit, Delacroix." Tony snarled, not backing down from the challenge, holding his ground. He was a couple inches shorter than Hunter, but a person wouldn't know it by the way Tony puffed himself up to meet Hunter nose to nose. Threatening.

Just fuck and get it over with already was what Eric wanted to say, but for some reason his filter was actually working at the moment, and he recognized that would be a very bad thing to let slip. Even if it would be a lot of fun. Instead, he shifted on the bed, groaning when it upset his bruised torso. Fuck. Vampires shouldn't be able to hit that hard under water, it had to be breaking some kind of law of physics. Bert would know. Or Hunter.

Hunter and Tony stopped their arguing to turn their eyes on Eric. Two different colors, the exact same fury. It would be sexy if Eric didn't feel like he'd been run down by a Buick.

"Oh, don't mind me," Eric said, pushing himself up against the headboard. The motion dragged against the cut on his back, threatening to tear it open again, but he ignored it. He also ignored the way an aura had settled over him in between the fight with Noah and waking up in Tony's bed.

In.

Tony's.

Bed.

Well, that didn't look good for him. But surely no one would be stupid enough to assume he was there because he wanted to be, when clearly it was because he'd gotten the tar beat out of him.

The room was a wash of strange rainbow outlines, like when a person stared at a light for too long then looked away, leaving an afterimage burned into their retinas. And there was a pressure building up behind Eric's eyes. It wouldn't be long now before he was saddled with another migraine. Because of course, *of course*, that would happen now that he was finally getting somewhere.

"Eric, hon," Hunter said, soft and soothing from where he'd appeared at the bedside, his hands hovering in the air above Eric's torso as if afraid to touch. "Tell me what happened."

Eric groaned, squeezing his eyes shut, hoping to will away the pressure and the halos, but all it did was make him see stars. He really needed to get his 'script filled if he was going to keep getting his ass handed to him by vampires. "In the morning. For now, take me home?"

"Yes, take him home. I've got a date in the morning, and I don't want my boyfriend showing up thinking I've—" Tony cut himself off, looking disgusted.

It raked over Eric's nerves, made him cringe away from the curl of Tony's lip, even though there was nowhere to go. The bed was under him, the headboard was behind him. He couldn't sink in to himself and hide away, even if it would make life easier.

Hunter shifted, uncomfortable, his ebony-brown fingers brushing too soft against the pink and bruised skin of Eric's ribs. He was lucky Noah hadn't busted one, really; it would have punctured a lung. Add that to the drowning, and Eric probably would have been a goner for real. "I probably shouldn't move—"

"Hun, let's just go." Eric shook his head and pushed himself away from the headboard. It hurt. It made stars dance in front of his eyes. But he wasn't going to stay where he wasn't wanted, not any longer. And he really didn't want to hear any more about the domesticity that was a breakfast date with Tony and Dash. It made his chest ache.

What the fuck was wrong with him? He should be over this by now. It had been two fucking months, and he and Tony had only been together for a couple of weeks. It wasn't anywhere near as long as he'd been with Kalla, and he'd moved on from her more quickly. Granted, he was younger then, and although the heart wasn't like a sore muscle, or a bone technically, it seemed that getting older made it heal slower. Like when he slept wrong and his neck ached for the entirety of the next day. Why should this be any different? Even if he hadn't thought his heart was involved.

Hunter watched him for a moment, dark eyes narrowed behind his glasses, reading Eric as easily as he did reports, and schematics, and ancient texts in languages Eric could never hope to understand. This could only be more embarrassing if fucking Ava were here to witness his humiliation too. *Fuck me.*

"All right," Hunter said after a long moment, and rose from where he'd been stooped by the bed to help Eric to his feet. Tony didn't do anything more than shuffle behind them, his hands clenching and unclenching—Eric could see them out of the corner of his eye when he looked back—as he followed them down the stairs and to the front door.

Eric looked over his shoulder for a moment, mouth open as if to say something. *Thank you* maybe. *I missed you. I'm sorry. Let me stay. Why didn't we work?* But none of those things seemed like a good idea, so he snapped his jaw shut with an audible *click* of teeth and let Hunter help him hobble out to the waiting truck.

Climbing up into the truck hurt like hell, even with Hunter holding gingerly on to his waist and taking some of his weight. But Eric wasn't going to let Tony see the pain register on his face from where he stood leaning against the door watching them. He'd shown enough weakness to someone who clearly hated him for one night, thank you.

They rode in silence until they cleared Tony's neighborhood, then—and only then—did Eric let himself fully relax back into his seat. Let himself close his eyes against the pain that had not just settled in his body but caught in his lungs like a stitch from running too hard.

"Are we going to talk about what happened back there?" Hunter asked. His gaze was heavy on the side of Eric's face, boring into him, trying to make him talk.

"No. We are not," Eric said, not even bothering to open his eyes. He didn't have it in him for a deep dive into how fucked up he was emotionally about Tony right now. He might not have that in him for a long while. They hit a bump, and the jerking of the car jarred the bruise on Eric's torso, making him wince. The perfect distraction. "I was supposed to meet Dash out there."

"Bert told me." Hunter's rings thudded hard against the steering wheel, a sure sign that he was agitated about something. But whatever it was, Eric didn't give him a chance to say it, because if he didn't have it in him to talk about the emotional issues he had with Tony, he sure as fuck didn't have it in him to withstand a heartfelt lecture from Hunter.

"There was no one on the dock at first," Eric started, then dove into the story at length. He paused once or twice to let Hunter posit a theory, but he didn't. Strange. Normally he would. But tonight, he was quiet. Deep in thought as he navigated the winding road from Ironport up to Moondale U campus in the mountains.

"So." Eric cleared his throat, shifting in his seat and drawing another wince. "What do you think?"

"I think you got real fucking lucky tonight, Eric. That's what I think." The words were angry, but the tone was tired. Like Hunter didn't have the fight left in him to get into another argument after he'd spent all his ire on Tony. Which was kind of a shame, really. Eric kind of liked that fire, missed it now that it was gone.

"Other than that." He sighed, turning to watch Hunter in the driver's seat, the streetlights illuminating his face in short bursts as they passed beneath them. His strong ebony-brown jaw was tight, working as if he were chewing on his words. Eyes fixed ahead. His fingers were wrapped tight around the steering wheel, hands placed at ten and two. Like the conscientious driver that he was. Because the only two things Hunter took seriously were driving and science. Science because it was his first great love. Driving because it was how he'd lost his mother.

"Other than that," Hunter repeated, the tone soft, like he hadn't meant for Eric to hear at all, like he was talking to himself. Eric didn't think he'd ever heard Hunter's voice so quiet before.

Fuck this weird night, he couldn't wait to get into bed and sleep it off. From the fight between Tony and Hunter—

"What were you and Tony arguing about before I came to?" Eric's eyes narrowed on Hunter, surveying his every movement, looking for some hint.

"Next question."

Eric huffed, poking his bottom lip out in a pout. "I hate that rule."

"And yet when you say it, I always let it go." Hunter shrugged. It had long been an understanding between them that when a topic came up they didn't want to talk about right that moment, all they needed to do was say "next question" and they could move on. "Unless you'd like to revisit the discussion of what happened between you and Tony back there?"

"No." Eric looked back toward the road, ignoring the way his chest tightened. He wanted to tell Hunter that nothing *had* happened between him and Tony back there, but he knew he couldn't without revealing too much of the heartache that sat heavy in his chest. No. He'd keep it to himself. Hopefully it would go away soon. Just like a bruise or a sore muscle. He rubbed at his chest where the ache sat, but it did nothing to alleviate the strange hollow feeling there.

He needed a distraction.

"So, about Noah." Eric turned to face Hunter again, ignoring the way it pulled on the butterfly bandages Tony had applied to keep his wound closed while he healed.

"What about him?" Hunter tapped his thumbs against the steering wheel.

"Do you think we could scry for him? I know he's not alive anymore, but . . ."

They pulled up outside of the dorm and Hunter put the truck in park before letting go of the wheel entirely to scrub at his face. He looked tired all of the sudden. Eric hadn't noticed it when he was driving, but now that Hunter wasn't solely focused on the road, Eric could see how his shoulders sagged, how he slumped in his seat. Goddess, Eric wanted to wrap Hunter up in a blanket and hide him away from all of this. From the blood and the teeth. All of them, really. None of his small family unit deserved this. They hadn't signed on for this war. They'd been drafted when they became best friends with an active Venator. It wasn't fair.

After a moment where it looked like Hunter was rubbing sleep from his eyes, he said, "We can try, but I'm not making any guarantees it'll work."

Eric reached over to take one of Hunter's hands, threading their fingers together and giving it a firm squeeze. "All I'm asking is that we try."

"All right." Hunter nodded. "But let's get inside before Ava and Kalla can't keep the kids in the house any longer. You know if they make it outside, they're only gonna get louder."

"Don't remind me." Eric groaned, turning to look at the six faces pressed to the window in the living room. They weren't even trying to be inconspicuous, and his head hurt already just thinking about the barrage of questions. "Why couldn't they just be asleep when we got back?"

"They were worried you died," Hunter reminded him, and Eric couldn't exactly complain anymore after that.

Chapter 13

THE MEMORY OF MARCELINO, soft and vulnerable, of his voice saying "I've missed you" like it was the truest thing in all the world, played on repeat in Tony's head all night. He couldn't have imagined that, right?

He didn't sleep. He tossed, and he turned. And he pressed his face into the pillow, some unconscious part of him wanting to see if he could pick up the smell of Marcelino's hair products on the fabric, a very conscious part wanting to scream into it. Marcelino left. He left. He made his choice. He could have stayed with Tony. He could have shown up sooner to that fucking house months ago when Tony had really needed him. But he'd left Tony there to be fed on, to be drugged. But—

The memories were distorted now. A hazy blur. He couldn't remember how long he'd been in the house anymore. Couldn't remember who had helped him to his feet. Tony tried to focus on it, tried to think through the distortion of time and vamp venom. It felt impossible. Every time he pushed, his ears rang, a sharp pain pounding in the skin just below his jaw. A burning like disinfectant in a vamp bite.

It didn't make any sense. And yet, Tony couldn't stop thinking about it, couldn't stop pushing. Where most people would have taken the pain as a sign to back off, to leave well enough alone, Tony McMahon had never been that sort. He had always been the sort to poke at a bruise, to ignore the pull of a broken bone, to pick at a scab. It was just the kind of person he was. He never knew when to leave things alone to heal. And he had revisited whatever he had been with Marcelino enough times that he was sure it would leave behind a lasting mark.

Good thing he liked scars.

And the more he picked at this partially healed wound, the more something didn't feel right. The more the memories came back in bits and pieces. There was something about Dash when they were in that house. Something feral, and terrifying—unlike when Marcelino was feral and sexy.

A conversation in the dark, the moon shining on . . . Fangs? No. That didn't make sense. That didn't—But it did. It made perfect sense. The bite marks. The lethargy. The way he couldn't really remember what had happened that night. It all made sense.

So when Dash's key turned in the lock at the front door, Tony was waiting for him, stake in hand.

The house was dark and silent around them as Dash slid off his shoes at the door and called a soft, "My darling, are you here?"

He didn't get past the entry way before Tony had him shoved up against the wall, the point of his stake pressed so hard into Dash's skin that on a human it would leave a red mark. It wasn't leaving any kind of mark behind on Dash's skin, red or otherwise. More confirmation of what Dash was.

"Came to your senses, I see." Dash smirked, the points of his fangs pressing into his lower lip. Tony didn't know how he'd missed them for so long when they were right there, staring him in the face. "Must be the Venator blood. Acts as an anti-venom. Helped you build up a tolerance. Fucking nuisance."

"Tell me why I shouldn't stake you right fucking now," Tony growled, pressing the point of the stake in harder against Dash's skin. It was beginning to poke through, creating a little hole that healed around the wood, making it easier and easier to push in. If he wanted, he could embed it entirely in Dash's neck, block his throat, make it difficult to swallow. It wouldn't kill him though. Only a stake through the heart would kill him. Didn't mean it wouldn't hurt.

"Because," Dash hissed. His eyes flashed blood red, presumably because of the pain. "You need me."

"I don't need you for shit, *leech*." The stake sunk deeper into Dash's neck, blood starting to drip, black and viscous, from one of the main arteries.

Dash hummed and tilted his head further back as if he could escape the press of Tony's stake into his skin. He couldn't. Well. Maybe he could, actually. He hadn't tried to fight Tony yet. Hadn't even so much as struggled. And yet, Tony got the feeling that Dash had the upper hand here. What was he missing?

His hand cramped, and he lost hold of the piece of wood. It slipped away to clatter to the ground, bouncing off his bare toes. What the fuck was that? Tony dropped his hand, shaking it out, trying to get his fingers to loosen back up, but they wouldn't. When he looked down at his hand to see what the fuck the problem was, he saw Dash's own hand clenched exactly the same way.

Dash was smiling, fangs on full display when Tony looked back to him. "Nifty little trick, huh? Consequence of the vampire blood in your system."

"I don't—I don't have any vampire blood in my system." But there was a memory, a hazy one, coming back into focus. Of his mouth open, tongue lapping at a wound on Dash's wrist in the dark. Of the taste of metal on his tongue, burning as it slid down his throat. His Venator body had tried to reject it, tried to make him throw it up, but Dash made sure he didn't. Kept him delirious and venom drunk long enough for it to sink into his blood stream.

"Not enough to turn you, no." Dash shook his head, pushing away from the wall and forcing Tony to take a step back. Away. Away. He needed to get the fuck away. Where a moment ago he'd been looming over Dash. Where a moment ago he'd had the upper hand. Dash leaned forward as if he might run his nose up the length of Tony's throat but stopped short. "But enough to control you."

"Control me." The words tasted like bile on his tongue, making his stomach lurch. How long? How long had this been going on? What else could Dash make him do? What else had Dash *already* made him do?

"Oh relax." Dash huffed, rolling his eyes like Tony was being some kind of dramatic teenager. It stung, but Tony couldn't source where that emotion was coming from. Was that him or was that the vampire blood in his veins talking? How much of what he'd felt for Dash over the last couple of months really belonged to him?

Oh. Fuck. Lu had been right. He *had* been high every time he came back from a date with Dash. High on blood and venom. He wasn't *happy*. He didn't like spending time with Dash. He was fucking drugged.

And that meant. . . that meant that when he'd thought he'd wanted to sleep with Dash he'd actually. . . fuck he was going to be sick.

"It's not like I can legitimately force you to do something you're vehemently against." Dash shrugged, heading further into the house. Like he belonged there. Like he'd been—like he'd been invited in. Fuck, Tony had invited him in. Dash had access to his home. *Lu's* home. Goddess, he was the worst guardian ever. "I can't make you kill Eric, if that's what you're worried about."

He wasn't worried about that before, but he sure as shit was now. "How can I believe anything you say?"

"What choice do you have?" Dash settled into one of the

chairs at the kitchen table, one leg crossing over the other, the picture of nonchalance. A king surveying his castle.

"You can't force me to hurt him, but you can do that yourself. You already have." Tony's nails bit into his palms where he'd curled his fingers into fists.

"What if I did? Why do you care? You broke that poor boy's heart."

Boy. How fucking old was this leech that Dash would refer to Eric as a boy? Fifty? A hundred? No. Older. Far older. He had too much control over his bloodlust to be that young. Too much control over the other vampires he had turned. But if that was the case, then how was Dash hiding out in Ironport? The place wasn't that big.

"No one fucks up Pretty Boy's face but me," Tony snarled.

Dash threw his head back and laughed, throat long and pale in the soft morning light. And Tony took his chance. He lunged forward with the spare stake he'd stored in his sweatpants pocket, using the momentum to—

To knock over the chair where Dash had been sitting a moment ago. Something sharp and cold pressed into Tony's throat, the bite enough to draw a hiss and a thin rivulet of blood. A kitchen knife, he confirmed with a glance to the knife block near the stove. "Ah, ah, ah. I wouldn't do that if I were you."

"Stake a leech?" Tony asked, baring his teeth. "Why not?"

"Because, my darling, like it or not, you and this leech are linked. If I die, so do you." Dash scraped the blunt side of the knife down the column of Tony's throat. "And it'd be a shame to waste all the work I've put into you, wouldn't it?"

"That's not true. There are no reports to suggest that killing a vampire would kill anyone in its thrall." But why would there be? The Huntsmen didn't give a flying fuck what happened to the vampires or the people they controlled—willingly or not. Their motto was the lives of the few for the survival of the many. And he remembered what he'd been taught about those under a thrall growing up. That they asked for it. That they wanted it. How much of what he'd learned was complete bullshit? All of it? And why had he never *questioned* it before now?

"Are you willing to test that, my darling? Leave Lu an orphan? Again? Leave your precious Eric and all his baby Venator unprotected?" The words came out a coo, but they sliced through Tony like a knife. Dash was right, he couldn't do that. Not to Lu, at the very least. Eric and the kids would probably be fine, but he couldn't do that to Lu. He'd promised her he wouldn't let her ever have to be alone again. Not after those few months in foster care.

"Then I'll just tell Eric what's going on. He and his little band of nerds can figure out a way around it." But even as he said it, he knew he wouldn't. Tony wasn't going to bring Eric and the kids into this. He couldn't. It would put them in Dash's sights too directly.

"You could, but I wouldn't suggest it."

"So what? I'm just supposed to stay with you? Let you use me as your fucking blood bag until you get bored of me and bleed me dry? And let you continue to do whatever the fuck you're up to in Ironport?" Not fucking likely. He'd find a way around this himself. Even if it meant having to off himself to do it. But that would be a last resort. It'd have to be.

"Yes, that does about sum it up, I think." Dash pressed the point of the knife into the soft skin beneath Tony's chin, making him tilt his head back further, giving Dash access to his throat. He felt the prick of his fangs, sharp and aching in his neck, this time.

"Don't put me under again," Tony all but begged. He needed to be in control of his mind. He needed to know what was going on. He couldn't—he couldn't bear not remembering everything that had happened between him and Eric again. "Don't put me under again, and I won't say anything. Don't hurt Eric and his brat pack, and I'll—I'll help you."

Dash hummed for a moment, the sound vibrating against Tony's throat. With a soft pop, lips left skin, and Dash whirled Tony around to face him, squinting blood-red eyes at Tony. "So you'd willingly help me? Do anything I asked? In exchange for this?"

"If you don't put me under again. If you don't hurt Eric or the baby Venator," Tony clarified. "If you do that, you can keep using my blood for whatever, and I won't tell anyone what's going on."

Time. He just needed to buy himself some time. To look into Dash's claims. To see if there was a way around all of this. There had to be. There *had* to be a way to counteract the vampire blood. All the magic in the fucking world? No way there wasn't a way to save his own skin and kill Dashfield fucking Chadwick.

Dash eyed him for a long moment, considering his options. Tony knew he didn't have the vampire fooled. Dash was cocky. Arrogant. A prick. But he wasn't stupid. He had to know Tony was up to something. And Tony wasn't stupid either. Whatever Dash said, he wouldn't hold off for long. This wouldn't buy Tony a lot of time, but it would buy him a couple of weeks. Hopefully enough that he could reach out to his contacts in Miami and do some of his own research.

"I don't trust you," Dash said, finally.

"I don't trust you either."

Dash barked a laugh, then he held out a hand for Tony to shake. "You've got yourself a deal, Tony McMahon. Truce."

"Truce," Tony agreed, shaking the cold dead hand of the cold dead fucker he was going to kill if it was the last thing he did.

CHAPTER 14

TAP. *Tap. Tap.*

Scrying for Noah was a bad fucking idea, Hunter was sure of it. So he was almost relieved when their efforts turned up nothing.

What good would come of hunting down Eric's best friend from high school who had been turned? All it would do was break Eric's heart. Maybe kill what was left of his spirit. Turn him into a zombie no better than the vampire Noah had become. No. It was better Eric didn't face that particular hurdle. Was taking the choice away from Eric fair to him? No. Maybe not. But Hunter didn't have a better plan at the current time.

Even if finding Noah was out of the question, finding the vampires and their nest was a must. A must Hunter couldn't actually *do* at this point. Because the Ghost Tracer wasn't picking them up again. Like they'd cloaked themselves. Or they weren't feeding off humans, thereby not creating negative energy. Maybe they'd decided to stick with the juice box method for a little while. Or maybe they weren't bringing their meals home anymore. Something.

Hence the *tap tap tap* of his rings on the steering wheel, and the low hum of old-school rock rattling around in his head. It was supposed to help Hunter relax. Supposed to calm his nervous energy. It wasn't doing either of those things. At this point, Hunter was beginning to wonder if anything actually *would*.

He didn't remember the drive to Moondale being this fucking long before. A half hour from the dorm, tops, depending on weather and traffic. But it seemed like so much longer than that when he knew what he was going for. Knew how the person he was going to see could turn him away.

Icarus Ashthorne was the genius behind the Ghost Tracer. A modern marvel. And if Hunter said he wasn't anxious about meeting a woman who put even his mind to shame, he'd be lying. It wasn't that he didn't think he could hold his own in conversation—he knew he could. But . . . Well, Hunter had never met a witch powerful enough to merge tech and magic that way. He was a little starstruck, to be perfectly frank. Which is why he was going alone, thanks Ava. He didn't need to be teased relentlessly for the next decade.

He was still fidgeting as he walked up the path to 157 Mourning Moore. Tugging at his shirt collar. Stuffing his hands into his pockets. Pulling them out again. Twisting the silver thumb ring around his finger. Futzing with his hair. How many little movements could he make before he reached the front door? Fuck.

The knock was too pointed, too sharp, but by that point Hunter had already done it. How did one knock on the door to the house of someone who was essentially their idol? Probably softer, less intrusively. He was fucking this up already.

A screech came from inside the house, then the door swung open to reveal a little girl. Her curly hair was up in two pigtails, resting on the crown of her head like puppy ears, and she was wearing a neon-green tulle skirt.

"Umm . . . Hi." Goddess, Hunter was shit with kids. How had he managed to endear himself to Chase when he was little? "Is your mom home?"

"Huaner!" a woman shouted from inside the house and poked her head around the corner. She had light-brown skin and a head of bright pink hair. "What have we said about answering the door?"

Huaner didn't look the least bit guilty; she just smiled toothily up at Hunter. "I didn't do it. The house did."

"Were you expecting someone?" another woman's voice asked, this one a little smoother, less gravelly than the first.

"I wasn't—Fu . . . dge. Yes, the kid from Ironport," the first voice responded.

"Does that mean I can come in?" Hunter asked Huaner at the same time the gravelly voice shouted, "Huaner, let him in!"

Huaner giggled and turned away from him, leaving the door open as she trotted back down the hall.

"Sorry. I kind of forgot I had a meeting scheduled today with everything else going on," the woman with the pink hair —Icarus Ashthorne, this must be Icarus Ashthorne—said as she came more into view. She was wearing a worn pair of black sweatpants and an oversized pale-blue sweater that looked like it might have been cashmere and expensive as hell. The outfit was mismatched, but as the other woman came into view, Hunter thought he understood why. The other woman had dark skin with plum-colored hair. She was wearing a pair of jeans and a sweater of the same material as Icarus's, but in a soft purple that seemed to fit her better than the one Icarus was wearing.

"I'll make some tea," the dark-skinned woman said, squeezing the first's shoulder as she passed.

"Thanks, Az," Icarus murmured back, her gray eyes following Az as she drifted down the hall. "What did you say your name was again?"

"Hunter. And that's fine, I'd forget about me too." Hunter frowned at himself. "If, you know . . . I wasn't . . . me?"

What the fuck was wrong with him? Why the fuck did he say that?! What a weird-ass thing to say to someone! Especially someone he was trying to impress. Well, that was probably half the problem. He was trying to impress her, and thus his brain-to-mouth filter had decided now was the perfect time to go on hiatus. Of course.

Icarus squinted at him for a moment, the corner of her mouth twitching a little. Then she said, "Follow me" and led him through the living room into a room that must have been her office. A large dark wood desk sat at the center, covered in so many papers that Hunter could hardly see the surface. How did she find anything? And the bookshelves that lined the walls—in the same black-stained wood—were stuffed so full, Hunter was amazed the books hadn't staged a revolt and headed for the floor.

"Miss Ashthorne," Hunter said, drawing his attention from the messy room long enough to take a seat in one of the plush emerald-green velvet chairs.

"Rus. Please." Icarus laughed a little, dropping down into the chair opposite him and curling one leg up into it with her. "I'm probably going to be changing my name any minute now, if Az has anything to say about it anyway," she murmured, as if she were speaking to herself, then released another soft laugh.

"What?"

"Nothing." Icarus shook her head, but as Az set down two mugs of something hot on the desk, he thought he saw a decidedly smug tilt to her lips. Rus's eyes tracked her every move, from the desk back across the room.

"I'll be in the kitchen getting dinner ready for the girls," Az said, her voice soft. Then she shut the door behind her, and Rus returned her full attention to Hunter. And wow, okay. If he'd thought it was unnerving having half of Rus's attention, it was absolutely terrifying once her gray eyes had settled on him entirely.

"You're not a kid" was the first thing Rus said once the door was closed. She narrowed her gray eyes to examine him more closely as if she could see down to the heart of him with just one glance. Maybe she could. Or maybe she was looking at his aura to get a read on him. Should he have done a cleansing ritual before he came? Should he have smoked? His aura was probably all fucked up from his anxiety. Damn it.

"I'm not," Hunter agreed.

"I was expecting someone younger. Given you said you were from Moondale U." Rus leaned forward on her elbows, pressing her face in closer to Hunter, her pale eyes going even more intense. How that was possible, he had no fucking idea. Goddess, maybe he *should* have brought Ava after all. She'd at least have taken some of the attention off him. Plus, she was much better at bullshitting her way into people's good graces than he was. Whereas when Hunter found himself on the spot as he currently was, he kind of froze up.

"I work there as a researcher." Why did he sound so stiff?

"That makes more sense," Rus said, nodding to herself. Her eyes fell to something on her desk, as if maybe she needed to remind herself what he was there to discuss. "Right. So"—she shifted in her chair, making it creak under her weight—"in answer to your question about the Ghost Tracer. Yes. I can alter the source code so it tracks vampires."

"Great! So—"

"But I'm not going to."

"What?" Hunter frowned. "What do you mean, you're not going to?"

"At least not on a wide scale." Rus sighed, running a hand through her short pink hair, getting her fingers caught in a couple of tangles before she pried them away to fiddle with the papers on her desk. "I'll do this for you," she said, tone carefully measured, like she was building up to something, "because I know Ironport has a vampire problem."

"But?" Because there was one-hundred percent a but in there somewhere. He just hoped it wasn't something ridiculous. Like she wasn't going to let him walk away with the app.

"But, like I said, I'm not offering it on a wide scale. This will only be accessible to your device, no others. It'll only work in Ironport. And I will monitor how it's used. I know the vampires in Ironport are causing a problem, but that's not the case all over the world. Vampires, usually in the wider world, don't. Yes, there are outliers, but that's the same with any species." Rus shrugged. "There are some really shitty witches too. Some of them even live in Moondale."

Hunter's frown ticked down further, making his glasses slide down his nose. He lifted a hand to push them back up. "I don't think I'm understanding what you're saying?"

Rus let out another long sigh and leaned back in her chair, her hands folded over her stomach. "I'm saying, most vampires don't kill, at least not in other countries. It's only really in the US that we have the kind of problem we're seeing in Ironport."

"That doesn't—" He swallowed, his fingers fiddling with the zipper on his jacket. He hadn't been raised in a Huntsmen family like Eric, Kalla, and even Ava had, but he'd read enough about their lore, their history to know that's not what the potential Venator were told. "No. They always kill. They never leave victims alive. The Huntsmen archives say so."

"I know that's what the stories say, but it's just not true. I knew a couple vamps in Ireland who actually had really healthy relationships with the hamlets where they lived. They were staples of their community. And there was a hive in Japan that hadn't had human blood in a century. They subsisted on wildlife, keeping the populations managed so they wouldn't kill the local vegetation."

Rus sounded like she knew what she was talking about, and who was Hunter to argue? He'd never been outside of the US. And even if he had, he wouldn't have searched out local vampires to see what they were up to. That wasn't something the Huntsmen community actively encouraged. In fact, as far as he knew, the Venator had orders to slay on sight.

"I can provide you with contacts, if you want them. Or even case studies some of my friends did," Rus offered. "I know this is kind of jarring, given how Ironport is, but—"

"Why would they do what they do here? Why would they kill people here? If they can live peacefully alongside humans in other places, why aren't they doing that *here*?" He was sinking, and not just because he was sliding down in the chair, his jeans leaving behind a path where they rubbed the velvet the opposite direction of all the other fibers. But also because it didn't make sense. Nothing about this made sense. If other vampires could act that way, why didn't the ones in Ironport? Why was Eric railing consistently against a tide of bloodthirsty leeches with no regard for life? Hunter could only imagine how much easier Eric's life would be if the majority of the vampires he came across left people alone and went about their lives.

"My best guess?" Rus asked. She had pulled her gaze away from Hunter so she could dig around in one of the drawers on the front of the desk. He didn't know if it was out of courtesy as he drowned in a sea of uncertainty, or if she was genuinely looking for something, and he didn't care. His hands already itched for his phone, to call Eric and Ava. To tell them what he'd found out. Would they believe him? And what would they do even if they did? Eric was under orders. He'd always been under orders. He'd always *be* under orders. He'd spend the rest of his life—which would probably be short if the Huntsmen had anything to say about it—hunting, and fighting, and killing. And then, one day, probably not too far from now, dying.

Hunter wanted to cry. His eyes burned with it. Goddess, he just wanted to go home and curl up with Eric. Let Eric soothe all of this away. Forget about it.

"Either the vamp leaders in America are just"—she paused, glancing up and over Hunter's shoulder as if to check that both doors to the office were shut—"dicks, or they don't have the same hierarchy that some other places have."

Hunter nodded, because he didn't know what to say to that. What could he say? He knew fuck all about vampire hierarchy, least of all what kind of system was in place in his own fucking city.

"Look," Rus said, finally returning her gaze to him, "I'm not saying this to freak you out."

A soft snort left Hunter of its own volition.

"I'm really not. But I want you to be aware of my reasoning for not letting someone go hog wild with this kind of thing. Vampires are just like every other species of folk, they're a mix of good and bad. They shouldn't be hunted to extinction just because of a couple of assholes. No matter what the Huntsmen seem to think."

"Okay." Hunter breathed out a long exhale, his shoulders dropping from where they'd inched up toward his ears without him noticing. "Okay."

"So I'm going to give you access to the data I've got about the vamps in Ironport, but you are not to share it with any of the Huntsmen. I had actually figured out how to track them months ago but wasn't looking to let anyone know. It's really about looking for the absence of life." Rus held out her hand, as if she wanted him to hand her something. "Unlife, as it were."

"Why?" Hunter had his phone out, but he still had to know.

"Because vampires tend to leech the energy out of the surrounding area. They act like miniature black holes. That's why so many people report—"

"No. Not that. I know that." Hunter waved her off. "I want to know why you're trusting me with this. Since it's clear you don't think it's a good idea."

"Oh." Rus stopped, a smile ticking up the corners of her

lips as her wrist flopped onto the desk with a *thunk*. "I've got a good feeling about you." She shrugged.

"And besides, like I said, I'm going to be monitoring the situation, and if you don't heed my instructions . . ." Her face fell and magic floated around the hand still extended in his direction. It was neon green and drifting like smoke, only faster, more pointed. With it came voices, whispers, moans, screams. And Hunter remembered, suddenly, that Icarus Ashthorne was a necromancer. Okay. Yeah. Fuck. He didn't want to cross a fucking necromancer. "There will be consequences. Have I made myself clear?"

"Yup. Super clear. Clear as clear can be," Hunter hurried to agree.

"Fantastic. Now give me your phone."

CHAPTER 15

SOMETHING A PERSON IS able to learn about their best-friend-turned-crush-turned-fuck-buddy-turned-best-friend-again-turned-roommate only by living with them: Eric Marcelino was afraid of spiders. And Hunter found it more adorable and endearing than he had any right to. Seriously, it wasn't good for the burgeoning resurgence of his early-twenties crush, and his poor, delicate heart.

He found this out by returning to the house after spending a few hours in Moondale going over the changes to the Ghost Tracer with Rus and her partner Az, to find Eric standing in the middle of the kitchen. All the lights were off. And he had a slipper held above his head like he was going to bludgeon someone with it.

"What're—"

"Sh!" Eric didn't so much as take his eyes off the floor to see who had come in, he just held a hand up to Hunter in a silent order not to move.

Hunter stilled, his pierced eyebrow raising in question. "Seriously, hon—"

"Sh!" Eric turned his head just enough to glare at Hunter out of the corners of his eyes, keeping most of his focus on the floor. "Where did you go, you little fucker?"

"What little—"

"SH!"

A spider crawled out from under the fridge a second later, breaking into an eight-legged run right for Eric. Who promptly screeched like a pterodactyl and jumped high enough in the air that he ended up on the island in the middle of the kitchen. The slipper he'd been brandishing like a weapon went flying, slapping against the kitchen table before it fell to the floor.

"Get it! Get it! Get it!" Eric screeched, pulling his legs up onto the counter with him as if the spider would reach out and grab them.

The spider—for its part in this whole melodrama—had disappeared again. Probably scurried into the living room to hide under the couch or something.

Hunter looked from Eric to the floor, then back to Eric, trying, and failing, to swallow down a laugh as he said, "It's gone."

"It's gone?! What do you mean it's gone?!" Eric leaned over the edge of the counter to look for the spider, his hands white-knuckled to keep him from falling off.

"I mean it's gone. It probably went to hide somewhere." Hunter moved carefully across the kitchen, holding his hands out to Eric. "Why don't you come down from there, and we'll talk about what I learned in Moondale?"

Eric blinked at him for a moment as if he didn't realize he was standing on the fucking counter like a girl who'd had too much Smirnoff. Then he seemed to realize and scrambled down, neck lightly flushed in his embarrassment. "Do you know what time it is?"

"It's not something that can really wait." Mostly because Hunter wasn't sure he could keep it inside of himself for much longer. He was excited, nervous, and anxious, all of it sitting like a ball of knotted yarn in his stomach, twisting, and turning, and forming more of a gnarled mess every second that ticked by.

With his feet on the ground again, Eric looked a little less crazed. He ran his fingers through his hair, as if trying to put it to rights, but all that did was make it significantly more tousled. It was a good look for him. It made Hunter want to drag him up to his bedroom and see how much more mussed he could make Eric. He shook the thought aside.

"It's, like, really late," Eric huffed, his arms crossed over his chest, defensive. As if he were trying to hide the fact that one itty bitty spider had just turned him into some kind of Victorian damsel.

Hunter glanced over at the clock on the microwave and sighed. He wanted Ava in on this anyway; she'd be the voice of reason they needed, no doubt. If it were left to him and Eric, he was sure they'd get into a fight over this. Or they'd both agree, and that might be worse. "It could *maybe* wait till tomorrow's project night."

"Good." Fluffy brown hair fell into Eric's eyes as he nodded. "Then"—he turned and headed for the stairs, his hips swaying a little, as if nothing at all had happened—"good night."

"Good night." But Hunter couldn't keep himself from watching Eric go. From smiling like a fucking idiot. Because . . . well, because Eric was an adorable dichotomy of a man. Strong, brave, and powerful in the face of vampires and monsters. But terrified of a spider and willing to show that fear to Hunter. Willing to let himself be vulnerable in front of someone else. It was . . . distracting, to say the least.

Hunter waited until he heard Eric's bedroom door creak closed, then he moved to squat in the middle of the living room so he could peer beneath the couch. He laced a bit of magic into his words when he called, "All right, come out, my furry little darling."

The spider peeked out from beneath the couch, tapping one of their front legs nervously. They weren't much bigger than a half dollar, certainly not large enough to warrant Eric's reaction. After a moment of Hunter *not* screaming at them, they seemed to decide it was safe to come out, and Hunter got a better look at them. A wolf spider. Not very old, if he were to guess.

"Hi there, little buddy," Hunter cooed softly, holding a hand out to them. "Sorry for all the shouting earlier. Ricky's not so bad really, he just has a bit of a fear of spiders. We're gonna have to work on that." He hummed approvingly as they crawled cautiously up onto his hand, coaxed along by a bit of magic to soothe them and keep them from biting. "In the meantime, let's get you back outside so he doesn't come for you with the slipper again, hmm?"

They tapped lightly on the meat of his palm in approval, and Hunter rose slowly from his crouch to head for the door. Once they were safely tucked away in one of the bushes, Hunter returned to the house, collected Eric's wayward slipper, and went up to bed himself.

Eric was finally making some real progress on the scarf he had started months ago. You know, now that the weather was turning warmer, because of course. But he wasn't going to let that stop him, because he needed to keep his hands busy or he was going to fucking throttle Hunter. Seriously.

"So what you're telling me," Eric said, the tension of the yarn in his hand way too tight. He was going to have to frog this row and start over. If he didn't, it would wind up looking like it was a stitch or two short. "That Ashthorne told us not to use the Ghost Tracer to hunt vampires."

"That's not what I said." Hunter sounded tired. His many rings glinted in the soft light of Ava's shop as he rubbed at the bridge of his nose, knocking his glasses out of his way with his knuckles. "At least, not exactly."

"What she said was, she's going to make sure we don't cause an extinction event using her tech," Ava piped up. Her own crochet project looked way better than Eric's. It was an afghan in creamy pastels, with intricate weave work on it. It looked more like a highland sweater than an afghan, and he wasn't sure how she'd done it. She kept promising to teach him how to use the long crochet hook with the bit of wire connected to it, but he needed to master plain old crochet first, he supposed.

"Fine. Then we can still use it to track down Noah?" Eric didn't know why he was obsessed with finding Noah and getting answers. Maybe because he still wasn't over seeing Noah leaning over him, venom dripping from his fangs as he hissed in Eric's face while Eric bled out on the sidewalk a couple months back. Or maybe because there was still a foolish part of Eric that missed his best friend. He knew it wasn't very *grown up* of him to miss people who'd cut him out of their lives. To look back on the Facebook memories from years and years ago and wonder what had happened. Where it had all gone wrong. Had he changed too much, or not enough?

"I don't think you can pin it down to follow one specific source," Hunter said, but the chair creaked under him, and when Eric looked up at him, he found Hunter staring intently down at the amigurumi spider pattern he said he wanted to make. It was actually kind of cute, which was weird considering how Eric felt about spiders.

"Have you tried?" Eric was sure if Hunter couldn't track down Noah, then one of the kids definitely could. Probably Bert. In fact, if Hunter refused to try, that would be his next stop. He should probably feel guilty about that, but it was hard to focus on the way the feeling crawled down his spine when his stomach hadn't stopped turning since Hunter told him about the vampires in other parts of the world. Something was off in his town, and he was going to find out what it was. Damn the consequences. Even if those consequences were Hunter not speaking to him ever again.

"Eric."

"Hunter."

Hunter sighed, brushing an errant curl from his face as he leaned his head back to stare at the vaulted ceiling of Ava's tiny shop. He looked tired. Like he hadn't slept at all last night. Or like the information he'd gotten from Ashthorne was wearing on him. Eric had to admit, it was distressing, knowing that maybe vampires weren't everything he'd thought they were.

It made sense that with the Huntsmen controlling the narrative, they would make the vampires out to be worse than they were. Dehumanize them. And hadn't Eric always seen the things he had in common with vamps? His enhanced senses. His easy charm. His strength. He saw so much of himself—and his Venator abilities—in vampires that it was hard sometimes to remember that they were killers. But then . . . according to Ashthorne, they weren't *all* killers. That just made this harder.

"If you two are going to fight, take it outside," Ava said when they had been quiet and staring at one another for too long. Which was entirely fair. Even if Eric and Hunter had never fought before, Eric could see how Ava wouldn't want that in her space. The negativity would probably fuck up her wards.

"We're not going to fight." Eric shook his head, looking back down at his scarf. They weren't going to fight because Eric was going to have one of the kids do what he wanted instead of trying to get Hunter to budge on this. Stubborn bastard.

"I don't like it," Bert said, but his fingers flew over the keyboard anyway, already making the changes Eric had requested. "What am I looking for again?"

"Go back to the night on the docks and see if you can find Noah's energy signature. Ashthorne said it should be like a little black hole. The absence of energy. Then follow it, if you can." Hunter was probably going to kill Eric for this. But he needed to find Noah. He needed answers. And Bert was the easiest to talk into doing something he knew he shouldn't. The hero worship helped, but Eric was also pretty sure Bert was the kind of kid who would do something he knew he shouldn't in the name of science alone. Like fucking Frankenstein or something.

"I don't like going against Hunter's recommendations," Bert repeated, like he thought maybe Eric hadn't heard him the first ten times. Eric had. He was just ignoring it because that was easier than dealing with the guilt that tingled at the base of his spine, threatening to bow his posture further until he curled up under the weight of it. Fuck. If this all went bad, Hunter was never going to let him live it down.

"We need answers, and I know I can get Noah to talk." He knew Noah. Had known Noah since they were in middle school. He could get answers from him. Maybe even a name.

"It's gonna take me a bit to do this." Bert was still typing furiously, hadn't taken his eyes away from the screen. "And if you tell Hunter that I skimmed the data off his phone to do it, I'm gonna kill you in your sleep."

Eric barked a laugh.

Bert looked away from the screen long enough to say, "I'm serious" before he returned to what he was working on. "I'll get you location data in a few days. Till then, keep your fucking mouth shut."

With a nod, Eric jammed his fingers through his hair and turned on his heel to leave Bert's messy room. Because Bert worked better when he didn't have people hovering over him. And because Eric had other shit to do, like get things set up for the kids' finals next week. Goddess, how had the semester gone by so fast?

CHAPTER 16

THE TEXT MESSAGE was from Tony's contact in Miami. Sage was a distinctly grumpy little fuck. They hated everyone and everything. They were half cryptid, half crotchety old biddy, all asshole. If Tony missed anyone from Miami, it was Sage. Even though they'd never been the type to go out drinking and partying like all Tony's other friends. Even though they mostly communicated through snarky text messages and memes. On the rare occasion Sage did deign to come out of their hidey hole—which Tony still didn't have the address to, because Sage was neurotic like that—they were always a lot of fun to be around. And they'd been there for Tony when he needed someone during his transition. Been there to pick him up from the hospital after his top surgery and help out with Lu while he was recovering. Sage was just . . . the best friend Tony had ever had.

Tony huffed, pressing his forehead into the punching bag he'd been wailing on for the last hour or so, leaving behind a sweaty smear. This was not a conversation he wanted to have via text, not really. And besides, Sage hadn't been answering for the last fucking week. They'd fallen off the face of the fucking earth again, like they did periodically, and been unreachable.

So he pulled up their contact and hit call again. Sage hit deny; he could tell because it rolled right over to voicemail. "Sage, you piece of shit. Pick up."

> Stop CALLING ME!

Tony hit call again. Sage hit deny again.

> I said stop it!

Tony growled, his hand tightening around the phone until the plastic case he had it in dug into his palm. The pain didn't ground him like it normally might have. Probably because he'd been stewing in his own anxiety for the last few days, and Sage was his only lifeline. Sage, who wasn't picking up their Goddess-damned phone, that absolute fucker.

Inhaling deeply, Tony forced himself to chill the fuck out, because breaking his phone was not going to help this situation. Then he texted back.

> I don't want to have this on written record.

> UGH! Fine!

The phone in his hand vibrated, Sage's contact image popping up on the screen. It was a piece of art Tony had done for Sage at one point, a watercolor painting of them in profile. It didn't even really look like them, but Sage had loved it and had used it for every avatar or profile picture since.

"If you'd answered my fucking texts *three days* ago," Tony

grumbled into the phone as he lifted it to his ear, "we wouldn't be doing this now."

"You'd have still wanted a phone call, you neophyte," Sage returned, blandly. There was no venom lacing their tone, no hint of annoyance, but that didn't really mean anything. They could have been distracted, or tired, or . . . literally any emotion was enough to make their tone go flat sometimes. "So what is it that was soooo important, it couldn't wait till I was done this coding project for—"

"What do you know about vamp blood?" It was better to get to the point right away with Sage, or they'd spend the next hour or two talking about whatever their latest project was, and Tony would never get his answer. Not because Sage didn't want to give it, but because they'd get off track. Which wouldn't be entirely Sage's fault—Tony had a thing about listening to people talk about something they loved that extended beyond people he wanted to sleep with. It was kind of nice to hear someone get animated over something. To know there were people out in the world who could feel that deeply about anything at all when sometimes he struggled to care about even getting out of bed in the mornings.

"Bury the lede much?"

"I didn't bury it! I started with it!" Tony pinched the bridge of his nose and went to sit on the floor, not wanting to get his sweat all over the chair Lu used to read when she was down there keeping him company.

"Mm-hmm." The tapping Tony heard in the background when he'd first picked up had stopped, meaning Sage was giving him their full attention. Tony shifted a little. "So what do you want to know?"

"Whatever you've got."

"Are you going to tell me why you're asking?"

"I'd really rather not." Because if Tony knew Sage, and he did—he was probably the only person who did—they would be on the first flight to Maryland if they knew what was going on with him. Tony could see them getting stopped by security now as they tried to board a plane with enough stakes and silver weaponry to equip all of Eric's little Venator class.

"Tony, Tony, Tony." Sage clicked their tongue in disapproval, and Tony imagined them shaking their head, the long floppy hair on top—dyed in a riot of colors last Tony had seen them, though it was probably different now—falling into their face to obscure their eyes. "You know I don't give information like that out for free."

"It's not for free. I put up with your weird ass."

"Yes, because insulting me is one-hundred percent the way to get you what you want."

"Sage, I don't have the time nor the fucking energy to deal with this shit today. Just tell me what you know about vamp blood."

"Well, if it's the *fucking* energy," Sage murmured, their fingers going back to typing on their keyboard, the *click-clack* near deafening. Tony wondered, not for the first time, how the fuck he'd ended up being friends with Sage. Especially when they didn't leave their house but once a month.

"Fuck you, just answer the question."

There must have been something desperate in his voice because, Sage sighed, and all sounds on the other end of the phone stopped as they fell into an unnatural stillness. The kind no normie could replicate. Tony had never gotten a clear answer on what type of folk Sage was exactly, but he knew damn well they weren't human. And that wasn't just because of the pointed ears. "Are you in trouble, Tony?"

Tony shifted, his tailbone digging into the hard cement of the basement floor. Sage couldn't see him, but he felt like their eyes were on him. Boring into him. Looking for answers. It was exactly how they'd looked at him the last time his father had gotten piss drunk and beaten the shit out of him. It was exactly the same tone of voice Sage had used when they planned how to get rid of Declan Brenner together, like two of the Chicks figuring out how to get rid of Earl.

"Tony," Sage repeated, their words measured, "are you in trouble?"

"I—I might be." Tony had never been able to lie to Sage. It was a part of their magic, probably some fae shit, that drew the truth out of him. Or maybe it was because their friendship had formed under duress, trial by fire. Either way, he'd always found it impossible to not tell Sage the Goddess's honest truth when they asked like that.

Sage swore, their words in a language Tony didn't recognize, but he knew what Sage sounded like when they were cursing a blue streak. This one was indigo. When they were done, they released a long slow breath that whistled on the way out. "Okay. Okay. Tell me everything, and we'll come up with a solution."

"Can't you just answer my question?" Tony asked weakly, it was exhausting bearing the weight of Sage's concern.

"Fine," they sniped. "Vamp blood has the power to turn anyone, even folk, even Venator, into a vampire, if enough of it is ingested in quick succession. Is that what you want to hear?" Sage's calm had evaporated, anger replacing it. Fear. They were afraid on Tony's behalf. He had enough good sense to be grateful for that, to be grateful someone gave a fuck about him enough to be afraid for him.

"And if it's not enough?" He didn't think he was turning. He didn't feel any different from how he had before Dash had started feeding him his blood. Maybe he was a little crankier, a little groggier, but that could have been caused by any number of things. The move. His sleep schedule—or lack thereof. The weather. It didn't have to be about the blood.

"If not, then you're under the vamp's thrall. At least until the blood burns off." Sage was giving him the facts. The bare bones. And Tony appreciated it. They were one person he knew he could always count on to give it to him straight, even if it would incite his temper.

"How long does that typically take?" *Please say not long.* Tony didn't know how much longer he could handle being under Dash's thumb like this. Then there was the matter of the deal he'd made. Of how he knew Dash wouldn't keep it for long. Because he was a vampire, and vampires couldn't be trusted. Leeches would always want to suck blood, no matter what they'd promised someone.

"That depends."

"On?"

"A number of things. The vampire's age. How much you were given. Your body weight. How much you'd eaten at the time." Sage sighed, their chair creaking under their weight. "If you could give me more information on this vampire and what happened, I could get you a better time frame."

Exhaustion clung to Tony's shoulders, making them sag lower. He needed answers. He needed a plan. He needed a way out. And Sage would be the one to give it to him—they'd been there to help before. But even as Tony opened his mouth to give Sage the answers they needed, to tell them the truth, the words got lodged in the back of his throat. Stuck there like a wad of under-chewed food. He coughed. Choked. Tried to force the words past his teeth. But they wouldn't budge.

After a moment of this, Sage hissed softly into the phone, "He's got your tongue tied up, hasn't he?"

Tony grunted a soft noise of affirmation because that's all he could get out. He leaned back against the wall, trying to breathe around the lump in his throat. When it finally died away, he swallowed down a mouthful of spit and regret. "So, an estimate?"

"Fucking bastard," Sage muttered to themself. "Has he done anything else?"

Tears pricked the corners of Tony's eyes at the memory of Dash's hands on him, his skin crawled. He needed to shower.

To scrub away the memories. A sound escaped him, a strangled whine.

Sage growled. "Let me meet this leech alone in an alley at a reasonable hour and I'll—"

"Sage." Tony pled, because he needed answers. He couldn't focus on what had happened to him, not right now, not until he had a way out.

Sage exhaled again, a long breath that made the speaker crackle in Tony's ear. "Anywhere from a couple of weeks to a few months."

"A few months?!" Tony shouted, his hand tightening around the phone again. "I can't wait that long, Sage. Not with—" The words lodged in his throat again, getting stuck there. His eyes burned, the corners dripping tears down his cheeks as he fought to breathe past the feeling of whatever hold Dash had on him, even now, even with him miles away. That bloodsucking motherfucker. Tony was going to kill him the moment he was able. Once he could breathe again, Tony asked, "Is there no other way to get it out of my system?"

"Well . . ." Sage sniffed, their fingers tapping against something that wasn't their keyboard—probably the desk or the arms of their chair, which creaked again as they shifted uncomfortably. "You could always try becoming a werewolf?"

"Excuse me?" Give up being a Venator. Trade the life he'd always known, the person he'd always been, for someone else. Change *again*.

"The werewolf venom would counteract the vampire blood," Sage said reasonably. But Tony could imagine them sitting at their desk, playing with the tips of their fingers, tapping their manicured nails against each other. "Honestly, it might not even take. It's not like Venator are bitten by werewolves frequently."

"What're the odds?" Tony chewed on the inside of his

cheek, wearing at a scar that cut a slash across the slick skin. Was this a chance he was willing to take?

"I wasn't serious, Tony." Sage sighed heavily, and when they spoke again there was a note of warning in their tone. "I have no way of knowing what your Venator blood would do with werewolf venom in it. Would you turn? Would it reject the venom like a body might a bone marrow transplant? How could having three different folk bloodlines in your veins hurt you? It could mess you up, like a lot, Tony. Don't—don't take it seriously."

"Right. Right. I'm not." But he was. Maybe it wasn't his main plan. But as a backup? As an escape hatch should he need it? Well, Tony had never gotten anywhere by being afraid to take a leap. "But if I were to try it . . ."

"I don't know," Sage said honestly. "There is no history of Venator blood mixing with any other folk, aside from the occasion when a vamp gets close enough to put a Venator under their thrall."

"So there's never been a Venator turned by a vampire?" That was interesting. Did that mean it was impossible? That thought made the ball of anxiety twisted up tight in Tony's belly unknot just a bit. If it were—

"Not that I know of. But that doesn't mean it's impossible, vampires have been able to turn almost every other type of folk. You should still not ingest any more of this vampire's blood, and not just because it gives them control over you." Sage sighed again. "Tony, I don't want you to become a case study."

"Don't worry. I won't."

"And yet, here we are." Tony could imagine Sage pinching the bridge of their nose, their eyes squeezed shut as they tried to keep from losing their shit on him. It wouldn't be the first time. It wouldn't be the last either. "Seriously. All you need to do is say the word, and I'll get on a plane."

"I know." Tony couldn't help the smile that tugged up the

corners of his lips at that. Sage might be perpetually absent. They might leave him on read for weeks at a time while they worked on a project. But when he needed them, when it felt like his life was going to shit, they were there. "I've got this covered."

"Yeah. That's what I'm afraid of."

CHAPTER 17

THE WRITTEN WAS the easy part of the final exam for Eric's baby Venator class—and they'd, predictably, passed with flying colors. Even the newbies, to his delighted surprise. But the physical obstacle course . . . Eric hadn't ever had a student pass it before. Not all of them had been as disastrous as Bert at the previous final, setting the course on fire in his clumsiness, but none of them had ever gotten above a D either. They hadn't been ready for hunting vampires, and the obstacle course proved that, especially as he'd run it himself multiple times.

He didn't know what he'd do if they *did* pass this time around. Would he stop teaching the class? Would he start taking them out on hunts? He still wasn't sure they were ready. Maybe *he* wasn't ready, really. They were just kids. Not even old enough to drink yet. Not even old enough to rent a car or book a hotel room. How could he, in good conscience, take them out into the field to possibly be sucked dry by a vampire? He couldn't.

"But you can't keep hoping they fail," Hunter said, as if he were reading Eric's mind. Or maybe Eric had muttered all of that out loud. It wouldn't surprise him. He tended to talk to himself when he got stressed, and right now his stress levels were at about a fifteen. To be clear, that was fifteen out of *ten*, not a hundred.

"I'm not hoping they fail." He kind of was hoping they failed. At least then he could say he wasn't taking them out on patrol because if they couldn't pass their fucking finals, if they couldn't prove to him that they could take on a vampire in a practice setting, why the fuck would he take them out into a real-world setting? He supposed the next step *would* be something like that, if they passed. A blood run at the hospital maybe. Or a night in the graveyard. Something easy. Something unlikely to get them killed. What kind of protections could he put into place for such a thing?

Hunter hummed softly. He was a gentle, warm presence at Eric's side on the couch as they watched the living room television set up to monitor his class's progress, its screen split into nine different smaller boxes. "You'll be proud of them if they pass."

He'd have to remember to send a thank you card to Dean Cochburn for the use of the abandoned dorm on the edge of campus. It was the perfect testing ground. Shame it would be torn down after this.

"I'll be afraid for them if they pass," Eric argued. It was true, he would be. Would the Council of Creatures ask for the test results? Would they want to send his kids into the field without his oversight and protection if they found out that they'd passed? Could he skew the results to make it look like they still weren't ready? Or would Janet want to see the tapes? Fuck the governing body, Eric wasn't sending his kids out into the field without him there to look after them and get them out of the trouble they'd no doubt get into. He just wasn't sure how he could ensure that would happen. Yet.

"Yes. That too probably," Hunter agreed readily. He knew, Eric knew that he did. It wasn't just that Hunter had been living with the kids for the past couple of months. It wasn't just that he'd been around Eric's baby Venator for years as their lab tech. It was also that Hunter had family in Eric's class. Chase Delacroix was a good kid. Quiet. Conscientious. Nervous. And Hunter didn't want him in the field any more than Eric did. His gene had shown up less than a year ago. He was in no way ready to be out fighting vampires. "But that won't erase the pride."

"No. It won't." Fuck. Eric hated when Hunter was right, and he was definitely right about this. Eric would be proud of his kids if they passed this test. He'd be thrilled to see how they'd progressed. But that didn't mean he wasn't absolutely terrified of what it would mean for them. Of how it would change their lives forever.

Hunter reached down, taking Eric's hand, threading their fingers together. The silver rings he wore on almost every finger pinched Eric's skin, but he didn't really mind. It was comforting. Grounding. To be slightly uncomfortable in a physical way instead of a mental way.

"I think it's a good idea that you turned this into a team test." Hunter gave his hand a squeeze, bumping his shoulder lightly against Eric's.

"I think so too." He had to resist the urge to lean his head on Hunter's shoulder. Keep himself upright in the face of what lay ahead. It was a struggle. It would be so easy to lean into the strength of someone else. To let someone else carry the load for a little while. But that wasn't who Eric was, never had been.

The plan to do teams could either blow up in his face or work in his favor. If they passed as a team, the Council of Creatures and the Huntsmen elders could realize that Venator worked better in units. That more of them survived and they were more effective when they weren't fighting alone. Or they could completely ignore the fact that it had been a team effort and decide to split his force up into smaller units and send them out alone, despite their Venator genes not being active yet. Eric would fight tooth and nail if they tried. He'd scream, and he'd rail, and he'd threaten to say fuck it and let the vampires eat all of Ironport. But he knew that in the end there wouldn't be much he could do about it. If the Huntsmen elders made a decision, he had no choice but to let it happen. No choice but to follow the mandate. They made the rules.

How different would things be if he made the rules. If there was an actual Venator in charge of these things . . .

"Shh . . . it's starting," Eric hissed, mostly to quiet his own racing thoughts as the first of his students came into view. It was Bert. Because of fucking course it was Bert. Bert would always be the first to run into danger, even if he was better suited to working behind the scenes. Stupid kid thought he needed to be just like Eric. Idolized him to a worrying degree.

Bert was flanked by Finn and Kate with Nik bringing up the rear of their little group, their hands already closed tight around the stakes they'd been tasked with making for themselves weeks ago. Because a Venator was only as good as their tools, and they couldn't trust anyone else to make what they needed. Or at least, not in Eric's case. Plus, it was better if his kids knew how to take what they found and turn it into something to be used against the monsters who would come for them. One never knew when they'd be caught without a stake. He knew that from experience.

"Heat signatures show two on the main floor," Chase reported, his voice calm and steady as it played from the speakers of the screen. He and Lu were in the van parked on the street, the command center in charge of watching their team's back and making sure everyone got out okay. "To your right."

"Roger," Finn replied, sharp and curt. She motioned to Bert and Kate, then broke off from the group to head toward where Chase had said the signatures were. "Nik."

Nik broke off from the group to follow her, his body turned slightly so that his back was to her, keeping eyes on every corner of the darkened room as they entered.

The fake vampires were waiting for them there. One tucked away behind a large wardrobe, the other sitting out in the middle of the floor. It wasn't exactly as good as a real-life situation. In a real-life situation, the vampires would have reacted the moment they heard someone enter their nest, and the kids hadn't been as silent as Eric had taught them to be. Instead, it seemed they were counting on their prey to be distracted. He would have to dock a couple of points for that, he thought, his pen scraping against the legal pad resting on his bent knee. They should know better. Should have come up with silent signals instead of the vocal ones they were using, even if they were one word.

The actors Eric had hired weren't as quick as a vampire could be, nor were they anywhere near as lethal, but the one who'd remained hidden still had Nik slammed against the wall before they managed to dispatch him, providing an opening for the one in the middle of the room to grab Finn and tackle her to the floor.

"Sloppy," Eric murmured to himself. "Very sloppy."

"Give them a minute. Maybe they have a plan." Hunter's voice was a soft rumble, his glasses reflecting the light from the screen when Eric looked over at him. But he was smiling. Like he knew something Eric didn't.

Eric's eyes cut back to Bert and Kate, who were no longer standing in the middle of the front room they'd entered through, so it took him a moment of scanning the screens to find them. They had circled around, using Finn and Nik as bait to come up behind the actors and dispatch them quickly before helping their comrades from the ground.

"First floor clear," Nik reported back to Chase, a little breathy.

"There is a basement on this place," Lu said, her voice almost drowned out by the *click-clack* of her fingers on the keyboard in the command center. "We tried to get heat signatures, but no dice."

"You'll have to split your forces," Chase murmured. "Do you need backup to watch the door?"

Kate shook her head a little. "Finn?"

"I've got the door." She nodded. "But we shouldn't break off into singles."

No. They shouldn't. He'd made this a team exercise so none of them would have to be alone in that house. And here they were debating whether they should split up. They were wasting time. Why didn't they plan this out beforehand? He'd given them the layout of the house. Lu and Chase had been able to watch the place for at least a couple of hours ahead of time. It was more time than he gave half his own missions like this. He made another note on his pad. They were going to have a unit on prep work next semester.

"No," Lu said, and Eric couldn't see her because he didn't have a camera set up in the van, but he could hear her moving, already pulling on her gear. "I've got the door. I don't want anyone going into that basement alone."

"How many are upstairs?" Bert asked.

"Three." Chase sounded like he was on edge now. Nervous. Hunter's hand tightened around Eric's again, the rings cutting into his fingers.

"I could take—"

"No," Lu cut Bert off, quick and decisive. "You're not taking three on by yourself. I'm coming in."

Eric blinked, surprised. He hadn't expected Lu to take up the role as leader. But he supposed he should have; Tony was like that too. He didn't let anyone railroad him with their own opinions. He just did what he thought was right. That was good. His kids needed someone like that—someone willing to make the tough decisions and say fuck it if it hurt anyone's feelings.

Bert huffed but didn't argue further. "How long?"

"Already on my way up the walk. Get moving."

"You heard the lady," Kate said, not giving Bert a moment to get into a huff about Lu taking the lead. "Finn, you and I will take the basement. Bert and Nik can head upstairs."

There was a collective nod, and off they went.

Chapter 18

THE TEST WENT on for another ten minutes, much less time than Hunter thought it might. Not that he had anything to base that on. He'd only been involved in one raid with Eric, and that had been a significantly larger property, with a significantly larger number of *real* vampires. Time also moved very differently when a person was involved in the raid versus watching it on a screen in a room safe at home. There was a weird distance between him and the events Eric's students were dealing with, only made larger by the fact that he knew the *vampires* were hired kids from the theater department.

Still, Hunter's hand tightened around Eric's as the test continued, his rings no doubt digging into Eric's knuckles. Eric didn't complain. He was sweet like that. Goddess above and below, Hunter didn't deserve him. No one deserved Eric Marcelino. Least of all someone who felt distinctly like they were using him as some warped kind of rebound.

The screens cut. Silence settled around them, slow and fuzzy.

"Is it over?" Hunter turned to look at Eric, who had his head bent over the pad perched on his knee, writing something down. It looked like maybe he was adding up totals. His lips moving as he did the math in his head. Hunter waited, watching, until Eric was done, then he asked again, "Is it over?"

"Yeah, it's over." Eric's pen tapped against the pad, his leg jiggling a little. Hunter couldn't read the expression on his face. A sinking sensation took over his stomach. Had the kids failed again?

"And? How'd they do?" He was almost afraid to ask. To find out that not only had his brother failed, but his whole class had. Would their failure be proof to the Huntsmen that Eric's classes weren't working? Would it be proof that Venator couldn't be trusted to hunt in packs, like Eric was proposing? Eric hadn't said what the consequences of their failure might be, but Hunter couldn't help but jump to the worst ones possible. He'd never been good at turning off the intrusive part of his brain that told him constantly that bad things were going to happen. This was just one more example of that. And the longer Eric took to answer, the more sure Hunter was that the kids were fucked.

Then Eric smiled, his eyes sparkling in the dim lights of the dorm living room, all proud mama bear and joy when he whispered, "They passed."

"They passed?"

"They passed!" Eric tossed the pad aside and lunged across the couch to throw himself into Hunter's lap, hugging his neck tightly, a whoop of celebration on his lips. Lips that were now terribly close to Hunter's. Closer than they'd been in years. Close enough that Hunter could see how chapped they were, bitten raw by Eric's anxiety about what the result of this test would be.

"They passed," Hunter couldn't help but laugh. He knew he should pull back. He knew he should guide Eric off his lap. He knew this was too much, too soon, too fast. He knew it wasn't right—the way his heart was in his throat. But it was hard to think of anything else with Eric's warmth pressed against the front of him. Then Eric's lips twitched into a wider smile, his joy pure, and whole, and perfect, and Hunter was helpless. Would likely always be helpless. Fuck, he hoped Britt wasn't watching from wherever she was.

"They passed," Eric whispered, his dark eyes flicking about Hunter's face, unsettled, unsure. Like a question.

Hunter leaned in and pressed his mouth to Eric's, hoping that was the answer he'd been looking for. It started off soft, just pressure, one pair of lips pressed against the other. Warm and light. Innocent. Chaste. But Hunter remembered very keenly the couple of times he'd been with Eric pre-Britt, and there was nothing chaste about the sound those memories elicited. A whimper, a whine.

Eric let out a soft laugh, a huff of warm breath against Hunter's lips, and opened his mouth. The first brush of his tongue against Hunter's—hot and slick—was like an electric current zipping through Hunter's veins and making every hair on his body stand on end.

Another sound ripped itself from Hunter's throat as he opened his mouth to Eric's gentle insistence.

"Relax. I've got you," Eric murmured softly, his voice a rumble in his chest that Hunter could feel where they were pressed together.

Hunter nodded, his nose bumping against Eric's cheek, and leaned in again, taking Eric's lower lip into his mouth, sucking on it gently and drawing a noise of pleasure from Eric. From there, Hunter lost himself to the push and pull. To the feeling of Eric's tongue pressing into every crevice of his mouth, tasting him, searching for something, running along his molars. He'd forgotten what it was like to kiss Eric Marcelino. Forgotten how addicting it could be. How Eric consumed a partner, ravenous for affection. How Hunter could get off on just this and a little rubbing against each other. Eric was thorough, always had been.

A hiss left him as Eric ground his hips down against Hunter's, the hardness building between them brushing against each other, making it difficult to get a coherent thought out other than *more. More. More.* And *Goddess above and below, he needs to be wearing less fucking clothes.*

"Hun," Eric mumbled, the word slurred by where he had his mouth pressed against the edge of Hunter's jaw. Dragging his teeth over the skin, rubbing roughly against it to bruise the bone.

Hunter grabbed Eric's belt loops, hard enough that he was sure they would tear, but he didn't care and it didn't slow down Eric either. The seams of his fly made Hunter ache, burning against his skin. He was going to be red all over. Hurting, and hard. And it didn't fucking matter, because all he could think about was the next place Eric would press his lips, or how his blunt teeth would feel digging into the meat of Hunter's shoulder.

The front door crashed open, smacking hard against the wall beside it, and suddenly the house was full of voices, full of kids. Victory and excitement.

Fuck! The kids!

Eric yelped and scrambled away, grabbing a pillow to try to cover his lap while he searched frantically for the legal pad he'd been taking notes on. His hair was a fucking mess, and Hunter wasn't sure how it'd gotten that way, because he couldn't remember touching it at all. Damn it. Now he ached to do just that.

"I'm gonna—" Hunter swallowed. His throat was raw. He stood, adjusting his pants as he went, hoping to hide the obvious erection making them too tight. "I'm just gonna go. You've gotta—"

"Yeah. I need to go over the results with them."

"Mm-hmm." Hunter nodded quickly and spun on his heel to head up the stairs, long strides practically speeding into a run as he tried to escape the heat, the excitement, of what he'd just done. Oh Goddess. What had he just *done*?

Fuck. Fuck. *Fuck.*

What the fuck was *wrong* with him? What the fuck was he thinking? Eric knew better. He did! He knew that Hunter was grieving. Knew that there was no space in Hunter's life for the mess that was Eric right now. It could never have been clearer with the way Hunter pulled himself back. With how his brows had disappeared into his hair. His eyes flicking around in a way that Eric had only seen when Hunter was distinctly freaked out.

So why had Hunter leaned in? Why had he kissed first?

"The heat of the moment. That's what that was. The heat of the moment." He was wearing a line in his carpet, pacing back and forth, his hands fisted in his hair. Ava was going to skin him alive when she found out what he'd just done. And rightly so. It was wrong. It was fucked up. *He* was fucked up. Fuck.

"Umm . . . is this a bad time?" Bert asked from the door. His hand was raised as if he'd been about to knock, or maybe he *had* knocked and Eric just hadn't heard.

"No. It's fine. Come in." He turned to flop down into the chair behind his desk, letting out a long, slow breath that didn't do anything to calm the anxiety twisting in his gut. Thank Diana he hadn't eaten dinner, or he probably would have thrown up. And how would that have looked to Hunter? He didn't want Hunter to think he was disgusted by him. Nothing could be further from the truth. But at the same time . . . Britt was most definitely going to curse him from whatever afterlife she'd ended up in. And he deserved it.

Every bit of it. He was a garbage person for taking advantage of his best friend's grief.

"Eric?"

"Huh?" He looked up at Bert, who had come in and closed the door behind him, his brow creased in concern. "Oh yeah, what's up, kid?"

Bert frowned, his forehead wrinkling more as if he was thinking about what to say. Eric was sure there was some desire in there to confront him about why he'd been pacing his room like a fucking maniac when he should be celebrating. He should have stayed downstairs and played *Mario Kart* with the kids. He should have let their excited energy seep into his fucking pores until the anxiety was burned away. But he hadn't. He'd come upstairs to stew and to cuss himself out, and to try to think of a way to fucking fix the mess he'd just made of his entire fucking life. This was going to blow up in his face. This was going to blow up in his face *so* hard.

"You good?" Bert asked after a long moment.

Eric shook himself. He needed to get his head out of his fucking ass. He didn't have time for it. Not with everything else that was going on. "Yeah. Fit as a fiddle." *Who the fuck says *that? "Did you need something?"

With a hard stare, Bert moved to stand closer to Eric, his eyes unblinking. As if he could make Eric come clean about something with a look alone. When that didn't work, he sighed, his shoulders sagging. "You'd tell me if something was wrong, right?"

"Yeah, sure, buddy." He wouldn't. Telling the kids what was going on in his personal life was a big no no, in Eric's book. They were his students. They were in his care. They should not have to deal with all the emotional drama that was his fucked-up relationship with another Venator, and the lab tech they all worked with. "So what did you come in here for?"

"I got the information on that vampire you wanted." Bert pulled a thumb drive from his hoodie pocket and held it out.

That. That was *exactly* what he needed. An out. Action. A fight. Something to distract himself from the mess that was him, Hunter, and Tony. Something to get him out of the fucking house where the licorice and anise smell of Hunter's magic and aftershave lingered.

Eric reached for it, and Bert tugged it away last minute. "Bert. Don't do this now. I've got shit to handle, you know that."

"I do, but . . . I want to make sure you're safe this time." His grip was so tight on the little hunk of plastic that his hands shook, the tips of his fingers turning pale. "I want to go with you."

"Out of the question."

"But I passed my—"

"With a team. And your personal score wasn't that high, Bert." Eric hated to ruin Bert's victory like that. But someone needed to bring the kid back down to earth. "But I'll take my earbud, I'll be in contact the whole time I'm gone."

Not that he hadn't done that last time, but still. Eric would make any promises he had to if it would get Bert off his back and keep him from coming along, and if it meant getting the fuck out of the house without someone trailing him.

Bert didn't let go.

"Bert, seriously. I won't be going out on the water. And I won't be letting anyone sneak up on me. This isn't a trap like last time, so I'll be fine. And you'll know exactly where I am. I'll even turn on the tracking data on my phone."

Bert eyed him for a long moment, as if weighing how sincere he was, then he held out the thumb drive. "If you get your ass in trouble, I didn't give this to you."

Eric snorted, snatching the drive and rolling his eyes. "Really, kid? Who's the adult here?"

"I'm serious. If Hunter finds out—"

"He's not going to find out." Eric grabbed his jacket from the back of the chair and shrugged it onto his shoulders on the way out the door. He didn't wait for Bert to say anything else, didn't wait for anyone to ask him where the fuck he was going. He grabbed his messenger bag and his keys, and headed for his car.

CHAPTER 19

THE SCREEN of the laptop was over-bright in the fading light, the blueness of it burning Eric's eyes where he sat in his car on a street outside of a closed apartment building. The streetlamps were out all along this section of town, washing the neighborhood in darkness. Which was going to make this hunt both easier and harder at the same time. The darkness would hide him, but it would also hide the vampire he was hunting. Couple that with the fact that he had no idea what the inside of that apartment building looked like, or how many vampires Noah might be traveling with, and it was a recipe for disaster. Not that that was going to stop Eric. Very few things could stop him once he set his mind to something.

"What do the heat signatures look like?" Bert asked, his voice a crackle in Eric's ear.

Eric rolled his eyes. "It doesn't matter. I'm not going in."

Though he'd thought about it. It would be so easy to race right in there and damn the consequences. But there was way too high a chance of being ambushed, and then having to stake the vampire he wanted to talk to. It wasn't worth the hassle.

"What do you mean you're not going in?"

"Exactly what I said, Bert, I'm not going in. He's got to leave for something. And from the data you gave me, he should be doing that in about twenty minutes, give or take."

"How do you know that?"

"Because that's his pattern. He's not going to break that." Bert had provided him with enough information to figure all that out. It was honestly astounding the kind of data the Ghost Tracer could provide. The woman who created it was probably some kind of prodigy. No wonder Hunter had been tripping over himself to repeat every word she said. Eric would have been jealous if he didn't know how Hunter could get about tech advances.

Okay, maybe he *had* been a little jealous. Maybe that's why he'd reacted the way he had to Hunter's news about the vampires. Just like he'd been a little jealous when he'd found out Tony had a breakfast date with Dash. It was all so . . . domestic. People never did domestic with Eric . . .

"Wait. You found a pattern?" Bert asked, incredulous, snarky, and more than a little insulting. Little shithead.

"Yes, *Humbert*." Eric returned the snark tenfold. "I found a pattern. In spite of what all you little assholes seem to think, I'm actually really good at my fucking job. I've only been doing this since I was thirteen, for fuck's sake."

"Yeah, but this was like a technical analysis. Don't you usually have Hunter do the technical analysis? You're more of the run in and stabby stabby kind of guy, aren't you?"

It wasn't an untrue statement. Eric *was* more of the sort to run in headfirst and ask questions later. But that was when he was looking to slay whoever was inside.

"You know what, Bert? Fuck you. How's that for finding a fucking pattern?" Eric groused, shutting the laptop he'd been staring at and tucking it back into the messenger bag in the passenger seat. He wouldn't need it now that he knew where Noah was holed up. He checked his watch. Ten minutes, give or take, if Noah stuck to his routine. Then he'd go out. What he'd go out to do, Eric didn't know. There still hadn't been any reports of vampires hunting in Ironport recently. But Noah had been leaving every evening at the same time and going somewhere down in the industrial part of town. The same area where Eric and Hunter had chased a whole flock of vamps down the street a couple months back. Was there a nest there? If there was, why wasn't Ashthorne's app picking it up?

"Okay. Jeez. Sorry. Didn't mean to offend," Bert grumbled.

"Yeah well, you really need to learn to think before you speak sometimes. Some day that mouth of yours is gonna get you in a fuckload of trouble." Eric ran his hand through his hair, fingers catching on the ends. He needed a fucking haircut. Add that to the list of personal care shit he didn't have time for lately. "We've talked about this, man."

Bert let out a long breath, and muttered another soft "Sorry," finally sounding chastened.

Good. Maybe he'd fucking learn something. Although, that was doubtful. Eric had laid into Bert numerous times about running off at the mouth without thinking like he did, and it had yet to stop him. The kid's brain-to-mouth filter was riddled with holes, or maybe it didn't exist. Eric wasn't sure which, but he'd keep on him about it because he didn't want Bert's mouth to get him fucking killed one day.

Movement drew Eric's attention to the front door of the apartment building, and he narrowed his eyes, watching as someone exited the building. The figure tilted their head just so, their face catching in the moonlight for Eric to see. "Right on time."

"Do you see him?"

"Yes. Now shut up. I've got to get this fucker in the car." Eric wasn't exactly sure how he was going to *do* that part. The plan he'd worked out was vague, and probably not going to work. He had the cuffs Hunter made for him months ago, but it'd probably be better if he could knock Noah out. And there hadn't been time to ask Hunter to design something for that purpose, even if he would have. Which he probably wouldn't, because Hunter had been clear that he didn't approve of this plan, like, at all. So he was on his own for this.

Bert said something, but Eric was too busy getting out of the car—hoping his door didn't squeal on the hinges—and making his way across the grass crunchy with late spring frost. In spite of how quiet he was, Noah heard him, or maybe smelled him, and froze.

Muddy blond hair fell into Noah's face, almost hiding his slate-gray eyes, but Eric felt the weight of Noah's attention on him. His chest rose and fell in slow, even breaths. Something left over from being human that Eric hadn't been prepared for. Most vampires he interacted with had been vamps for long enough that they'd gotten rid of those biological impulses, let them be worn away by time like sand under the tide. It was one of the markers he looked for when trying to spot a vampire in the crowd: an unnatural stillness.

But Noah was his age.

Their birthdays were a week apart. They'd celebrated them together for years. First with video games and ice cream cake, then with stolen beers and girls who lied about where they were. All of that had ended when Eric started dating Kalla, though. Because Kalla Regan was upright and serious. She didn't party. She didn't drink. She was the kind of kid who everyone knew would be going to an Ivy League when they graduated. It made Eric want to be better, to try harder. Noah hated that. Hated how he changed.

"Don't make this harder than it's gotta be, man," Eric whispered into the still night, almost afraid of what his voice might disturb should he speak too loudly.

Noah's head tilted for a moment, the hair falling away from his eyes to reveal that they'd narrowed on Eric. Assessing. Probably trying to figure out if he could run from Eric and actually get away. Then his mouth twitched into a bit of a smile, the kind of smile he'd worn right before he was about to crash his fucking car into Eric's on *Mario Kart* or drop one of those stupid turtle shells, just enough to show off some fang, and he took off. Running backward at a lope so he could keep his eyes on Eric, never once checking to make sure he didn't back right into a light pole or a parked car, but still inhumanly fast.

It was a weird flex, but Eric was impressed.

"Fuck," Eric hissed, and started after him. He didn't know if Noah *wanted* to get caught, or if he was fucked up from the transformation enough to not realize the danger Eric posed him, or maybe he was simply that cocky. He always had been an arrogant little fucker. But it only took a block or two before Eric tackled him to the ground.

"You motherfucker," Noah hissed. Nails like claws swiped Eric's cheek, sharp enough to draw blood. Eric took a knee to the stomach, the exact move Noah had used to nearly kill him last time, but there was no water to get into his lungs now, to impede his movements. He got a hold of one wrist—the bones fine and brittle, the skin too thin under his touch—and got the cuff on it.

The other hand was still flailing about. Landing blows on Eric's chest, his face. Scratching him. Trying to push him off. Drawing blood. But Noah was weaker than he'd been a few days ago. Maybe from lack of blood. Maybe from the magic in the cuff dampening his innate otherness. Whatever it was, Eric managed to get him cuffed entirely and drag him to his feet.

"Now," he said, brushing his cheek on his shoulder and hissing at the sting of it, "are you going to come quietly?"

"Go fuck yourself, Marcelino," Noah spat, but he'd largely stopped struggling. Eric wondered if he couldn't anymore. Because he'd used what energy he had on that backward running stunt, which yeah, had looked cool, but had obviously been a fucking waste. Or maybe there was something else. Maybe Noah meant to be caught . . .

No. He'd deal with that later. Whatever it entailed. First, he wanted answers.

"Maybe later." With a roll of his eyes, Eric dragged Noah back toward his car, ignoring the way he dug his heels in and tried to fight it. He wasn't kicking at least, and Eric was going to count that as a win. Well, he wasn't kicking until Eric bent to get the back door open, and Noah scrambled against his hold. Kicking and struggling, and nearly pulling free. Eric took a deep breath, hating the guilt that crawled along his spine like syrup, and slammed a wolfsbane-coated dagger into Noah's chest. Noah grunted once but fell still, his head hanging so his hair obscured Eric's view of his face.

Inhaling deeply to quell the rise of acid in his stomach, Eric threw Noah into the back and climbed into the driver's seat again.

"Did you get him, Eric?" Bert asked, his voice a crackled hush in Eric's ear. Like he was trying to be quiet. Maybe all the other kids had gone to bed.

"Yeah, I got him." Eric tapped on the wheel, his eyes flicking to Noah in the back seat as he pulled away from the curb. This didn't feel right. None of this felt right. It was too fucking easy. "I'm going dark for a bit, kid."

"That wasn't part of the deal!"

"I remember the deal. My location tracker will stay on. But you're not gonna want to hear what comes next." *Eric* didn't want Bert to hear it. He didn't want the kids to know what he was capable of, what he'd do to keep them safe. And he didn't think he'd ever be able to look them in the eye again if they knew how he'd tortured someone to get answers.

"Eric, you prom—"

Eric didn't let him finish. He pulled the bud out of his ear and put it back in its case in the messenger bag on the seat, effectively ending the call. When he glanced back at Noah, he was sitting up, coherent again. *Damn, should have used more wolfsbane.*

"So, you gonna tell me what all of this is about?"

Noah met his eyes in the rearview mirror and shot him another sharp-toothed smile but didn't respond.

In fact, he was quiet the whole way to Eric's parents' house. They hadn't been there in ages, so they wouldn't notice, and he still had a key. He'd taken to using it as a bunker of sorts years ago. Tucking extra munitions there just in case. He knew it was silly, there was no reason for him to need something like that. Not when he had the house on campus—the one at 1106 Moonshadow Way. But there was something about having his own space away from everyone else that no one knew about. Bert would know about it now, thanks to the location tracker. But there wasn't much choice. He wasn't about to take Noah back to the dorm and deal with him there, and if he turned off his location tracker, Bert would call in the calvary.

Chapter 20

WHEN ERIC PULLED up outside of the house, he saw Noah's brows lift in amusement, but he still didn't speak, just let Eric lead him inside and throw him down on the couch. No dust floated up from the uncomfortable piece of furniture. Because even if his parents hadn't been home in probably close to five years—too busy traveling the globe with their golden boy—they had staff come and clean it every other week. It was the work of a moment to cuff Noah's ankles too, keeping him in place for the most part.

"Well," Noah said, shifting around a little, as if he were trying to get comfortable, "this brings back memories."

"Yeah, it does." Eric came to sit on the coffee table in front of him, his knees spread wide. The duffle he had slung over his shoulder clattered against the wood when he set it down and unzipped it. He removed the items one at a time, setting them on the coffee table so Noah could see. Stakes. Silver. Knives. Pliers. He'd been at this long enough to know what would work on a vampire, and he was going to use all that experience to get answers.

"So we're really doing this, huh?" Noah asked.

Eric didn't look up from where he was arranging everything in a neat row, as if the fact that they were all at a right angle to him and evenly spaced could make them less of what they were—implements of torture—before kicking the empty duffel under the coffee table. "Yeah. We are."

"You sure you got it in you, King Ricky?"

"Guess we're about to find out." Eric shrugged and grabbed one of the silver-tipped blades. His movements were precise, leaving no room for Noah to pull away or for himself to back out as he leaned forward and pressed the point of the blade into Noah's knee. It sizzled, burned, even through the pant leg.

Noah howled, his legs twitching. Trying to kick out, to get away, but the cuffs held fast. When he couldn't escape, he fell over onto his side, curling his body back against the couch cushions.

"You can make this stop," Eric said, pressing harder, swallowing against the bile rising in his throat. Goddess, he was going to puke. He wondered if the silver would burn clean through the bone, eat away at the rest of Noah's leg. Eric had never tried this before, never wanted to make a vampire's death slow. He didn't want to *now*. But desperate times.

"You didn't even ask a fucking *question*!" Noah snarled. His leg jerked, and the knife clattered away from Eric, hitting the edge of the end table then skidding across the carpet.

"That was a warning." He needed to separate himself from this. To step back from it. If he didn't, he'd never finish. But it was difficult to do that when the vampire looking back at him had been a friend at one point in time. Fuck. A friend. He was *torturing* a *friend*. What the fuck was wrong with him? His hands shook as he reached for the stake. It was one of the silver-tipped ones, rough but effective. "What do the Chadwicks have to do with this whole thing?"

Noah snorted. The skin of his leg was slowly healing over, but a hole gaped in his jeans now, greasy blood and char marks leaving behind a black-brown stain. "I don't know what you're talking about."

"One of them sent you to the docks that day," Eric

insisted, his hand tightening around the stake. Maybe Noah wouldn't make Eric hurt him again. Maybe he'd give him an answer without it. But even as Eric thought it, he knew he wouldn't be so lucky. He never had been before, why would he be now? "Are they working for the head vamp? Is the whole council in on it, or is it just the Chadwicks? How deep does this thing go?"

"Dude." Noah laughed, wiggling in his seat once he sat up. "That's more than one question."

Eric growled. His patience wearing thin, only made thinner by the churning of his stomach. He needed to get this over with. Get answers, and get the fuck out of there. The ghosts of his parents' house hung heavy around his neck, weighing him down as he leaned forward and pressed his face into Noah's space. He settled the point of the stake just above Noah's heart, the silver burning a hole through his thin T-shirt. It was completely inappropriate clothing for the weather, but Eric supposed vampires couldn't feel cold the same way living creatures could.

"Who are the Chadwicks working for?" Repeating the question made Eric want to grind his teeth. He spent half his life repeating himself over and over with the kids, trying to get the message that they needed to be concerned for their safety through their thick skulls. He didn't particularly want to have to do it with an adult.

Noah seemed to know that, seemed to relish in the annoyance he found on Eric's face. "What's wrong, King Ricky, don't like being treated like you're not top dog anymore? Sucks to suck, doesn't it?"

"Fuck you, Noah. Just tell me who the fuck turned you." The stake had worn a hole through his shirt and was starting to press into the skin. Soon, soon it would go through the bone, burning a hole the whole way. Noah's only reaction was to wince, making Eric think that perhaps the previous reaction had been embellished to some degree. Did vampires not feel pain? And if they didn't, what did that mean for Eric's line of questioning?

Noah leaned forward more, the stake going in deeper. Not much further, and it'd press into his heart, turning Noah into nothing more than a pile of dust. The Roomba would pick him up when it ran later, and the cleaning staff would take care of what was left on the couch. Nothing would be left of Noah. Nothing would be left of Eric's friend, nor his friendship. It was like shredding a piece of his childhood.

"Do it," Noah challenged. Blood dribbled from the wound, slow and sluggish, staining his shirt. It would drip onto the couch and leave behind a mark that not even the best cleaning products would be able to remove. Eric's parents would have to buy a new couch the next time they came home to Ironport. If they ever *did* come home.

"Answer me!"

"You can't, can you?" Noah's smile widened, showing off two razor-sharp fangs, the markers of what he'd become. "Never did have the balls to do the hard stuff, did you Eric? That's why Kalla left you. That's why your Nonna died. That's why *everyone* left you behind. Because you're nothing."

"Just tell me who the fuck sent you, Noah!" His hand was slick with sweat, the stake going slippery in his grip. He was going to drop it. He was going to drop it and prove Noah right, *exactly* right. Because he was a fucking failure. Because he was only good at one thing, just the one—staking vampires—and it seemed he couldn't even do that right these days.

"Fuck. Off." Noah snarled, then he lunged, knocking the stake from Eric's grip. His hands went for Eric's throat, latching on tight to cut off the air from his lungs. Eric had a moment, just one, to think *Oh, the cuffs broke* before his back slammed against the coffee table hard enough that it gave out under his and Noah's combined weight.

They'll have to replace that too. They're gonna be pissed.

Eric choked, coughed, tried to suck in air past the tight grip Noah had on his throat, but he couldn't. Darkness swam in front of his face. Noah hovered above him, so much the same boy who had once shoved Eric's face into his birthday cake, and also so very different. The two images blurred together, the past Noah and the current one. Eric couldn't tell if it was that, the lack of air, or the bruises along his back that made his eyes burn.

"See?" Noah hissed. Saliva dripped from his mouth, his fangs extending as he leaned down closer. Eric was going to pass out before the bite even came. Did Noah mean to kill him this way? With his bare hands? "You're weak. You were always so *weak.*"

He wanted to object, to tell Noah that he wasn't, but there was no air to do it and he wondered, as his vision began to tunnel, if there was any truth to it. Maybe he *was* weak. Maybe he always had been.

"And when I'm done with you, when you're nothing but a dried-up corpse," Noah whispered, dark and promising into Eric's ear, "we're going for the brats."

Eric blinked hard, and his hands, which had been fighting ineffectually to shove Noah off, reached for one of the coffee table legs, stretching his arm out till it burned to grab on to the splintered wood. It wasn't nearly pointed nor sharp enough. It would do the job.

"You leave my fucking kids *alone,*" Eric snarled with the last breath in his lungs. He jammed the piece of wood up through Noah's chest. Blood poured from the wound, more than Eric thought he'd ever seen come from a staked vampire.

Noah's gray eyes went wide, stunned, his fingers loosening on Eric's throat enough for Eric to suck down a breath. Then he looked at Eric, directly in the eye, and murmured a soft, broken "thank you" right before he erupted into a cloud of dust.

Coughing, retching, choking, Eric struggled to sit up, and

when he did the world spun under him. He leaned over and heaved up everything he'd had in his stomach onto the floor. There wasn't much; it was all bile, yellow, and waxy tasting.

Thank you echoed in his head, over and over again. The look in Noah's eyes burned into his brain. Like Eric was freeing him. Like Noah hadn't wanted this. He hadn't *wanted* this! Eric didn't have to kill him. He could have helped Noah. He could have freed him. He could have done *something*. But he hadn't. He hadn't really even tried to talk to Noah outside of torturing him.

What good was he if he couldn't save anyone? What good was he if he couldn't help the people who were close to him? He and Noah weren't friends anymore, true, but they had been once upon a time. Once upon a time, they had been inseparable. They played T-ball and then baseball together. They went on double dates. They were on the swim team together. They drank together. Noah had bought Eric his first weed. Noah had been there when Eric's Nonna died. Had come to the funeral and sat beside him when his parents didn't show up. Noah had been . . . He had been Eric's best friend for so many years. A constant.

And now . . . Now he was dust. A pile of ash that the Roomba would pick up and dump in the bin come morning.

"Eric! Eric, open the fucking door!" Someone banged on the front door. Eric didn't know how long they'd been there, knocking, trying to get in. The light outside had shifted. It wasn't morning yet, but he could tell that some time had passed while he sat there in the remains of his best friend, watching as the blood on his clothes dried, turned flakey and hard. Trying to remember what he'd said to Noah the last time they'd spoken, before Noah had become a vampire. It had probably been something horrible. They hadn't ended on good terms. Goddess, if only he could take it back.

"Eric!" the person shouted again, then there was a bang, like a gunshot, the door smacked against the wall loudly, and

Kalla came into view. "What the fuck, Eric? Why didn't you answer?"

Eric looked up from the pile of . . . of Noah, the ash sliding off his lap as he shifted, smudging it into the carpet, and frowned at Kalla. "I killed him."

"He was dead a long time ago, Eric. He was a vampire."

"No. No. I killed him, Kalla. He was my friend, and I killed him."

"Come on, we've got to get you back to the dorm." She grabbed his arm, long mahogany fingers curling tight enough that he felt her nails cut into his skin, and yanked. He didn't move. Couldn't. Could only look up at the blur that was her head of cobalt-blue locs.

"I can't leave him here. The . . . the fucking *Roomba* is going to suck him up. Like he's . . . like he's . . ."

"Fuck," Kalla muttered to herself, stepping away from him and letting go of his arm. He lost track of her after that, but he could still hear her in that vague, fuzzy way as his fingers tried to scoot together what was left of Noah, ignoring the fangs because they weren't part of the boy Eric had known. Tried to scoop him up. If he could just . . . if he could just take some part of Noah back to his family. Maybe bury him the way he ought to have been. The way he deserved. Maybe then Eric would be able to let him go. But . . .

But also maybe not.

CHAPTER 21

THE TEXT WAS ATTACHED to an image of Eric's forest-green beamer parked on the curb of a dark street. Eric was behind the wheel. Tony could see him via the light of some large electronic he had perched on the passenger seat, either a laptop or a tablet. It washed his face in a sickly blue, making him look like a ghost.

Tony swallowed roughly, his fingers trembling a little as he tapped on the message bar and began typing.

Not that it really mattered. If Dash had a picture of Eric, then he could get to him. And he'd already proven that even places previously thought safe weren't. The campus. The little shop Ava owned, that Eric and Hunter liked to frequent. Dashfield B.M. Chadwick was everywhere in Ironport, and Tony was coming to realize he wasn't ever going to stop. Not until someone stopped him.

Tony didn't know, but he was sure it was likely to get someone fucking killed. Likely Eric himself. And if not him, then definitely one of the kids. Tony wondered if he zoomed in on the shot, if he could figure out where Eric was, and if it would matter at all. Whatever he was doing there, he was going to do it. Whatever Dash planned for him, there was no stopping that either.

Should I go say hi?

What did it mean that Eric was sticking his nose where it didn't belong? Tony knew he didn't have long before Dash decided Eric was too much of a nuisance and got rid of him. He had just been planning on Eric not doing anything to fucking *speed up* the process.

Even if offing Eric hadn't been part of the plan in the beginning, where Dash wasn't going to stop, neither was Eric. Trying to get either of them to behave in a way that would buy Tony enough time to burn the vampire blood from his system was too much to hope for.

Sage had been clear. Werewolf venom might not actually combat the toxins of the vampire blood. It *could* cure him. It *could* do nothing at all. It *could* make matters *so* much worse. But Tony needed a backup plan. He needed a solution before these two trains ran headfirst into each other and took him down with them. And if he didn't wind up having to use the venom, that was fine too. He needed to do *something*. Sitting around and waiting was making him antsy. And who knew what would happen if he didn't have some kind of failsafe in place.

Isn't it time for a feeding?

That was a surefire way to derail whatever Dash was planning, hopefully. It wouldn't stop him, but it might distract him long enough for Eric to get the fuck away from there. Goddess, how was he supposed to keep Eric safe if he was going to run off half-cocked like this?

Is that a distraction?

Is it working?

The three little dots that meant Dash was typing appeared. Disappeared. Appeared again. This was a gamble, and Tony knew it. He knew he was flirting with the devil by opening a vein for Dash to keep him away from Eric. Dash could very well try to give him blood again while he was doped up on venom. But he didn't have any better ideas currently, and the longer those dots blinked one after the other on his screen, the tighter his chest felt. Like those days before he'd figured out how to bind correctly and was doing it all the wrong ways. The longer he waited, the shallower his breaths grew, until he wasn't sure he'd ever take a full breath again.

I'll be there in ten.

Relief washed through Tony in a shudder, making his shoulders sag and his body go lax against the counter where he'd been making a snack for himself and Lu when Dash texted.

Lu was watching him, her green gaze burning and fierce on the back of his neck.

"Was that that fucker?" she asked as soon as his phone clicked down against the countertop, and Tony realized—not really for the first time, but it still hit him like a fucking truck out of nowhere—he couldn't have her here. She couldn't be *here*, not when Dash came, not if he had to take the werewolf venom. Maybe—fuck. Maybe not ever again! He'd invited Dash into their home. It wasn't safe for her here, not anymore.

It wouldn't be so long as Tony's name was on the deed. He needed to get her out. Now.

Okay, Tony, just breathe.

"Yes, it was my boyfriend," Tony said, but the words tasted like bile and burned at the back of his tongue. Fuck. He was really doing this, wasn't he? He was really going to kick his baby sister out. It was for her own good, he reminded himself. It was the only way to keep her safe. Because he could handle Dash, but he couldn't have her there when he did. "Do you have a problem with that, *Louisa*?"

"I think you *know* what I think about him," she hissed. He could hear her stool squeaking under her as she shifted on it behind the island, like she was getting up to stand. But he wouldn't turn around to face her. He couldn't. She might see the truth of what he was trying to do in all this, and then she'd try to save him. Because she was brave, and stupid, and noble. And he couldn't have that. He couldn't.

"And I think if you have a problem with my *boyfriend*"—Goddess, he hated that word, it made his skin crawl. He might never be able to use it again after this—"then you can fuck right off. Go live with Marcelino and his fucking brat pack for all I care."

"Or you could just break up with that piece of shit!" The stool squealed across the floor as she stood, clattering onto the tiles in her rush to get at him. The slap of her slippers accompanied her stomping into the kitchen proper until she stood beside him at the stove, her eyes narrowed into slits. "He's a bastard, and you know it."

"If I want your opinion, I'll ask for it, *Louisa*." She hated that name. He knew she hated that name. Their father had picked it, naming her after an aunt who was just as much of a belligerent bigot as he was. But it would rile her up. Make her seethe. Probably send her out of the house. He had ten minutes to do just that: get her out of the fucking house. Or at least have her on her way out when Dash got there. He needed to speed this up.

"If you're saying it's him or you," Tony said, every word a blade, slicing him open, leaving him bleeding, and doing the same to Lu. Goddess above and below, she was his sister. His best friend. The only person in the world who truly understood all the shit he'd been through. And she trusted him to take care of her. Had put her faith in him when he'd signed the guardianship papers. And now here he was, spitting in her face. Treating her like she didn't mean anything to him. It was for her own good. It was the only way to keep her safe. He had to keep reminding himself of that or he'd chicken out. "Then I choose him."

Lu stopped breathing, her body stilling to a statue, and they stood on the precipice, on a knife's edge, waiting for the pin drop. He could feel her watching his every movement as he stirred the rice dish he'd been making. Some of it had burned to the bottom of the pan in his inattention. It made the room smell smokey and a little acrid. Not that it mattered. It was going in the trash the moment Lu was out of the house anyway. He wouldn't be able to eat.

"I choose him," Tony repeated, making sure to keep his tone level. It would hurt more if this didn't seem like a decision he'd made in anger. Would cut deeper if it seemed like he simply didn't care about her anymore. But fuck if his eyes weren't burning. He hoped the movement of the spatula hid the way his hands shook. "Pack your shit. Call Hunter. And get the fuck out."

"Tony—"

"You heard me. Now."

There was a sharp inhale, the slicing of a blade into her gut, and then she spun on her heel, her long red hair whipping out behind her to nearly smack him in the face. She stormed up to her room.

He waited until he heard her door slam on the second floor, then he pulled his phone out to send off two quick texts.

> Make it twenty.

To Dash. And:

> I need you to come get Lu and take her to campus.

To Hunter. He knew he didn't have any right to ask that of Hunter. Hunter wasn't his friend. But he also knew Hunter was like Eric; he would do anything for the baby Venator Eric had in his class. While at the same time, he was different from Eric and he wouldn't stick his fucking nose into what was going on between the two siblings again. Probably.

Not that Tony thought for one single second that this wouldn't get back to Eric eventually. But maybe not until after Tony had his backup plan in place.

> What's going on?

He could try to tell Hunter the truth. He could try to lay it all out for him and hope to the Goddess that Hunter had a solution that didn't involve possibly turning himself into a fucking werewolf, but there wasn't a snowball's chance in hell that Hunter wouldn't tell Eric everything. Even if Tony asked him not to. Even if Tony could get the words past the lump in his throat. He didn't know much about their relationship, or Hunter in general, but he knew enough to know Hunter couldn't keep a secret for shit. Especially not when it came to Eric.

It was a little jealousy inducing, really. Tony remembered —now that the thrall was wearing off—what he and Eric had been like. He remembered how sweet Eric could be. How they had seemed to fit in a weird way. Two sides of a coin. Two halves of a whole. He also remembered that night in the car when Hunter had told him that getting into an accident and putting himself in the fucking hospital wasn't the way into Eric's pants. Like he knew from experience. Like he'd tried a number of methods to get Eric into bed. And even if Tony had felt so often that what he and Eric had was something special, that they could really work, he saw too how *Hunter* and Eric would work. How they wouldn't be two opposites that happened to work together. Hunter and Eric were tertiary colors where Tony and Eric were more complementary colors. They worked well in some situations but in others they clashed.

Hot date.

A lie was better than the truth. Or at least he hoped so.

Dash?

Yeah.

She hates him you know.

So she's told me.

Look can you come get the fucking brat or am I putting her on a bus?

I'll be there in five. Hold your fucking horses.

"Hunter is coming to get you!" Tony shouted up the steps where he could still hear Lu throwing shit around in her room. "Hurry the fuck up!"

"Fuck you!" Lu screamed back. Something thunked on every step on the way down, and when he looked over his shoulder, he found her dragging her duffel across the foyer, scratching up his floors. Her face was red and splotchy, like she'd been crying but had hurriedly tried to hide it because she didn't want him to see.

That was fine.

That was okay.

No.

That was a lie.

That was such a fucking *lie*.

All he wanted to do was scoop her up in his arms and tell her everything. Make it clear why he had to do this. Not that he actually *could* what with the compulsion still clinging to his every cell, but even if he could . . . Well. Tony knew his sister, and he knew that if she was aware of what was going on, she'd try to help. He also knew that if she did that, Dash would make her pay for it. Would make them both pay for it.

"I hope you packed your toothbrush!" Tony forced his voice to be even, to sound like he didn't fucking care, even as his chest constricted and his lungs screamed for air. The smell from the food turned his stomach, making his spit feel thick and stringy in his mouth.

Lu didn't respond, she just held up her middle finger and dragged her bag outside to wait for Hunter. The door slammed behind her, leaving Tony in the silence of an empty house, and a moment later Hunter's truck pulled up outside, the lights casting shadows into the kitchen in their brightness.

Tony watched, not moving from the sink, as the shadow of Lu moved to throw her bag into the back of the truck and then climb in. He waited until he heard the slam of the door and the grumble of the engine as Hunter threw it in reverse.

Then he crumpled, leaning over the stove and breathing in deep, his stomach roiling at the smell of the burned food. He reached over to turn off the burner but couldn't get up the motivation to pitch the pan, so it sat there as he backed away and headed for the fridge for water.

He'd fix this. He'd fix this and Lu could come home.

HUNTER WAS HALFWAY BACK to campus with Lu glaring silently out the passenger-side window when his phone started buzzing in his pocket for the second time that night. The screen on the dash showed Kalla's contact info.

"Fucking wonderful," Hunter muttered to himself, reaching over to tap on the screen and answer the call before returning his eyes to the road.

"I need you to come get Eric," Kalla said before he could even say hello. Her tone was crisp, a little annoyed, the way it got when she was having a minor freakout over something. Because being pissed was better than being vulnerable in Kalla Regan's book.

"Come get him from where?" But already Hunter had his turn signal on to head into a side road and get himself turned around back toward Ironport. He didn't know where Eric had been all night, but he had his suspicions.

A long breath left Kalla, making the mic crackle, and Hunter imagined her running a hand down her face. "His parents' place."

"Why did he go *there*?" Hunter didn't even want to think about what kind of shitstorm that meant he was walking into. As far as he knew, Eric hadn't been back to his parents' place since he'd gotten the job at Moondale U a few years back.

And even before that, he hadn't spent much time there, choosing instead to crash on friends' couches where he didn't have to live with the cold emptiness of the Marcelino house. He couldn't even call it a home, because from what Hunter knew of it, it'd never been one. It was all a performance. Minimalist decor. Clutter-free white walls. Carpet that looked brand new. More a showroom than a home. Growing up, Eric hadn't even been allowed to have a fucking pet.

"I don't know." Kalla sounded tired. "But I can't get him to leave. I've tried. He won't listen. He's just . . . he's just sitting in the middle of the living room." She was quiet for a moment, breathing into the space between them, and Hunter felt like he was holding his breath, his lungs burning with the effort as he pulled back out onto the highway. "When I got here, he said he killed Noah."

"Damn it." Hunter gripped the wheel tighter, his knuckles turning white. Something was sitting on his chest all the sudden, making it hard to breathe and even harder for his heart to beat.

"Who's Noah?" Lu asked, her head turned to look at him, eyes glinting in the streetlights.

"Who's in the car with you?" Kalla's voice had gone sharp, accusing. "Do you have the kids?"

"Just Lu. Tony called me to come pick her up. He said he had a date. I'll have you take her back to campus while I deal with Eric." He didn't have a whole lot of other choices in the matter. He had to get Eric out of that house, and he couldn't leave Lu with Tony. Not after he'd fucking kicked her out. "You good for a bit more of a ride?"

Lu shrugged, turning back to the window. "Better than spending time with my asshole brother and his piece of shit boyfriend."

"Cool." Hunter relaxed a little into his seat, thankful there was no one else on the road. It meant he didn't have to deal with all the anxiety that came from having other drivers around him. He didn't think he had the bandwidth for that on top of everything else in that moment. "Kalla, I'll be there in twenty-ish?"

"Okay," Kalla said with a long, slow exhale. Which meant she was probably trying to keep from saying something cutting. Goddess above and below, Hunter needed to stop spending so much fucking time with Kalla; he was finding it way too easy to read her lately. "I'll see you when you get here."

"Yeah. Just . . . try to get some water in him?" There wasn't much else Hunter could offer by way of direction or suggestion, not till he was there. Kalla wasn't equipped for an Eric Marcelino who was dealing with a break like this one. She wasn't really one for feelings and had always found Eric's to be too messy, even when they were together. It's why they didn't fucking work. Eric might not hold a grudge against her for that, but Hunter had for a while. He was over it now, but it had been a rough couple of years.

"Will do." Kalla hung up a moment later, the line beeping through, and Hunter returned his attention to getting to the Marcelino house. Until a thought struck him.

Bert and Eric had been a little chummier than usual lately. Whispering and tucking themselves away into rooms where no one could overhear. They'd been up to something, not a doubt in Hunter's mind. So, he pulled over on the side of the road, tapped the screen on the center console, and called that little shit.

"Hunter!" Bert sounded excited, on the verge of bouncing like a kid in a bouncy castle at the idea of one of his favorite people calling him probably. "What can I do for you?"

"You can tell me where the fuck Eric was tonight." Hunter didn't pull back onto the road. It wasn't a good idea to drive angry, and fury simmered low and slow in his gut.

"Wha—what do you mean?" Bert's voice broke a little, a clear indication he was hiding something.

"I mean," Hunter said, tone measured but deadly. He wasn't playing this fucking game with Bert, there wasn't time for it. "You two have been awfully secretive of late. Whispering about shit and stopping as soon as people walk in the room. Don't think I haven't noticed. And now he's got Noah, and I want to know what the fuck you two have been up to."

"I uh . . ." Bert cleared his throat, clearly stalling for time.

"Humbert. Explain."

And then it all spilled from Bert in a rush. "Well Eric asked me to use the Ghost Tracer data to track Noah so I did and then he kind of went off to hunt him down and now I guess he's found him so yay that it worked but also boo that you're clearly very pissed at me and I'm sorry I did this without your permission Hunter I know it was wrong to clone the app off your phone and I told Eric that you were going to be super pissed when you found out but he just wouldn't let up and really who am I to tell Eric Marcelino no?"

Hunter grunted, his fingers tightening on the steering wheel. "I'll deal with you later."

Bert let out a startled *meep* just before Hunter hung up.

When he looked over at Lu she had her head turned to look out the window, as if she'd tried to give him some privacy during the call, or maybe it was because she was still stressed by whatever happened between her and Tony. "You okay kid?"

"Yeah. Fine. Let's just go."

"Okay."

Hunter nodded and pulled back onto the road.

When he finally pulled up outside, he looked over at Lu to make sure she hadn't fallen asleep on the drive, but she was watching out the front window with wide eyes.

"This is Eric's house?" she asked, tilting her head to try to take all of it in at once, which was impossible, because the Marcelino house was fucking huge. Large enough that Eric had been able to fit their entire graduating class into it senior year for the biggest bash Hunter had ever seen. The cops hadn't even been called—there was so much space between the Marcelinos and their nearest neighbors.

Hunter remembered looking at it exactly the same way that night. Like Eric was the luckiest little shit in the world because he had so much space, a pool, a billiards room, a library, a liquor cabinet, and *no* parental supervision? Fuck yeah, that was a teenager's wet dream. It was only years later, after he'd gotten to know Eric, that he'd learned that the Marcelino family house wasn't anything of the sort. It was a haunted house, echoing with the emptiness of a childhood of loneliness.

"This is the Marcelino house. This isn't Eric's anything," Hunter responded. "Kalla's gonna take you up the mountain to campus while I deal with Eric. Grab your bag."

Lu frowned at him, her freckled nose wrinkling like she wanted to ask him what the fuck that meant, but when he raised his pierced brow at her, she merely shook her head and clambered out of the truck. Her bag hung heavy off her shoulder, knocking against Hunter's leg on their way up the walk to where Kalla sat on the front stoop. Her fingers were tapping quick and nervous against her knees, and Hunter could almost picture her chain smoking while she waited, if she were a smoker. When she saw them coming, she pushed off from her knees to stand.

"He's in the living room," she said, coming out to meet them a couple of steps from the front door.

"Did you get him to drink anything?" Hunter rubbed at his face, his rings cold and hard against his cheeks. How was he supposed to fix this?

"A little, but it doesn't seem to be helping. He's practically catatonic." Kalla frowned at him, her eyes apologetic as they flicked from him to Lu. "You ready to go, kid?"

Lu's gaze shifted from Hunter to Kalla then back, and she huffed. "Doesn't look like I have much choice."

"You don't," Kalla agreed, heading back down the walk to the driveway where her car was parked without a backward glance. Rolling her eyes, Lu followed her, not saying a word.

Hunter waited until they had pulled away before he knocked lightly on the door. "Eric," he called softly, not wanting to sneak up on him when he was in a state like Kalla had described. "Hon, I'm coming in."

A soft noise of assent came from the direction of the living room, and Hunter followed it till he was standing on the plush carpet, his feet sinking into the fibers. Eric sat in the middle of what had once been a coffee table, dust scattered all around him, blood drying on his shirt. He looked lost, an expression Hunter was painfully familiar with from when it had rested on his own face while he tried in vain to put the blood back where it belonged. Begged to turn back time. Wished for a different outcome. Eric's brow was pinched, his eyes focused somewhere in the middle distance. His hair was a mess, like he'd been running his fingers through it over and over again, and a bruise was forming on his throat as if someone had tried to strangle him.

"Eric, honey, I need you to look at me," Hunter said, keeping his tone level but firm as he came around the couch to squat off to Eric's right, carefully telegraphing his movements so Eric didn't lash out at him on accident. "Come on, Eric, let me see those beautiful eyes."

Eric didn't look away from whatever he was staring at. He just shook his head. "I killed him, Hunter. I killed Noah."

"I know, baby, but I still need you to look at me. Please." His gentle pleading must have gotten through to Eric because Eric's honey-colored eyes finally met Hunter's. They were red rimmed, blinking lazily in an exhaustion that likely went bone deep. Hunter was familiar with that too. Grief was a tiring thing. "There he is," Hunter murmured softly, fixing Eric with a gentle tilt of his lips, an almost smile. "How you feeling, hon?"

"I don't . . . I don't know." Eric's words were stilted, robotic almost. They didn't sound anything like the Eric Hunter knew and loved. The one who was always animated, always expressive.

"That's fair." Hunter nodded. He reached out, careful again to make sure Eric saw him coming, and brushed some of the dust from Eric's cheek. "What can I do for you? How can I make this better?"

"Can you . . . can you get the broom? I um . . ." Eric looked away, his gaze fixing on the dust. "I want to bury him. The right way."

Hunter nodded again, his knees cracking as he stood and headed for the broom closet off the kitchen. He grabbed a fancy glass container holding dried pasta on the way, dumping it in the bin, and returned to find Eric trying, in vain, to scoop the dust up into his hands. It slid through his fingers, a soft whimper leaving him every time it did.

"Hey," Hunter called softly, kneeling beside Eric and taking his wrists in his hand. "Hey, let me do that, okay? I've got him."

Eric took a shaking breath. "Okay."

It was so eerily the opposite of the events of a few weeks ago. When it had been Hunter hunched over someone he loved, trying to protect her, trying to bring her back when there was no way to do it. Then not leaving her side for a single moment, and Eric not leaving his. It made something sharp jab into Hunter's chest, claw at his throat. The reminder of that loss. His eyes burned. But he sniffed back the grief and focused instead on the moment. Eric needed him, and breaking down now would only slow this process.

"Why don't you go to the bathroom and get cleaned up? I can grab you some clothes from the truck?"

"No. No, I want to stay with him." Eric's hair fell limp into his face as he shook his head. "I can stay with him, right?"

"Yeah, honey, you can stay with him. Just come sit over here, out of the way." Hunter guided him gently over to the armchair standing catty-corner to the couch and helped him sit. "Do you think you can fill me in on what happened while I work?"

"No."

"Okay. Then how about I turn on some music?"

"No."

"Okay." Hunter took a deep breath to steady himself. It didn't really work, but at least it gave him a minute before he started sweeping up the ashes of some asshole he'd gone to high school with and scooping them into a glass pasta jar. "Should I just be quiet?"

"You don't have to."

"I'll be quiet," Hunter said softly as he brushed a small pile of ash into the dustpan. There would be some left in the fibers, of course there would be. There was no way he could get it all out of the carpet, even with magic. But he'd do his best. For Eric. Not for Noah—who had been a real piece of work and had dropped Eric the moment things started getting hard. He'd once slammed Hunter so hard into his locker, Hunter got a fucking concussion. Noah had been known to take cell phone pictures up girls' skirts. No. This wasn't for Noah, who was objectively a trash human in high school and hadn't grown out of being a trash human in adulthood where he drank too much, beat around his girlfriend, and then finally became a bloodsucker. This was for Eric. Who looked like he might fall apart at any second.

"Okay."

A quick glance at Eric to make sure he was at least sitting up and coherent, not catatonic like Kalla had said, and Hunter settled himself more firmly to the task of cleaning up the mess as best he could.

CHAPTER 23

WHEN ERIC finally emerged from the fog of his mind, he was in Hunter's truck, leaning against the passenger-side door, his shoulder pressing hard against the door frame as they took a turn. The sun was just peeking around the mountain, poking through the trees, which had begun to get their spring leaves on them. Warmer weather was on its way. It should stir hope in his chest, but the only thing coming to life there was regret, guilt, and nausea.

Eric looked over at Hunter and frowned. There was a smear across his jaw, and his nails were crusted in something dark where he had them wrapped a little too tight around the steering wheel.

"Where are we?" The words came out croaky, catching in Eric's throat like he'd been either screaming or crying.

"Almost to campus," Hunter said, gentle and low. As if he was afraid that speaking too loudly would spook Eric.

Which . . . Eric supposed it very well might. It was kind of hard to tell what his own mental state was like in that moment. The pain was a profound numbness, making it nearly impossible to feel his fingertips where they brushed against the cold lid of the mason jar in his lap. He tapped them against the metal and found that even the pressure was dulled to almost nothing. *This is what shock feels like, isn't it?*

He needed to get his mind off it before he did something irrational. Like scream until he was hoarse just to feel something.

"We need to have a service for Noah."

"We will. But not until you get some rest." Hunter's tone left no room for argument.

Clearing his throat, Eric returned his focus to Hunter. "There was someone else at the house tonight. Who was it?"

"I had to go pick up Lu from Tony's." Hunter frowned, his nose crinkling enough that it raised his glasses up a little. Eric had always found that motion adorable. Liked the way it made Hunter look almost like a cartoon character. But he didn't feel any of those warm fuzzies right then. Right then, a cold emptiness emanated from somewhere in his stomach, but it was hard to pinpoint. Maybe he should eat something. Maybe that would fill the void. Or make him throw up. It was a toss-up. "He umm . . . he kicked her out?"

"Oh well, she's always welcome at—wait. What?" Eric squeezed his eyes shut once, then opened them again and lifted a hand to scrub at his ear. He was sure he'd heard Hunter incorrectly. Tony wouldn't, couldn't, kick Lu out of their house. Right? Tony McMahon was a lot of things, an asshole being one of them, but he wasn't the sort of person to kick his seventeen-year-old sister out on the street. Even if he did know she had a place to go. That wasn't who he was. Eric knew that. Their relationship had been short lived, but he knew *that*. "Did you just say Tony kicked Lu out?"

"Yeah. He said he had a hot date and told me to come get her. I didn't get much out of her on the drive over, but I got the feeling they had a fight."

The blinker was loud in the ensuing silence while Eric tried to work that out. He twisted it around and around in his mind, but it didn't fit with what he knew of Tony. Didn't track. Maybe it was a message? Maybe it was a sign that Tony didn't feel safe? It had to mean *something*. "We have to turn around."

"What?" Hunter turned to look at him as he pulled into a spot out in front of 1106 Moonshadow Way, slamming the truck in park. "No, we fucking don't. We have to get you inside and put you in the fucking shower and then bed. You're in shock, Eric."

"We need to check on Tony." Where were his keys? Eric lifted his hips, digging through his pockets. Why he thought they might be in his jeans when he didn't feel them digging into his thigh, he didn't know. But it was always a good place to start, in his experience. When they weren't there, he started shuffling through his jacket. "Where are my keys?"

"I have them." The keys jingled when Hunter pulled them from his own pocket and hung them from his finger to show Eric. Eric reached to snatch them, but Hunter pulled his hand away, closing his ebony-brown fingers around them to hide them from view. "You're not going anywhere."

"Yes. I am." He turned to look outside, and frowned when he didn't see the beamer. "Where is my car?"

"You left it at the Marcelinos'." The words *the Marcelinos'* came out a little rougher, a little sadder than the rest of the sentence, and Eric kind of hated how Hunter knew what it did to him. Knew what that house had been like for him. But he also appreciated that someone had seen what it was like there, and it made them sad. The hand still around the wheel squeaked as Hunter gripped it tighter, as if he was trying to keep himself still, steady, lest he run off into the night and track down Eric's parents to give them a piece of his mind for everything they'd put their son through. It was sweet. Unnecessary, but sweet.

"Well then, you'll take me." There was a pleading, whining thing crawling up Eric's throat, making a home for itself in his chest. He needed to check in. He didn't know why. He couldn't explain the urge. But it buzzed through him, making every moment he sat in Hunter's truck not doing that a struggle. Impatience crept in at the edges, making him irritable, irrational. If Hunter didn't give him his fucking keys, Eric might very well snap at him. Which he knew, rationally, was not the best response, but it was hard to turn off the anger simmering under his skin.

"No." Hunter licked his lips and turned his focus once more to Eric, meeting his eyes, challenging. "I won't."

"We need to check on him, Hunter! He's in trouble. I know he's in trouble. I can feel it. He wouldn't do that to Lu. He wouldn't treat her that way. Not if it wasn't for her own good, not if it wasn't to protect her." Desperation had crawled in along with the impatience, made a home for itself beneath his skin. Panic. Oh fuck. He was *panicking*. Eric's heart beat hard against his rib cage. His lungs inflated, deflated, and inflated again in quick succession like he was taking in air but it didn't have the oxygen he needed in it.

"Eric. Eric, look at me." Hunter let go of the wheel entirely so he could reach for Eric's hands and take them in his own. He squeezed, his rings biting into Eric's fingers, his knuckles, bringing him back to the present. He leaned in closer, pressing his forehead to Eric's hard enough that Eric was sure it would give him a headache. But it was a good pressure, a grounding pressure. It helped make his lungs feel like they were getting enough oxygen again. "You need to take care of you for about half a minute. Okay? You've been through some shit tonight, and you need to take care of yourself."

"But Tony—"

"We'll check in with him tomorrow. After you've gotten cleaned up. After you've had some sleep. All right?" Hunter was staring at him, his eyes so close that Eric couldn't meet his gaze directly. He had to dart between one eye or the other to look at him. That was also going to give him a headache. But he didn't fucking care. Because it was nice to be this close. It was nice to share this space. He felt safe here with Hunter. When was the last time he could say that? Not since . . . not since Tony showed up to the funeral and ripped his fucking heart from his chest.

"Tomorrow? We'll go tomorrow?"

"I'll drive you there myself, hon," Hunter swore, giving Eric's hands another careful squeeze.

Eric nodded, his nose bumping against Hunter's, then he took a deep breath and dove in, pressing his lips to Hunter's so hard, he felt their teeth clack together. Hunter was still for a moment, like he wasn't sure what to do, like he wasn't sure if he wanted it. Shit. Maybe Eric should have asked. No. He *definitely* should have asked.

Eric started to pull back, to give Hunter the space and time he clearly needed. The space and time Eric kept *forgetting* was necessary for a person to grieve. Fuck, he was a terrible friend, wasn't he? Jumping Hunter's bones when he was clearly still—

"Nuh-uh," Hunter mumbled against his lips, his teeth biting down on the lower one as his hand moved to fist in Eric's hair. Eric hissed through the burn of it against his skull but didn't fight the hold, leaning into it instead. "You're not going anywhere. Not this time, hon."

"But you're—" He cut himself off, diving in again. Lapping his tongue against the piercing in Hunter's lower lip, murmuring at the taste of cold metal. What was he going to say again? That Hunter was still not over Britt. That Eric couldn't afford to be a rebound. That Eric wasn't over Tony. That they needed to get inside. That—oh, fuck it.

He turned to put Noah carefully on the back bench, then his fingers found Hunter's belt loops and he tugged, pulling Hunter over the center console into his lap. All long, gangly limbs, and laughing mouth. Hunter's rings clacked against the window, his wide palm cutting through the steam they were quickly building. Once he had his balance, he reached for Eric's fly, fumbling. And Eric had just enough sense to grab Hunter's wrist and stop him.

Wide brown eyes glanced up from where Hunter had been focused on his task a moment ago, brows raised in question. His lips were puffy from the kiss, breath coming in short pants. The ring in his right eyebrow glinted in the yellow streetlamps. Goddess, he was something, wasn't he? "Do you not . . . ?"

"I do!" Eric rushed, heat crawling up his neck. "Goddess, do I ever. But. But do you? I mean, Hunter . . ." He sucked down a breath, tried to force his brain to work, to think of words, when all it wanted to focus on was the way Hunter's lips looked, the way his breath felt brushing against Eric's mouth. He could have those fingers wrapped around his cock in less than a minute if that's what he wanted. And it *was*. It was so much of what Eric wanted. He needed this, he knew he did. Otherwise he wouldn't sleep, wouldn't be able to get himself to calm down. It was the perfect distraction. But not at the cost of Hunter's peace. "Britt."

Hunter took a deep breath, leaning until his back hit the glove compartment. The space between them was chilled with early spring air, making goosebumps rise on Eric's skin, but he ignored it. Because they needed to talk about this. Eric couldn't get into another relationship with someone where he didn't talk about shit like this. Where he rushed in. He couldn't have his heart broken for a fourth time. A repeat performance of losing Hunter so quickly after Eric had lost someone else would tear him up, leave him shredded. It wasn't something he could afford to let himself feel, not right now, not with what was happening in his city. Fuck. This was such a bad idea. Why the fuck had he thought—

"Eyes up here, Big Ricky," Hunter said, flicking his wrist so he could point at his eyes. Eric followed the movement, and what he found on Hunter's face made his shoulders relax a little. Hunter didn't look upset. He didn't look guilty or unsure. He looked resolute. Like he always did right after he'd made a decision. It was an expression Eric had become intimately acquainted with over the years, but usually it was in the lab right before Hunter did an experiment that he half expected to blow up in his face and singe his eyebrows off. Was Eric going to singe his eyebrows off? Maybe.

"I'm lookin'," Eric said when Hunter was silent for too long. "What am I lookin' at?"

"You're looking at me saying I want this." Hunter kept his words even, his tone steady, and never once broke eye contact. "You're looking at me saying that yeah, maybe we're rushing into things a bit, but this feels right. You're looking at me saying yes."

"Yes?"

"Yes." Hunter nodded, his lips twitching into a smile.

"Then can we—" Eric gestured to the space between them again.

"Goddess, yes," Hunter gasped and leaned in again, his mouth hard on Eric's, his tongue already brushing along the inside of Eric's cheeks, his teeth. He tasted like stale coffee and root beer hard candies, and Eric liked it. Goddess above and below, he *liked* it. It was so fucking weird, and he knew that, but it was all Hunter.

The cool night air hit his cock, and he lifted his hips at Hunter's urging, letting him pull his jeans down until he was sitting bare assed on Hunter's leather seats. He fumbled with Hunter's jeans, not willing to take his mouth away from where it had moved to worry a bit of skin beneath Hunter's ear—his curls tickling Eric's nose—long enough to see what he was doing. Hunter swatted his hands away for a moment to do it for him with a soft huff of laughter.

"Stop laughing at me, you asshole," Eric grumbled against Hunter's ear, making him shiver. A smile tugged at his lips, a laugh crawled up his throat. Happiness, sharp and real, came with it, making him feel like he might choke on it. Goddess, it had been so long since he'd been happy like this. Months.

"I'll laugh at you if I—" A groan cut off Hunter's words as

Eric finally got his fingers wrapped around Hunter's shaft, giving it a threatening squeeze before thumbing at a bead of pre-cum on the tip.

"Shut up and come here." Eric guided him closer, careful not to pull too hard, until their cocks lined up, brushing against each other.

"I thought I was the one in charge here," Hunter joked, leaning in for another kiss. Eric hummed against his lips, his hand tightening around both their lengths, gliding up along them and drawing a hiss from Hunter and a shiver from himself. Goddess. It wasn't going to take long to get him off this way, and he didn't even have the excuse of a long dry spell like he had with Tony. What the fuck was wrong with him? He supposed grief did weird things to people.

Hunter shifted, his hips grinding so their cocks brushed in Eric's grip, fucking up his rhythm. But it didn't matter. It sent a zing up Eric's spine, making his toes curl in his shoes where he'd braced his feet on the floorboards to give himself leverage. Lips moved against his, nipping, and suckling, and moving to his chin, to his neck. Eric tilted his head back, let Hunter set the pace with the shifting of his hips as his teeth sank into Eric's skin over and over, leaving behind marks and drawing gasps.

After a couple of clumsy attempts to sync up, Hunter growled and swatted Eric's hand away, taking over entirely. His hand pumped over them both as he thrust against him. His rings were cool, heating up slowly, and the callouses from years of working in the lab or playing guitar rubbed rough against Eric's sensitive skin. Just different enough, just new enough, that with the sharp pinch of Hunter's teeth on his earlobe, Eric went over the edge quickly. Spilling across Hunter's length and fingers, soiling their clothes.

Hunter gasped, his hips jerking again, and he followed right after, leaving his hand a sticky mess. Tilting his head back down, still panting, Eric shot Hunter a hazy sort of smile and asked, "Feel better?"

"You don't think I still have those wipes in my glove box, do you?"

"Not if you've been carting around the gremlins." Eric laughed softly, the sound breathy and a little broken, but Goddess he felt so fucking *light* all the sudden.

"Fucking hell," Hunter muttered, and wiped his hand on his shirt.

CHAPTER 24

THE NIGHT MARKET was not at all what Tony had been expecting. First of all, it wasn't even *at* night.

"That's just because that's what time you're going, you dingus," Sage chided, and Tony imagined them rolling their eyes. "You could have gone at night if you'd wanted to."

"I have patrol at night," Tony reminded, tapping his foot on the cobblestone street at the start of the market. He wasn't even sure how he'd gotten there really. If he were asked to repeat the directions Sage had whispered into his ear while he walked and knocked along alley walls until he found the right brick, he wouldn't be able to. He just knew that once he'd done exactly as Sage said, a path opened onto a busy cobblestone street that looked like it was straight out of an old fantasy novel. And where he'd left Ironport on a cold and rainy day, he came through to someplace bright and sunny, not a cloud in the sky. So clearly it had been some kind of portal. "Where the fuck even am I right now?"

"Don't think about it too hard," Sage advised. "It'll just make your head hurt."

"Ah, it's one of those metaphysical bullshit planes the fae like to use, isn't it?" A snort left Tony and someone walking past him cut him a sharp look. He caught a glimpse of pointed ears through their long pale-green hair. "Sorry."

"You need to learn when to keep your mouth shut," Sage grumbled from the other end of the line, their chair creaking under them a little. "One of these days, you're going to get your ass cursed."

"It's rude to threaten your best friend with hexes." Tony tugged down his T-shirt and started through the crowd, his eyes flicking about the stalls. There were folk of all kinds. Witches, and goblins, and everyone in between. Selling everything from sleeping draughts to funnel cakes.

"Not my best friend, and that wasn't a—"

"Only friend then."

"I'm friends with your—"

"Lu doesn't count, she's fucking seventeen." Tony grinned a little to himself, knowing full well that Sage could hear it in his voice. It was nice to be away from Dash, to be out somewhere and talking to someone he actually liked and cared about. Someone who didn't expect anything out of him for the moment. Sage was a good friend. The best friend. Goddess, Tony didn't deserve them.

"Do you want to talk about—"

And like that, any good mood he might have been having was gone. Washed away by the guilt, the regret, and the disgust. Would he ever be able to get Lu to forgive him? Should he even try? He didn't deserve her forgiveness for what he'd done. Even if it was to keep her safe. He should have told her what was going on. They should have worked through it as a family. But he couldn't. And not just because he was worried about what she might do, but also because he could still feel the words clinging to the inside of his throat. Unable to get them up or down every time he thought about them. "I think you know the answer to that question."

Sage let out a long, slow breath; it made the speaker crackle in Tony's ear as he pushed past a gathering of witchlings who couldn't have been older than Lu. He wondered where they were from. If they'd popped in from somewhere local, or if this night market was accessible all around the globe. He'd ask Sage if they didn't sound so fucking frustrated right now.

"Where's your contact?" He needed to get in and get out. Dash was likely going to be back from work soon, and Tony needed to be there when he returned or else he'd get suspicious. Dash deciding to stay over for the foreseeable future had put a fucking dent in all of Tony's plans. And he wasn't sure how to get him to leave. He'd tried making himself as obnoxious as possible. Smoking in the bedroom. Leaving his dirty laundry on the floor. But none of those things seemed to bother the fucking leech.

He'd just gotten up, gotten ready for work, had a quick drink off the bite on Tony's shoulder that had scabbed over, and left. Tony was dying to tell someone about it. To let Sage know what kind of trouble he was in, but he couldn't. Sage would probably have some elaborate plan that would wind up with Dash nailed into a coffin and buried for the rest of eternity until he eventually dried up like a fucking prune. Would serve him right.

"You'll know her when you see her." Sage hummed softly, their fingers tapping lightly against some surface in the background, likely their desk. Tony didn't know if he'd ever seen them away from it, not really. And when they were, they usually had a tablet out. Unless of course they were helping him set up a way to kill his father. But that was neither here nor there.

"Is she a werewolf?" Wouldn't that be weird? Buying venom off the werewolf who had produced it? Tony hoped not; he didn't think he had it in him to deal with that level of awkward right now. Not that he was being given much choice. "Does she sell a lot of wolf venom?"

"Yes, she's a werewolf. Where the fuck do you think the venom comes from, Tony?"

Fuck. So this was going to be weird. Great.

"It's only as weird as you make it." Sage snorted. "And yeah, she sells a bit of it. It's not just used for turning wolves, you know? There are potions witches can put it in, and it can act as an antidote for a few poisons. Which you'd know, if you actually sat down and read a book on magic every once in a while."

Tony huffed, rolling his eyes as he side-stepped a small fae woman with one of those wire shopping trollies people used for the grocery store. She had it stacked full of things from books to potion ingredients. It looked like she was stocking up. He wondered if she'd be reselling any of it. "I have no use for magic books when I can't use magic."

"Tony." Sage sighed, likely leaning forward to pinch at the bridge of their nose in exasperation. "We've been over this. You're of the folk. Just because you can't use magic directly like a witch or a fae doesn't mean you shouldn't be aware of what different magical elements do. It might—"

"Right, right. Save my life one day. You keep saying that but—"

"But you called me the other day asking for an antidote to vampire blood, which you might have known had you already done your own research," Sage sniped.

"You said there was no record of anyone having ever done this before."

"There's not. But you'd have known that werewolf venom can be used for . . ."

Tony tuned them out as he continued to scan the crowd. There were a lot of people there for a Thursday afternoon, but he supposed normal shopping rules didn't apply to magical markets that set up shop in pocket dimensions or whatever the fuck this place was. It took a couple of minutes, traveling the never-ending street of stalls before he saw her: a tall, broad-shouldered woman with steel-gray hair and deep-brown skin. She met his eyes over the crowd and her eyebrow twitched upward, as if she knew exactly who he was and what he was there for. Well. Sage had probably told her.

"I think I see her," Tony said, cutting off whatever tangent Sage had gone down.

"Good. Try to be nice. She can be a bit of a bitch on the surface, but she's actually a huge sweetheart. And since she'll be your sire if you wind up having to become a werewolf, it would behoove you to have a good relationship with her," Sage pled. Their words were logical, and yeah, Tony knew that. But the werewolf in question had mad resting bitch face, and Tony wasn't exactly above poking the bear a bit. Never had been.

"Well, you look thrilled as fuck to be here," he told her, ignoring the groan from Sage in his earbud.

"I said be *nice*," Sage hissed. Tony ignored them.

"Let me guess," she drawled, her arms crossing over her chest as she leaned back on her heels. "You're Sage's Venator."

"What gave it away? The great muscles? The sculpted jaw? The—"

"The stake stuffed into your fucking pants like you're an idiot." She pointed, and Tony looked down to find that yes, he did have a stake stuffed into his pants pocket. Not that he'd really thought he would need it where he was going, but it was hard to leave the house these days without one. Knowing what Dash was doing to him was making him increasingly paranoid. His hair pins would have been a better option, but he hadn't been able to find them earlier, and he was kind of in a hurry. He'd have to remember that for next time.

"Right. That." Tony's neck heated a little in embarrassment, but he pulled his jacket closed to cover it and lifted his head back to glare at her. "Look, this doesn't have to be any weirder than it has to be."

"You were the one making it fucking weird." She shrugged, then held out a hand. "I'm Lowell."

"Is she really pissed at you?" Sage asked in his ear.

"No. I think I just made a friend. I'm gonna go." He hung up without another word, stuffed the earbud into his pocket, and held his hand out to Lowell for her to shake. "Tony."

Lowell's grip was tight, grinding his bones together as if she either didn't know her own strength or it was a test, a bid for dominance. Tony didn't so much as wince; he just held on tightly and waited for her to be done. After a long moment that left his fingertips tingly, her lips twitched into a smirk, and she dropped his hand. "I'd say welcome to the pack, but I know your situation, and you might not actually be joining."

"Even if I did wind up turning, I'm more of a lone wolf anyway." He flexed his hand as he returned it to his side to try to get feeling back into his digits.

Lowell huffed a laugh. "Sure, that's what they all say."

"Look. Do you have what I need, or not?" Tony shifted on his feet, refusing to let his eyes move from where they met Lowell's. She must be the lead of her pack. There was no other explanation for how she acted. And he had nothing against her, but he didn't think he wanted to be her underling.

"Impatient little shit, aren't you?" She turned to dig through a cooler stored behind her table and held out a vial to him. "It has to be injected. It cannot be drunk, or eaten, or otherwise ingested. Am I clear?"

"Because it would make the venom non-viable. I know. I'm not an idiot." He hadn't known that, actually—Sage had told him. But Tony wasn't about to back down in front of this woman. He could tuck his tail between his legs and tell Sage all about how nervous he was later. For now, he needed to stand his ground.

"Sure you aren't." Lowell held the vial out to him, and he took it.

Despite it having been in a cooling bag a moment ago, the silvery liquid burned hot in his hand. The way a freshly pulled vial of blood might. He tucked it into his pocket, out of sight, and hopefully out of mind as well. Now. If only he didn't wind up having to use it, that'd be peachy.

Lowell tipped her head to the side, her eyes flicking over him quickly, assessing, as she drew in a deep breath, likely scenting him. Then she said, "I'll see you around, Tony."

"Yeah. Well. Let's hope you don't." Tony grunted and turned on his heel to head back the way he'd come. Once he was sure he was out of earshot, he hit call on his phone and asked, "Why didn't you tell me she was fucking scary?" as soon as Sage picked up.

"Figured that wasn't super relevant to what you were asking. Plus, if you do really need it to counteract vamp toxins, you're gonna want some strong werewolf shit. Lowell is the strongest werewolf I know." Sage sounded like they were shrugging. "Did she give you what you needed?"

"Yeah."

"Good. Then you have a plan B. Let's just hope you don't have to use it."

"Fingers cross—" Tony's phone started vibrating in his hand, and he pulled it away from his ear to check the caller ID. Dash. "I gotta go. That's him."

"*Him* as in, the vampire who's got you under his thrall?"

Yes was on the tip of his tongue, but Tony couldn't force it off and out into the air. The thrall wouldn't let him. He choked on the word, coughing and releasing a strangled noise of agreement.

"Okay. You need to get that so he doesn't suspect anything," Sage said softly, their words gentle. "But if you need me, I'm a text away. Okay? I can be on a plane in under an hour. And I will not hesitate to drive a stake through his fucking heart myself."

Tony didn't know how that was fucking possible, nor did

he know how to express his gratitude for the sentiment. So he just grunted again and hung up to answer the call from Dash.

"Tooooony," Dash sing-songed, "where are you?"

"Running errands. I'll be home shortly. I was thinking curry for dinner, should I pick it up on my way?"

Dash hummed, soft and leading, in agreement.

CHAPTER 25

IT WAS GOING to be fine. Eric was overreacting. This whole thing was just a trauma response. There was no reason to really think that Tony was in trouble, that Eric needed to go in there and save him like some kind of white knight. And Tony probably wouldn't even like that. He'd think it was fucking gross. Even still, Eric decided he needed to check, or he might never fucking sleep again. This wasn't a rescue mission, it was just a check-in. Just to see.

He and Hunter loaded into his car, because Hunter wasn't letting him go anywhere by himself after what happened the night before, and drove over to Tony's. Hunter spent the entire ride fidgeting and rambling. Jumping from topic to topic. About his experiments. About how he wanted to chat with Ashthorne some more about the Ghost Tracer. Eric couldn't really follow it, and not just because he was stressed but also because Hunter had hardly finished two sentences before he was off on another tangent. It was how he got when he was nervous or upset, and that didn't make Eric feel any better. Couple that with the fact that his lower back was all fucked up from sharing his twin bed with Hunter, and Eric was in a terrible fucking mood.

Fuck, if that was going to become a habit, they were definitely going to have to swap rooms, even if Hunter's room didn't have an ensuite bathroom. Eric's was too small for a larger bed, and he couldn't in good conscience squeeze them both into that twin bed for another night. Not if he ever wanted to be able to stand up right again. Fuck getting old, it was for the birds.

When they pulled up outside Tony's, a slick red sports car sat in the spot next to Tony's Mustang. It was electric and still had temp tags on it. Because Dashfield Chadwick could fucking afford to get a new vehicle every other year if he so chose.

"Slick ride," Hunter murmured with a whistle.

"Well," Eric said, running his fingers through his hair and likely making it even more of a mess than it already was, "he's driving an electric car. If he *is* a vampire, he's at least trying to save the environment."

Hunter snorted. "Nah. That's a dick-mobile if I've ever seen one. Like . . . I thought Tony's was, but this is way worse. I mean, look at it. It doesn't have a fucking spot on it. He's probably got someone who washes it every morning for him."

The comment drew a soft laugh from Eric that eased some of the tension in his shoulders. "Yeah. It kinda is, isn't it?"

"Do you think he's compensating?" Hunter turned a feral smile on Eric, his teeth glinting in the afternoon sunshine.

"Shut up." Eric huffed another soft snicker and gave him a shove. He'd thought for half a second last night that waking up next to Hunter this morning would be awkward. That something would hang over them that would make every interaction from now until the day he died weird. But it had been normal between them. Hunter had grumbled and whined and kicked him in the fucking spleen until Eric rolled out of bed to go to the bathroom. And when he was done, he heard Hunter downstairs starting the coffee machine and making breakfast for the kids, as if nothing at all had changed between them. The breath that had been trapped in Eric's chest when he'd first woken up had whooshed out of him in a rush.

"You shut up." Hunter snickered, reaching for the door. "Come on, you're stalling."

Eric grumbled and grabbed his own door. He was stalling. He was one-hundred percent stalling. But that didn't mean Hunter had to fucking call him on it. Asshole. "Let's just get this over with."

A soft sound of agreement came from Hunter's side of the car as he slid out into the chilly afternoon air. It was warming up little by little. Soon it would be summer and they'd all be sweltering, but for now Eric pulled his scarf more tightly around his neck and hoped it would ward off the goose-bumps that prickled along his skin just from looking at Tony's house.

He couldn't place the feeling, didn't know where it came from, but something was off about the place. Once it had been cheerful and happy, warmth flooding his gut at the idea of getting to spend time with Tony in his own space. Getting to see how Tony kept his room neat as a pin, never a sock out of the hamper, but also covered their living room in soft fluffy blankets for him and Lu to use whenever they needed. In the short time Tony had been there, he'd made the townhouse a home for him and his sister, and Eric had been fucking enamored at the thought.

But the house didn't feel that way now. No warmth radiated off it. No homey-ness. Just the stillness of a residence that had been left empty, stagnant. And a scent lingered in the air on the way up the walk. Something he could almost recognize but couldn't directly place.

It was a relief to have Hunter at his side, his hand brushing against Eric's as they walked up to the front door. Warm, and alive. He glanced over at Hunter, meeting his dark eyes for a moment, then he rang the bell.

The door swung open almost as soon as he rang it, like the

person on the other side had been waiting for him, watching him. Well. That explained the way the hairs on the back of his neck had lifted and refused to lay back down.

"Well, well, well. Look who it is," Dash said, leaning his body long and languid against the door frame. "My darling! Your ex is here!"

Eric's stomach twisted. Hunter leaned subtly closer, lending his support. It didn't really help. Nothing was likely going to help. Because Eric was terrible at breakups. Terrible at facing down his ex when he still felt raw. And wasn't that fucked up? He was sort of something with Hunter, and there he was standing beside Hunter and losing it over the way Tony ambled up to the front door, his neck a patchwork of love bites. Red marks covering almost every inch of his lightly tanned skin.

"What do you want, Marcelino?" Tony asked, moving to stand beside Dash. There was a twitch, so subtle Eric might have imagined it, on Tony's face as Dash slipped his arm around his waist and pulled him in closer.

"You kicked out Lu?" Eric blurted, instead of everything else he wanted to ask. Like, *What the fuck is Dash doing here? How long are you going to keep dating this asshole? Do you know he smells like a fucking graveyard? Why did you leave me? What did I do wrong?* None of those questions would get them anywhere. They would just expose his soft underbelly, which he'd learned when he broke up with Kalla was never a good idea. It was a surefire way to get himself hurt.

"I didn't kick her out." Tony rolled his eyes, his long hair falling into his face. Eric's fingers twitched to brush it away from his cheeks, to hold it away from his neck so Eric could bury his face there. What the fuck was wrong with him? Why was he still feeling like this?

"That's not what she said," Hunter said. He'd stuffed his hands into his pockets, rolling his shoulders back to make himself appear bigger, broader shouldered, than he was. Eric knew the posture well. He'd seen Hunter do it any number of times when he was trying to puff himself up to deal with something he was anxious about.

"Yeah well. She's a dramatic little shit." Tony shrugged. He pushed off from where he leaned against Dash, standing up taller as if he and Hunter were about to have it out right there. Planting his feet.

"Then what happened?" Eric asked, hoping to head off the brewing tension. If he could get through this interaction without someone throwing a punch, he'd be happy.

"I refused to raise her allowance, and she threw a fuckin' fit." It grated on Eric's nerves how cool and unaffected Tony sounded. Eric didn't think he'd ever heard Tony's tone like that before. Especially not when it came to Lu. She was his best friend. His baby sister. The person he'd moved several states away to look after. Eric knew what Lu meant to him. But to hear him talk about her now, he didn't care.

"So we can bring her back?" Eric was gambling. His gaze narrowed on Tony's features, looking for a tell. He probably should have been paying attention to Dash too, considering everything that had happened so far. But it was Tony he was worried about. Tony who he thought was in a dangerous situation.

There was a moment of panic. A slight widening of Tony's eyes as they flicked to look at Dash and then back to Eric. If Eric hadn't been looking for it, he'd have missed it. Tony covered it quickly enough, his arms crossed over his chest, his shoulders curling forward to make himself smaller, to hide, his face going impassive, unreadable. And when he said, "Do whatever you fucking want, man. But she's probably not gonna want to come back," he sounded annoyed and gruff.

"She can stay with us until she cools down," Hunter volunteered. Eric wasn't sure if he sensed the tension and was trying to defuse it, or if he had seen what Eric had. But Eric was glad he was there to speak when Eric didn't know that he could. When it felt like his heart was twisting in his chest at the way Dash guided Tony in again, and Tony went willingly.

"Yeah. Sure. Whatever man." Tony tilted his head, leaning it against Dash, his hair falling over his shoulder to cascade down his back, and that's when Eric saw it. His eyes narrowed, homed in on one of the red marks in particular. It wasn't a love bite or a hickey. It wasn't a bruise left over from Dash being a little too rough. No. It was—it was still fucking bleeding. From two little puncture marks. *Fang* marks.

Eric's heart kicked in his chest, slamming against his ribs, and he leaned in closer involuntarily to get a better look. To make sure he was seeing what he thought he was seeing. Yeah. Those were definitely *fang* marks! And now that he was closer, his torso leaning over the threshold of the house, he got a better whiff of the scent he'd picked up outside.

Death. Decay. Blood. Blood. *Blood.*

Vampire.

"Dude, what the fuck is your problem?" Tony asked, giving him a little shove so Eric stumbled back. He sounded angry, but when Eric looked him in the eyes, he saw that Tony's pupils were dilated in fear, his gaze flicking all over the place, looking for the nearest threat. His chest heaved. "Get the fuck out of here."

"Yeah. I'll . . . We should get back." Eric swallowed roughly, taking another step back. He jerked his head so he could examine Dash, look for the signs.

Dash smirked, one lip peeling back slightly to show a flash of what might have been fang or might have been an overly pointed incisor. It was hard to tell with how quickly it happened, between one blink and the next. Just like how his eyes might have flashed red, or it might have been the light from outside. Might have been Eric's imagination.

Eric inhaled deeply again, sucking down the smell of corpse, and knew he wasn't seeing things wrong. He wasn't imagining them.

Dashfield B.M. Chadwick was a fucking vampire.

The realization sent Eric spiraling. All the memories he thought he had of Dash from their time growing up. Playing together. Going to school together. It all came crashing down. Why would he have had algebra with Dash when Dash was three years younger than him and Janet? Why would he remember Dash sharing a limo with them to prom when Dash was too young to go?

Now that Eric was looking at all these memories, they didn't make sense. None of them made sense.

Tony was in deep fucking shit.

Hunter grabbed him by the hand, pressing his cool, dry palm to Eric's overheated one, the grip firm as he wheeled them around and dragged Eric back to the beamer.

# Chapter 26

"I'M GOING to ask you this once," Dash said, not turning from where they were still watching Eric and Hunter through the window on the door. Eric looked upset, frazzled. Hunter looked harried. Something had set them off. Nothing that Tony had said, he knew that. But they'd seen something. They'd noticed something. They knew what was going on, and it put Tony in more danger than ever. "What did you tell them?"

Dash's grip on Tony's hip had turned punishing, the nails growing to points, digging into the skin, drawing blood. Fucking vampires and their fucking fingernails. It was weird how they had the ability to make a part of their body grow like that. If Tony had more time and wasn't in the circumstances he was in, he might want to study it, to understand it better. But Dash wasn't about to sit down and let himself be subjected to an in-depth interview about his physiology. Pity, really. The better the Venator could understand the vampires, the better they could all get along. Maybe? Probably not. The Venator would never get along with vampires. It wasn't how they'd been raised.

"Tony," Dash hedged. A note of warning rang in his voice. Tony shook himself, trying to focus through the haze of vampire venom coursing through his body, leaving him tingling. He wished Dash would stop doing that. There had to be a way for him to bite without leaving the venom behind. Or maybe there wasn't? Another thing the Venator had no understanding of.

"They're probably just worried about Lu." Tony shrugged, pulling out of Dash's hold. He needed space from the cloying–graveyard flower scent that lingered on Dash's skin. It made him want to vomit. And now that he thought about it . . . *that* had likely been what tipped Tony off. Did Dash not know that Venator had a keen sense of smell? Did he not know that Eric could smell a vampire from a mile away? Or had he merely forgotten the bit of spellwork that hid him? He hadn't slid back on that gaudy necklace he always wore. Maybe that was the source of the cloaking. If Tony could get it away from him—

Dash grunted, disbelieving.

"They're busybodies. You should know that, you've been around here long enough." He headed for the kitchen, gulping down air to try to clear his head and his lungs. It didn't do much; the smell of Dash had invaded every room in his little house. Seeped into the walls. Tony might never get it out. Might never be able to stay there again once all of this was over without remembering everything that happened while he was under Dash's thrall.

"Marcelino does like sticking his nose in where it doesn't belong." Dash hummed in agreement, his presence a cold pressure at Tony's back as he followed Tony about the kitchen. Tony did his best to stay two steps ahead, out of reach. "So he was just worried about his baby Venator then? Nothing else?"

"Definitely." Tony didn't believe it though. Eric had seen something, had smelled something. He knew what Dash was, there was no doubt now. All Tony could hope was that Eric kept his fucking nose out of it long enough for Tony to burn away the vampire blood in his system. He needed to call Sage and ask how he'd be able to tell. Dash hadn't given him another display of his power, not since that first day when Tony realized just how much control Dash had over him. He supposed that periodically trying to tell someone what was going on would be a good marker. In the meantime, he needed to keep Dash from confronting Eric. "You've got nothing to worry about."

Dash made a soft noise, but Tony couldn't tell if it was in agreement or something else.

Fuck.

Maybe he needed to accelerate the plan a little . . . Get himself out before Eric did something stupidly noble that would get them all fucking killed.

"Okay," Hunter said, throwing the beamer into park in an abandoned parking lot. It was for one of the small parks in the area with a playground and a ball field, left vacant during the colder months when parents kept their kids indoors. His stomach was a writhing mess, hands too tight around the wheel even though he wanted to reach for Eric, to pull him in close. "What the fuck was that?"

"I'm gonna put a stake through Dashfield fucking Chadwick, that's what the fuck that was." Eric growled, his hands balling into fists on his knees, opening and closing, opening again. As if he could get them around Dash's throat and squeeze until there was no life left in him by sheer imagination alone. He lunged for the door. Hunter reached out to grab his wrist and stop him from opening it.

"Whoa buddy," Hunter said, giving Eric's wrist a tight squeeze and using his free hand to pull his face around until they were looking at each other. What Eric planned to do after he opened the door, Hunter had no fucking idea, but he was pretty sure he didn't want to find out. "No. You're not."

"Yes. I am," Eric seethed. His jaw was tight under Hunter's fingertips, grinding his teeth in his fury. "We'll all be better off for it."

"Okay." Hunter nodded, placatingly. "Can you at least tell me why?"

Hunter had some idea. A vague sense of wrongness. A chill up his spine. He was nowhere near as tuned in to the world of the supernatural as someone like Eric, but he had his own instincts, even if he was a less powerful witch. He couldn't pinpoint the feeling, of course. For all he knew, it might have just been there was a wonky ley line in the area. But the house had felt wrong. The energy all fucked up by something.

"He's a vampire. No." Eric shook his head, forcing Hunter to drop his hold. "He's *the* vampire. And I'm going to fucking drive a stake through him."

"All right, slow down." Eric hadn't moved for the door yet, but Hunter didn't think that he wasn't thinking about it. So he tightened his hold on Eric's wrist until it had to be near painful. "What do you mean *the* vampire?"

"He's at the heart of all this shit. He's the one running it." Eric shook under Hunter's hands, his heart beating so hard and so fast that Hunter could feel it under his fingers without even trying. "He's in *charge*!"

Hunter forced himself to breathe. One of them had to be calm in this situation, and it clearly wasn't going to be Eric. "Eric. Think about that a minute. Dash has been around for ages. He was born here. He's—" But wait. That didn't feel right. Did it? "We went to—"

"Did we?" Eric pressed, his eyes wide and wild. "Did we go to school with him? Can you remember what classes you had with him? Who was his homeroom teacher?"

Hunter floundered, his mouth opening and closing. He

cast his mind back. Tried to think. Hadn't he been in English with Ava at one point? Wasn't he in Mrs. Fornash's homeroom? But even as he thought that, Hunter realized he couldn't imagine it. Couldn't see Dash there, walking the halls of their high school. That couldn't be right.

"Who did he go to prom with?" Eric leaned in closer, his forehead bumping against Hunter's. If Hunter wasn't careful, he could drown in that intense tilt of Eric's brows. Goddess, why did he have to be so fucking pretty when he got like this? "Why do we think he was in classes with us when he's younger than us?"

"He's not—"

"He is! Hunter, he's at least three years younger than us, that's what Janet always said. He's her younger brother. Right? Then why do we think he walked with us?"

"It's a spell," Hunter whispered, and as soon as the words left his mouth, the places he thought he remembered Dash inhabiting disappeared. He was no longer there in the hallway. No longer sitting in the back of the class. "A cloaking spell?"

"Maybe? Maybe it's a mass thrall? I don't know." Eric shook his head, leaning back again, his back hitting the door behind him hard enough that it thunked. "Whatever it is, I can't tell how long it's been in place."

"Do you think it's failing now? Or is it because we've seen his true colors?" Hunter scrubbed at his face, pushing his glasses up into his hair where the nose pads caught in the strands, making him hiss.

Eric shrugged, which Hunter supposed was fair. He didn't have a whole lot of magical knowledge. Really, that was a question Hunter should have been able to answer. But he'd never been terribly good at magic; maybe that's why he'd never advanced in his power. Or maybe he'd moved around too much. Or maybe he came from a family of low-level witches. He'd never really figured it out, and sitting down to think too hard about it just made him feel incompetent sometimes.

"Right," Hunter said, letting out a long, slow breath and brushing his hands through his hair, knocking his glasses into the floorboards. He cursed and bent to retrieve them. "Okay, next question. How long do you think he's actually been here? And how is he able to walk around in the *sunlight*?"

"I don't know." Eric chewed on his lower lip, his fingers tapping lightly against his legs. He looked like he was about to fly away again. Run off into the street and hunt down Dash all on his own. Goddess, Hunter wondered sometimes if he needed to put Eric on a fucking leash. "But I know a way we can find out. Call Ava. We're gonna go mayor hunting."

Hunter let out a loud groan and bent forward to press his head into the steering wheel. "I want to go on record as saying I think this is a bad idea."

"Noted." Eric shrugged, turning back around in his seat and buckling himself in. Hunter wasn't sure when he had unbuckled, but he was glad Eric hadn't decided to just roll out of the fucking car before they'd stopped. He pulled out his phone to dial Ava.

He put the phone on speaker so Hunter could hear as Ava opened her mouth to say hello, and was cut off almost immediately by "How would you feel about inviting your ex out to dinner on a double date?"

"I'd say my current girlfriend wouldn't like that," Ava responded without missing a single beat. "What the fuck do you want me to ask Janet out to dinner for?"

"I think she's a vampire."

"Oh sure. Yeah. Then let me just invite her out for fucking pasta while I leave my non-bloodsucking girlfriend at home diddling herself. Do you think garlic would kill her?"

Hunter choked on a laugh, and Eric rolled his eyes. "It's not a real date. It's a trap."

"I realize it's a fucking trap, Eric. I'm not stupid. But that still doesn't mean I want to do it."

"I told you this was a bad idea," Hunter added, but Eric waved him off before returning his attention to the phone.

"Look. You don't even have to be there, it's just—"

"Oh, fuck off if I'm not gonna be there while you stare down the mayor and accuse her of vampirism. I'll see you at seven. You better make something good. Something with looooads of garlic." Then Ava hung up and Eric dropped his locked phone to his lap.

"Well," Eric said, tone thoughtful. "That gives us a few hours to get shit set up. We should take care of Noah's burial first."

Hunter hummed his agreement and turned out of the parking lot.

Eric had chosen to bury Noah in a spot on the outskirts of town, far enough away from the water that Noah would have no fear of being swept away by the current, but close enough that if his spirit returned to this spot, he'd be able to look out across the water to where Virginia lay on the other side. There was a beach within walking distance. One where Eric and Noah had camped out a couple of times. Building up a fire to ward off the cold and littering the sand in beer bottles.

It was a good memory. One washed out with age. Eric had been fifteen, maybe sixteen at the time. Content to be the king of Ironport High. Relishing in his status as the team captain of literally every sports team he was on. Loving the way girls fell all over him. He'd used his Venator charm a bit too much then. Because why shouldn't he use the gifts given to him by the Goddess? If he had to deal with the bad parts of being a Venator, he should be allowed to relish in the good parts too.

Pre-Kalla. Pre-getting his head out of his ass. Pre-realizing that no matter how good he was at sports, no matter how many friends he had, he was never going to fill the gaping hole in his chest left behind by his family.

"Do you want to say something?" Hunter asked. He stood just behind Eric, his hand tight in Eric's own. The marker they'd used to denote the gave didn't look like anything more than an old bit of driftwood.

"No." What was there to say, really? Noah had been his friend. And then he wasn't. And now he was dead.

"Okay." Hunter gave his hand a little squeeze. "I'll put a ward on it to keep people from fucking with it."

"Thanks." Eric sniffed, scrubbing at his eyes. They were burning, but he couldn't seem to get them to water at all. Like they'd dried up.

Hunter hummed and bent to press his palm to the soil. The ink on his arm writhed, answering the call of the witch using it, and a little Baltimore Checkerspot Butterfly spread its wings, lifting from Hunter's skin to flutter in the air. The sun danced against its dark-brown wings, making the orange and white spots stand out even more as it glided on an unfelt breeze to rest atop the piece of driftwood stuck into the ground. It flapped its wings once, twice, and then it melted into the wood, leaving behind a dark blurred stain that might have been a butterfly or a bit of still-wet mud.

"I'll have to refresh it every once in a while," Hunter said.

Eric nodded and pulled him to his feet and into a fierce hug. He knew Hunter had never liked Noah. Most people hadn't. Noah was a complete and utter dickhead to people outside of his circle. Had even been that way to Eric once they stopped being friends. But Hunter would do this, for Eric.

"Let's go home," Hunter said after a moment of simply holding Eric close.

Eric made a soft noise of agreement, and let Hunter lead him back to the car.

CHAPTER 27

"YOU DON'T REALLY HAVE to go on patrol, do you?" Hunter sounded a little whiny. He was following Eric around the house while Eric gathered his things for the evening's "patrol." Well, it was a patrol, technically. Eric was going to walk around Ironport and hunt for vampires. But he had a very specific vampire he was going to hunt and possibly stalk from Tony's house onward. That still counted, right?

"I do." It was less to do with the fact that Eric needed to make sure the people of Ironport were safe—he was pretty sure Dash wouldn't make his move yet—and more to do with the fact that Eric felt itchy under his skin. If he sat still for a moment longer, he'd probably start screaming at someone. No. It was better he went out for patrol and burned off the nervous energy before he had to deal with Janet and all the complicated bullshit that came with her. He needed to be tired to deal with that. To lack the energy to get himself worked up.

"You don't really, though," Hunter insisted. He circled around Eric where he was trying to finish gathering the weapons the kids had scattered in the command center, and fixed Eric with his best puppy-dog look. "Don't leave me alone with Ava when she's like this. You know how she gets."

"I do. Why do you think I'm going out?" Eric teased, giving him a nudge to get past him to the table where he gathered up a couple of the freshly made stakes the kids were working on.

Hunter made a sound like a deflating balloon.

"Look," Eric said, leaning in to brush a kiss to Hunter's downturned mouth, "I won't be gone long. I just want to blow off some steam before I have to have dinner with Janet. Okay?"

His shoulders hunching forward, Hunter leaned in to press his forehead to Eric's. "A couple hours?"

"At most." Eric buried his hand into the curls at the base of Hunter's neck, brushing his nails lightly over the skin in a way he knew Hunter liked. "The lasagna is in the oven. Take it out when it beeps and put in the garlic bread. Instructions are written down next to the stove."

"I can't read your handwriting," Hunter protested, but it was a weak excuse and they both knew it.

"Bert can. He'll help. Now"—he pressed another kiss to Hunter's forehead, lingering for a moment, enjoying the closeness before he pulled away—"I need to go so I can make it back before Janet gets here. You do not want to be left alone with Ava *and* Janet. Do you?"

"Definitely not. In fact, let me carry that to the car for you." Hunter took the duffle that Eric had been carrying easily over his shoulder and dipped a little under its weight. "Fuck, what do you have in there? Bricks?"

"Yes. My vampire slaying bricks." Eric chuckled, shaking his head as he grabbed the bag and pulled it onto his own shoulder again. "Come on, you can still walk me out, handsome."

"If this is how you were when Kalla broke up with you, no wonder it took so long for you to become friends again," Kate said, her tone all judgment in Eric's ear. He kind of wished he could wrench the earbud out and stomp on it, but the kids would have a heart attack, and he didn't want that. Then they'd drag themselves, Hunter, and Ava out into the city to hunt his ass down. "I never took you for a stalker."

"It's not stalking," Eric grumbled back. It wasn't. He wasn't following Tony around Ironport, he was just following Dash down the street to see where he went when he left Tony's. Dash, who he now *knew* was a vampire. Dash, who he now suspected was behind fucking *everything* that had been going to shit in Ironport in the last few months. What Dash's overall plan was yet, Eric didn't know. But he was going to find out. He just needed to follow him long enough to see where the fuck he was going. Maybe Dash would lead him back to the nest. Or maybe he would lead him back to some kind of base.

"Sure seems like stalking to me." Kate sounded like she was chewing gum while on the phone with him. Eric had expressly forbidden them from eating in the command center after the last mess they'd made of the place—crumbs fucking everywhere—but he supposed he couldn't get on her for chewing gum. So long as he didn't find it stuck to anything, anyway. Even if it did annoy the living shit out of him. All of his kids knew it too, including Kate, but Kate liked to do things to push people's buttons. To see how far she could go before someone snapped at her and she ran whining to her sister, the sheriff. "I guess at least you're not stalking your ex. That'd be really desperate. Although this does have a whiff of jealousy to it, doesn't it?"

It kind of did. If, you know, Eric wasn't so sure that Dash was a vampire. *If* he wasn't dead positive that Dash was in charge of everything. Then yeah, he could one-hundred percent see how this would reek of jealousy. And sure, even with those things factored in, it did still kind of smell like it. Because maybe jealousy was coloring his opinions and his motivations a little. But Eric wasn't going to give that thought the time of day—he had other things to worry about.

"Why are you on call tonight? Where the fuck are the rest of the gremlins?" He'd take literally anyone else at this point. Even Bert, who'd spend the entire time overanalyzing every-thing that went on. Or Chase, who would probably sit silently. They were all better than fucking Kate, who didn't know how to filter her nasty thoughts. They were going to have a discussion about that at some point. Her mouth was just as likely to get her in fucking trouble as Bert's was.

"Downstairs keeping Ava and Hunter from killing each other." Kate sounded like she shrugged, her clothes rustling against the mic. "They told me I was making things worse."

Eric grumbled softly. Kate Regan definitely would have made things worse. The only way that the tension between Ava and Hunter could reach a boiling point any quicker was to add in *Kalla* Regan. Thank the Goddess he hadn't had to call Kalla to help with the setup for Janet. That would have been a whole other set of problems that Eric didn't think he had the time or the energy for right now.

Especially as he was having to follow Dash on fucking foot because he was worried about the noise of his car giving him away. He hoped Dash didn't hear the way his heart pounded against his rib cage. Eric was as silent as he could be, planting his feet carefully on the slick ground, staying close to things he could tuck himself behind if need be. Goddess, his stalking skills were rusty. It'd been so long since he'd last had to do this.

"Are you scared?" Kate asked, out of nowhere. Or maybe it wasn't out of nowhere. She'd been yammering for the last couple of minutes that Eric had gone quiet—maybe some-thing had led to this. It was always hard to follow her train of thought.

Even harder when he looked down one moment to kick off a plastic bag that had skittered across the walkway like a fucking tumbleweed and gotten caught around his ankle, only to look up and find the street in front of him empty. Dash had been there a moment ago. And now he was gone. There was no alley. No turn off. No doorway for him to tuck behind. Nothing. He was just there one moment and gone the next. Like he'd fucking disappeared. Which was ridiculous because vampires couldn't just disappear, despite what the movies liked to say. They couldn't turn into bats, or wolves, or smoke. They couldn't scale buildings. And they sure as shit couldn't just disappear.

"Fuck. I lost him." Eric stopped, rubbing at his face a moment, wishing he'd worn his glasses instead of his contacts. The breeze was drying his eyes out. "And to answer your question, no. I'm not scared."

"Maybe you should be," a voice whispered into his ear, the breath cold, raising the hair on the back of his neck.

Eric whipped around and came face-to-face with Dashfield Chadwick. He didn't even have time to ask how the fuck Dash had looped around behind him before Dash had him by the throat, slamming him hard into the cement wall of an alley off to his right. It set his ears ringing.

"Oof, that's gonna cause a migraine," Eric grunted, reaching for the stake in his pocket and coming up empty. Had he dropped it? Had it fallen out? Had—

"Looking for this?" Dash held up the stake with his free hand, the other still holding Eric firmly by the neck against the wall. Eric's vision was starting to dot with darkness. He was going to pass out if he didn't get a full breath soon. That would really make the migraine unbearable.

"Yes. Actually. I was." Eric planted his foot on Dash's stomach and kicked him away, gasping down a breath and dashing for the stake, which clattered out of Dash's hold. He didn't make it. The vampire had the upper hand. Supernatural speed and all that bullshit. He tossed it away, and Eric saw it hit the ground just before it was run over by a car and shattered into splinters. "Fine then. We're gonna do this the hard way."

"We are," Dash agreed, his smile too big, fangs poking the skin beneath his bottom lip. Now that Eric was seeing it, he wasn't sure how he had missed it all this time. How he'd thought Dash was human, a Huntsman without a Venator gene. It was so obvious now. Red eyes flashing in the dark.

Eric didn't give Dash the time to ready for another attack. He lunged, knocking his shoulder hard into Dash. Cement dust fell where he smacked the wall on the other side of the alley, but it didn't do more than piss Dash off. He grabbed Eric by his wrist and twisted, pinning his arm behind his back, shoving him face down into the debris of the alley.

"This is how you like it, isn't it?" Dash hissed into his ear, using whatever vampire strength he had to hold Eric against the ground.

"Fuck off."

"No. I don't think I will." His tone was soft, almost conversational, as he ran his nose up the length of Eric's neck. "I could do to you what I've done to him, you know. I could feed you my blood. Make *you* my pet."

Eric grunted, jerking his arm, but there was no freeing himself from the grip Dash had on him. If he moved too far, the bone would break and he'd really be fucked. "Is that what you did to Tony?"

"Hmm . . . yes," Dash murmured, and the next thing he dragged down Eric's neck was a fang with enough pressure behind it to scratch. "But I think I'll just feed from you. Venator blood is very tasty, and your boy doesn't taste as . . . untouched as he once did. Do you think if I keep going, I might turn him?"

"Get the fuck off me!" Kicking did nothing. Eric couldn't

get the right angle from where Dash had shifted to put his knee in Eric's back.

"No. Don't think I will." He sank his fangs into Eric, and Eric got a rush of venom so strong it made his head spin.

Venom had never worked on him before—it didn't make sense. Why now? Why was he sinking? He felt . . . separated from his body. Like everything was happening to someone else. Like when a person's hand falls asleep and suddenly no longer feels attached to their body, except . . . all over.

"What the fuck?" Eric slurred into the ground, his struggling ceasing.

"You like that?" Dash hummed, lapping at the wounds on Eric's neck. "That's elder venom. Nothing like what you're used to. Your Venator system can't fight it off like it can youngling venom."

Kate chattered in his ear, but he couldn't focus on it. All he could focus on was tilting his neck, making it easier for Dash to give him another dose. To sink him deeper. Goddess, it felt good. It felt like he wouldn't ever have to deal with anything again. Not the pain. Not the heartache. Nothing.

"You hear that, little Venator?" Dash asked close to the comm, and Kate had gone eerily silent. "Your darling teacher likes it."

"You tell that son of a bitch," Kate said, her tone carefully measured, deadly, "that I'm gonna enjoy seeing you dust him."

"Hmm . . . Good luck with that. Better get here before he bleeds out. I'm not closing the wound, and oh, it is a gusher," Dash bragged. He pulled away, the pressure keeping Eric grounded gone, and Eric felt like he was going to float off into space. A balloon let loose from a children's birthday party. "See you around, Eric. I'll tell Tony you said hello."

TONY WASN'T PACING. He wasn't pacing. He wasn't—

Fuck it. He was pacing. Wearing a hole in the carpet. Going back and forth, back and forth. Like a caged fucking animal. A big cat trapped in a tiny pen in a tiny circus in a tiny backwoods town.

Maybe he should have thought about that before, when he decided to make that his backup plan, his failsafe. All he'd thought about was the fact that it might very well kill him, or it might not work at all. Two of the three options were that he wound up fucking dead, and honestly, that might be preferable at this point to having to sit back and watch Dash do whatever the fuck he wanted to this town.

Tony didn't even particularly like Ironport. It wasn't sweet and quaint like the town to the east. Moondale was a nice little place, nestled between water and mountains, protected from the dirt and stink of the bigger cities by Ironport itself. But Ironport. Ironport took on all those things: the sprawl, the people being pushed out of DC because of gentrification, the big businesses, the corporate greed. It was too much like

Miami, and at the same time so much smaller. The perfect breeding ground for vampires, really.

But even if Tony didn't much care for the place, it was Eric's home, and that meant something to him. It also had accepted him and Lu when they'd needed a place to go. Welcomed them, begrudgingly. He'd protect this fucked-up not-town-not-city with his fucking life.

> I don't know, Tony. No one has done this before.

If a text could sound exasperated, that one did. Tony could practically hear Sage's eye roll in his head. It didn't help that Sage had said as much over and over during the last couple of days. Tried to caution him against doing anything rash. Like that would work—they both knew that no number of careful warnings was going to stop him from doing something stupid as fuck. Especially not where the safety of his sister was concerned.

> It could be instant. It could not take until the next full moon.

> No way to know.

> Super helpful.

> inject yourself and we'll both find out.

Tony huffed a soft laugh, rolling the syringe between his fingers on the table. It was one of the ones he usually used for his T. He'd filled it up as soon as Dash left, debating with himself if he should do it now or hold off a little bit longer. See if he still had a choice. But the longer he thought about it, the less choice he felt like he actually had.

> don't do that. I was kidding.

The front door slammed, and Tony stuffed his phone into his back pocket.

"Honey, I'm home," Dash called. There was glee in his voice. Self-satisfied and arrogant. Tony wondered momentarily what would happen if he injected Dash with the werewolf venom instead. But if it killed Dash, then it would likely kill Tony by extension, or so Dash said anyway. And there was absolutely no way for Tony to test that theory without consequences.

When Dash rounded the corner at the top of the steps, he was flush-faced and his eyes gleamed red in the low light. He looked . . . satiated. Stuffed full.

"You've been out feeding," Tony accused, his hands tightening into fists at his sides.

"Of course I have, my darling," Dash cooed. He leaned in close to run his nose along the side of Tony's face, murmuring gently as if he could coax Tony in, soothe his ruffled edges. But the charm that had been there in the beginning, the good looks and the smooth words, were all gone now. Tony saw Dash for exactly what he was. A monster. "And after all," he said, pulling back, his face splitting into a smile so chilling, so predatory, it sent a shiver down Tony's spine, "you got a taste of him. Shouldn't I get to have one as well?"

Tony's stomach dropped out through his feet, and cold overtook every limb, every extremity. He couldn't feel his fingertips anymore, wasn't sure if they even still existed. "A taste of who?"

That smile turned cruelly delighted, curving up the corners of Dash's lips in an unnatural way, like something out of a fucking horror movie. Like a fucking snake about to unhinge its fucking jaw and swallow him whole. Tony refused to hunch, to cower, even as his vision darkened and his stomach gave a sickening twist.

"Eric Marcelino, of course. Your little boyfriend." Dash licked his lips.

Now that Tony was looking, he saw blood on Dash's dark shirt. Not a lot. A few drips. But it glistened in the low lights of Tony's bedroom. Tony took a step back, needing to distance himself from that. "Where is he?"

Dash shrugged, unconcerned, and advanced, his eyes glowing redder than Tony thought he had ever seen them before. And why shouldn't they? Dash was full to the brim of Venator blood. The boost that would give him . . . Fuck. Tony needed to get out of there before Dash did something stupid.

"Was he alive when you left him?" Tony took another step back, thinking carefully about how close he was to the open window. He slept with it open, and thank the Goddess that he did because Dash was blocking the fucking exit. His fingers shook as they closed around the syringe. Could he inject himself before he made it out the window? Would it disorient him? Would it put him in more danger? He didn't know. Sage had been supremely un-fucking-helpful.

"Yes, but who knows how long that'll last. I did take quite a lot. And I didn't close up the wounds, like I've been kind enough to do with you." Dash stepped forward again, the distance between him and Tony closing at an alarming rate. The only thing keeping Tony from panicking and doing something really fucking stupid was that he needed information. If he was going to get to Eric and save him before the blood loss took him, he needed to know where he was. He needed to know how bad off he was. "I really have been almost sweet, with you."

"Fuck you, you have," Tony spat, unable to stop himself.

"You know what, you've been rather mouthy lately. I think it's time for another dose." Dash's words had turned almost idle, thoughtful, as he dragged a fang across his own wrist, then lunged for Tony, his arm outstretched as if to force Tony to take in his blood.

Tony grabbed the lamp from the nightstand and slammed it as hard as he could against Dash's skull, bending the long metal neck of it but taking Dash down for a moment as well. Not long. Just the second it took for Tony to jam the needle into his thigh and press down the plunger. It burned cold fire through his veins, making him cry out and shiver. He nearly lost his balance, nearly went to his knees on the floor next to the momentarily incapacitated vampire. It was likely sheer stubbornness that kept him standing.

After the initial rush, Tony had just enough sense to stumble to the window and throw himself out, falling into a boneless heap from the second story. He missed anything that might have severely injured him, but the dead grass and the compacted dirt underneath didn't cushion his fall at all. He laid there for a moment, trying to catch his breath, staring up at the slowly fading light until he heard "You little bitch! I'm going to suck you fucking dry for that!"

He rolled to his feet and started running.

He lost track of time and direction then. Just running on instinct as he put as much distance between himself and Dash as he could. He didn't even realize he was making his way toward Moondale U campus until he came upon the sign sometime later. It could have been hours. It could have been minutes.

It had gotten darker, but the sun hadn't set yet, and the adrenaline was running so high that Tony honestly wouldn't be surprised if he outran a fucking car. Not that a Venator had ever done that before. But a Venator had also never shot themselves up with werewolf venom before. Only the Goddess knew what the fuck it would do to his system.

The initial buzz wore off right as Tony walked up the path to 1106 Moonshadow Way—Eric's little dormhouse. He stumbled, the ground swerving around beneath him. But the door was in sight. The door that would provide him with safety and comfort. The door where Eric was.

His knees gave out on the stoop, his stomach lurching until bile and sick rose burning in the back of his throat. The spit in his mouth turned stringy and thick, making him gag. But he swallowed it down, breathed deep through his nose, and reached for the doorbell. Since when were there two?

His vision must have gone double. Tony squeezed his eyes shut, dragged in another breath, and opened them again. It took him a second to find the right button, but when he did the bell was loud enough to deafen, leaving his ears ringing.

"Fuck. That's gonna take getting used to," he grumbled, his voice echoing in his ears, garbled and too loud like when he used to cover his ears as a kid while his parents shouted at each other and he could somehow still hear them through it. Of course it might kill him before he got used to it. Maybe all of these were signs of his body shutting down.

The door opened, and he fell inside where he'd been leaning against it, his shoulder hitting the floor hard, drawing a groan from his lips. He grumbled, "Fuck me. Couldn't you have been more *careful*?"

Or at least he tried to, but his jaw was locking up from the shudders racking through him. He didn't know rightly what it sounded like.

"Tony?!" whoever had opened the door asked.

He rolled onto his back and tried to look up at them through blurry eyes, but all he could make out was a dark blob. It could have been any of Eric's kids. Most of them were brunette, except for his sister. Where was Lu? He'd recognize Lu even in this state, right?

"What the fuck. What the fuck. What the fuck," one of the others was muttering over and over again.

"Get him to the couch, shut the door. Hunter, Ava, and Eric will be back soon," another ordered, the voice a little higher, sterner. That might have been Lu. It sounded kind of like her. Maybe not the voice, but the tone.

"Lu," he mumbled, holding a hand up to reach for her, but she swatted it away.

"I'm still mad at you."

And you know what? That was fair. She had every right to be pissed at him for what he did. He'd be pissed too.

"Just get him to the fucking couch."

There were hands on him. Lifting. Tugging. He was on his feet again, but there was no weight on his knees. Distantly, he felt himself being dragged along, the toes of his boots skidding across the floor, catching on the rug right before he was flopped down onto something soft. The couch probably. But maybe the rug was really squishy. He couldn't say he'd ever really noticed before.

"Bert, go get the med kit. Nik, call Hunter, let him know what's going on. Finn, we need all the blankets you can find, he's fucking freezing." Tony didn't think he'd ever heard his sister so self-assured and commanding before. It was kind of awesome. He was definitely going to tell her that—you know, when he could get his jaw to unlock.

"What about me?" someone else asked.

"Go heat up some water. Not boiling, only as hot as you can stand. We've got to break this fever. Chase will help you."

There was a murmur of agreement from the whole group before they left to fulfill their tasks, then silence as Lu put something on top of him. The softness of it brushed his cheek. The blanket from the back of the couch maybe.

"What the fuck did you do to yourself?" she asked, a shake to her voice now that no one else was there to hear. Tony wanted to tell her it'd be all right. That now they would all be safe.

But when he opened his mouth, what came out was, "Dash was giving me his blood. I was under his thrall." And he knew then that the werewolf venom had done its job. Whatever else it might do to him, it had at least managed to let him speak the truth.

"So what? This is a detox?"

Tony grunted as another wave of shivers hit him. It wasn't

not a detox. He struggled under the blanket, getting caught in it as he reached for his phone.

"What the fuck are you doing? Sit still," she snapped, shoving him down by his shoulders.

"My phone. Look at my phone." He rolled again, nearly falling off the couch, but Lu shoved him back again.

"Fuck. Fine. Just sit still." She helped him roll onto his side and pulled the device from his back pocket, then held it up to his face to unlock it. "What am I looking for?"

"Sage."

It took her only a couple of seconds to find what he was talking about, then she smacked him with the full force of her anger on the shoulder. "Werewolf venom?! You fucking idiot!"

Tony grunted, but his jaw had locked up again and he couldn't say anything to defend himself before the brat pack was back and hovering over him.

CHAPTER 29

HUNTER HAD no idea how much blood Eric had lost by the time he found him. No idea how far gone he was. He had some vague idea what had happened, given Kate's screaming. She tended to overreact, but he'd never seen her that frantic, that afraid, before. All smugness and bravado dropped. It scared Hunter more than he could explain, made his heart stutter in his chest, skip a beat in terror.

But what made his heart stop almost entirely was seeing Eric's feet in the low light of the alley, not moving. His stupid too-clean Reeboks gleaming in the night. A noise ripped itself from Hunter's throat, like a heart rending, or a cat who'd had its tail trod on. Then he was running. Running to get to Eric. To make sure he was still breathing. To make sure his heart was still beating.

"Hunter, slow down," Ava called, but she had to know she couldn't stop him. "We don't know if it's safe."

Hunter didn't answer. He didn't give a fuck. Fuck safety. Fuck protecting his own neck. He wasn't going to leave Eric in the alley to bleed out alone, and cold, and scared, and in the dark. He wasn't going to do that. There were a lot of things he'd do, but that wasn't one of them.

Eric didn't so much as twitch when Hunter fell to his knees beside him. But his heart was still beating, Hunter found when he pressed his fingers to Eric's pulse. His chest moving in short, shallow gasps. He was alive. He was *alive*. And that's all that mattered to Hunter right then.

"We need to get this closed up," Hunter said, pressing his palm into the bleeding wounds on Eric's neck. They weren't gushing, but that probably had more to do with the weakness of his heartbeat than the severity of the wounds. "Ava?"

Ava looked like she wanted to argue with him. To tell him this wasn't what her magic was for. But then something flashed behind her eyes, maybe the same reminder that had settled into Hunter's mind the whole drive over. Britt, surrounded in her own blood, bleeding out, her heartbeat stuttering, slowing, stopping. Nothing they could do. Nothing they could try.

It wasn't too late for Eric. He was a Venator. He was built for this kind of trauma. Built to spring back from the brink of death. Ava just needed to close up the places where he was bleeding, and he'd be right as rain.

"Ava. Come on," Hunter pleaded, adding more pressure to the wound. Eric was a dead weight in his arms, his head lolling to the side to show off the deep punctures left behind by Dash, still dribbling lazily. They should have closed by now. Why hadn't they closed? Had Dash done something to them? Injected them with some unknown vampire toxin that slowed the healing? Hunter would have to look into that later. After he'd kept Eric from bleeding to death.

Ava took a breath and scooted closer, heedless of the blood soaking in through the knees of her jeans, and she set to work. Light flooded the small alley, making Hunter's eyes burn. He chose not to look at the debris, blood, and trash sprawled around Eric. Chose to ignore that if they'd been a few minutes later, this was where Eric would have died. Instead, he focused on Eric's face. His skin too pale. His lips slightly parted. But his eyes were open, glassy as they stared up at Hunter.

"It's gonna be okay, hon," Hunter promised, his touch

gentle as he brushed hair away from Eric's sticky forehead. "You're gonna be okay."

Ava's magic zipped through the air, sunshine bright and twice as hot. If Hunter hadn't seen her work it a million times, he might have been mesmerized by the way a stitch witch could form a needle and thread out of only magic, could mend anything, even skin, if they focused enough.

It would burn. Would sear the flesh in its heat. Ava's magic always did when she was upset like this. But Eric didn't wince. If the sheen in his eyes was anything to go by, he likely couldn't feel it.

"How much venom do you think Dash gave him?" Hunter whispered, almost choking on the words as Eric's skin turned somehow clammier under his touch. Did they have any of the antidote left? It would make Eric sick, but it would be better than him trying to work through the withdrawals on his own.

"Too much. We're lucky he didn't OD." Ava shook her head. She pulled back a moment later, her magic fading to a dull glow, just enough to see by. "We need to get him back to the house, where it's safe."

Hunter chose not to remind her that the house wasn't really safe. Campus wasn't, anyway. That's where Eric had been stabbed a couple of months back. It wouldn't help. Right in that moment, she needed to feel like there was a place they could take Eric that Dash wouldn't be able to get to them. A place that was protected. And yeah, the house was warded, but so was the campus, and a vampire had gotten past anyway.

"Just help me get him to the car." Hunter bent to scoop Eric up into his arms, struggling a little under his weight, and followed Ava back to the car.

Hunter hadn't been able to sit down since they got back to find Tony on the couch of the dorm, sleeping off werewolf venom, according to the kids.

Werewolf venom.

What the fuck.

"Where did he even *get* that?" Hunter asked, brushing his hands through his hair and nearly knocking his glasses from their perch on his head. He was starting to understand Eric having regular migraines. How did he deal with this shit all the time?

Bert shrugged. "Didn't say."

"Right. Super. Brilliant. Next question, where the fuck are Lu and Finn?" They should not be separated right now. Not when both their protectors were fucking incapacitated. Ava had managed to weave some thicker wards on the house, and Vanessa Cochburn had called to assure them that no vampires would get on campus without her knowing—aside from Janet, who still had yet to show up—but none of that eased Hunter's mind. This could all still go to shit so quickly, it wasn't even funny.

"Library," Nik volunteered. He'd taken to twisting his oversized T-shirt into a ball against his stomach, his fist so tight in the fabric, it looked like it might be cutting off circulation. "Lu wanted to do some research on werewolf venom, and we didn't think she should go alone."

"That might be the smartest thing you little dumbasses have done all night," Ava said. She was sitting on the coffee table that rested between the sofa where Tony was sprawled and the recliner they'd propped Eric into, minding both of them in her way. Even if she was furious at them, by the look of things.

Kate opened her mouth to fire something back, but Chase trod on her foot to stop her, and Hunter shot him a look of thanks. They didn't need a Regan-style argument on top of everything else. The only thing probably keeping the peace right now was the fact that no one had thought to call in Kalla. Hunter thanked the Goddess every day for small miracles.

"How long have they been gone?" They shouldn't be wandering around outside in the dark by themselves. But Hunter couldn't send any of the other kids after them, and he wasn't about to leave Eric's side either. See, this right here was why he'd make a terrible guardian. Why Eric was so much better at this shit than Hunter. Eric would know what to do in a moment like this. It was what he excelled at: knowing what the fuck to do.

Hunter never had to know how to handle a crisis. Never had to think about what orders to give who. Because Eric had always been there. And when he wasn't, Britt was. There was always someone *else*, someone more capable. An adultier adult. Goddess, what would Hunter do if he lost Eric too?

"Huh?" he asked when he tuned back in to the conversation. One of the kids must have answered him, but he missed it in his own panic.

"About an hour." Bert sounded like he wasn't worried about it. And maybe that was an indication that Hunter shouldn't be either. But he couldn't seem to turn his worry *off*.

"You should text them, check in," Ava said, always the voice of reason. Good. At least one of them was.

"I don't really think—"

The doorbell rang, and they all stopped what they were doing.

"Who the fuck is that?" Kate whispered into the silence, taking a step toward the door as if to position herself between the possible threat and her fallen teacher.

Hunter logged that away to tell Eric about later before

stepping past her, a hand on her shoulder. She held up a stake to him, silver tipped, that she'd maybe just had in her pocket? Hunter didn't know. He didn't fucking ask Venator where they stored their stakes all the time. It was better not to know sometimes how many weapons the people around you had on them at any given moment.

"Thanks, kid," he murmured softly, and stepped into the foyer littered in shoes and jackets from the kids. He reached out with his magic to open the door, letting it creak inward as he stayed tucked into the shadows. His heart beat loud in his ears, unsteady, unsettled. His grip around the stake too tight, digging splinters into his hands. But he waited. He waited, and he watched.

"Hello?" Janet called into the house, her head appearing through the crack between door and frame. Tension wrinkled her forehead, made her look angry, or upset.

"Come in," Ava called from the living room—an invitation —and the tension eased from around Janet's eyes.

So at least the needing to be invited in bit isn't a myth.

She stepped into the foyer, shutting the door behind herself, and dipped her head to slide off her shoes. Hunter grabbed her by the collar during her moment of inattention, slamming her back against the wall, and held the stake to her eye.

"You're going to tell me everything about that so-called brother of yours, or I'm going to ram this thing through your eye socket and find out if it has to go through the heart after all." He was breathing hard, his chest moving in uneven pants, but he kept steady, the point of the stake poised in front of Janet's too-blue eye, ready to make good on the promise of violence. She didn't look nearly as terrified as he wanted her to.

"I wouldn't test him, Jan. We've been through some shit tonight," Ava warned from where she was now standing behind Hunter. Her presence a firm reminder that he wasn't in this alone. That he didn't have to be scared because he had his friend and the kids to back him up even if Eric was currently out of commission.

Janet eyed Hunter for a long moment, one blond brow raised, then she shrugged. "I was going to tell you guys everything tonight anyway."

"You were?" Hunter frowned but didn't lower the stake. He wasn't going to be fooled into letting his guard down.

"Dashfield has taken this shit too far," she said easily, relaxing back against the wall. Then her eyes flicked to the stake. "Do you mind?"

"Actually, I do mind," Hunter replied, his tone light and conversational as he pressed the stake in closer. "In case you didn't hear Ava, we've had a really fucked-up evening, and I'm not in any kind of mood—"

"Hunter," Eric's voice broke through Hunter's rage, making him still. "Let her come in and tell us what she came to tell us."

CHAPTER 30

"ALL RIGHT, JANET," Eric said, settling back into the recliner. He clenched his jaw, grinding his teeth together to hide the way the room still spun slightly at the motion. He didn't need Hunter thinking he was incapable, or Janet thinking he was weak. It would leave them open for attack, and he couldn't afford that. Not with Tony still sleeping off whatever the fuck he did to himself. "You wanted my attention. You've got it. Talk."

"I wouldn't say *I* wanted *your* attention." Janet rolled her eyes. She'd crossed her arms over her chest and settled into the other overstuffed recliner, hooking one leg over the other like a neat businesswoman. But all Eric saw was the petulant little girl who had once thrown a fit because her mommy and daddy didn't get her the right Barbie for her birthday. She wanted Malibu Barbie, not President Barbie—even then, the Chadwicks were training her for politics. "You're the one who invited me here, after all."

"Cut the shit, Chadwick," Ava growled. Her expression was murderous, like if the room weren't full of children, she might see if her sunshine magic could burn Janet to cinders the same way they'd been led to believe the sun would. Eric would have to get a straight answer about that eventually, but for now, he needed to know what the fuck Dash was up to. All the lies he'd been fed growing up could wait.

"Is it *Chadwick* now? A couple hours ago it was *baby*," Janet cooed, leaning forward a little so they could have an arguably scandalous view of her cleavage. Eric would have been impressed if Ava didn't let out a snarl that had Hunter taking a step forward to put himself bodily between the two women.

"Janet," Eric said admonishingly.

"Oh, all right." She huffed, leaning back again and giving her blond hair a flip. "So you know the prophecy, right? The one about the end of the Venator?"

Eric made a soft sound of acknowledgment. He knew about it, all right. He lived it every day. Worried he'd meet a Venator with the surname Mac Mathghamhna, and it would all be over. The world as he knew it up in flames, and him helpless to stop it. Because the fucking prophecy had been so vague, given no indication of what was to come, that he couldn't even fight against it. All he had was a name and the axe constantly hovering over his neck.

"Well"—Janet shifted a little, the leather squeaking under her—"Tony here is from the line of Mac Mathghamhna."

"No. He's a McMahon. I should know, I've seen his sister's records." Eric frowned. This whole business was giving him a fucking migraine, and he probably shouldn't mix his meds with the venom still pulsing through his blood.

"McMahon. McMahon. McMahon," Hunter muttered to himself, chewing on the side of his thumbnail.

"I had the kids do family trees this semester. Lu and Tony's goes all the way back to the McMahon Venator of Ireland. There was nothing about—"

"McMahon!" Hunter burst out, making Eric hiss and cringe away from the volume. His ears crackled a little. "Sorry." Hunter grinned sheepishly at Eric, before continuing. "McMahon is an anglicized version of Mac Mathghamhna."

"Give the witch a gold star," Janet cried, all condescension.

Hunter flicked her off.

"Okay," Eric said, to keep them from breaking out into another fight. "So Tony is the prophesied Mac Mathghamhna, which means we're about to completely fuck the Venator system into oblivion. What does that have to do with that old fuck pretending to be your brother?"

"Because"—Janet swapped which leg was on top, her arms moving to the arm rests as if she were making herself very comfortable—"when the Venator Huntsmen structure collapses, there will be a power vacuum. The vampires have their own prophecy that says that because you and Tony make it crumble, you fill the void and wind up in charge of everything. Vampires and Venator alike."

Eric's mind went blank and he blinked, perhaps a little too rapidly, as silence descended on them all, the only sound Tony's deep breathing as he slept on. Slept on while Eric's world tilted on its axis. While Eric's brain tried to reboot itself. Because this? All this bullshit? It was because of him. Because of some stupid fucking prophecy.

Then he was laughing, the sound loud and grating, ripped from his throat. It was a gasping, barking thing. It made his own ears hurt, and his ribs—which were probably bruised after his fight with Dash—ache. But he couldn't stop. He didn't know if he ever would. He might laugh until he was sick. He certainly had already laughed until tears were streaming hot and fast down his face.

"I think you broke him," Bert said, fear in his voice.

"Eric, sweetie," Hunter called softly, his rings cold on Eric's cheeks as he pulled his face down from where he'd thrown his head back, forcing Eric to look at him. It didn't make the laugh go away. It was still there. Clawing up his throat, leaving it raw. "Honey, I need you to breathe."

Eric nodded and took a deep inhale, then another, following the cadence of Hunter's breaths. It eased some of the hysteria, made the laugh die away slowly until it was just a broken, sobbing thing, then nothing at all. Nothing but blurry eyes and an aching body.

"That's it. Good job." Hunter leaned in to press a kiss to his forehead, the warmth easing some of the ache. Or it seemed to, anyway. Once Eric was able to take a full breath on his own, without Hunter coaching him through it, Hunter smiled gently and pulled away.

He didn't go far. He took Eric's hand, threading their fingers together and giving it a firm squeeze to let Eric know he was there, always right there. Warmth spread from his palm all the way up Eric's arm, warding off the chill that had lived in his bones for so long now, he hardly noticed it anymore.

"So, so, so. Let me get this straight," Eric said, when he was sure what came out of his mouth wouldn't be another laugh. "Dash has been trying to kill me because he wants to take over being head of the Huntsmen, Venator, and vampires?"

"That's about the size of it, yeah." Janet shrugged. "At first, he was content to just let things play out. He figured he'd kill you once you'd become the elder, or the councillor, or whatever you're meant to be. But that was taking too long, so he decided to speed up the process."

"Cool, cool, cool." Eric scrubbed at his nose with his free hand, grateful for the grounding grip of Hunter on his other. He might float away if it weren't there. Float away, or scream. Or laugh. Or cry. Or vomit all over the floor. He couldn't really tell right now, and it was better not to find out. "Well tell him he can have it. I don't fucking want power. I don't have the time or the energy to keep track of my class of six baby Venator, much less the whole of Huntsmen and vampire society. He can have it."

"Oh, Eric." Janet sighed, and she genuinely sounded kind of sorry now. Like she was about to break bad news. Like she'd tell him all over again that his parents weren't making it to his tenth birthday party despite them promising him they would. Why they'd left her to break the news to him, and an adult hadn't done it, he didn't know. But he remembered hating Janet that day. Hating her and wishing her own parents wouldn't make it for her party. They did, of course; the Chadwicks were always more hands-on with their children than the Marcelinos were with Eric. Maybe they knew even then what a disappointment he'd be. "You know that's not how prophecies work."

"Well, they don't fucking work the way he's trying to make them either!" Nik protested. Eric was amazed the kids had been silent this long. Maybe they were afraid of Janet. She was the mayor, and a vampire, and from one of the most influential Huntsmen families in Ironport. Or maybe Ava had threatened that if they didn't stay silent, she'd force them to. Either way.

"Well, it sort of is," Bert interjected. The other kids shot him betrayed looks, but he shrugged. "It is. If you kill the target of the prophecy, you can supplant them. That's the one rule."

"Right. So I just have to die then. For this whole thing to be over." Eric leaned his head back against the recliner, letting out a long, slow breath. His chest felt like it was in a vice. It was amazing he was able to breathe at all.

Hunter squeezed his hand again.

"We're not going to let that happen," Ava said. She met Eric's eyes from across the room, where she was standing by the door to the kitchen. Her hands were gripped tight around one of Eric's ridiculous mugs—the one shaped like a gingerbread house, which he distinctly remembered stuffing into the back of the cabinet when the season had turned. She must have gone digging. It was her favorite. She always said the shape of it was the best for keeping things hot. He thought she was full of shit. She just liked the pink icing roof.

"Agreed," Hunter murmured softly, brushing his thumb over Eric's knuckles.

"Why does all this matter anyway?" Chase asked, his voice soft but clear. It cut through the room, settling silence over the adults. It was a fair question.

"What?" Janet frowned. "What do you mean?"

"Well, why does he want to bring about the end of the Venator? Why bring them and the vampires under the same leadership? Why not just wipe out our entire race?"

Janet sighed, brushing hair back from her face. "Because it wouldn't solve anything. The vampires tried to do that years ago, and it turned into what it is now. A war that never seems to end. They don't want that, or at least, some of them don't. The elders, the ones that matter, want peace. What *I* want is peace. That's why I did this, you have to understand. We want the Venator to go back to what they used to be."

"And what's that?" Eric pressed.

"A police force of sorts. Born and bred to keep rogue vampires in line. To make sure they don't kill humans needlessly. I know we were taught growing up that vampires are just leeches. That they can't control the instinct to hunt, to kill, but it's not true. Dash turned me a decade ago, and I've never killed anyone. I can walk down the street of Ironport without once being tempted to bite one of my constituents. Well"—she laughed a little, showing off her fangs—"at least not any more than a human would be tempted to bite someone they found very annoying."

"Ha. Ha," Ava muttered, but didn't interrupt any further.

"Okay, say I believe you." Eric wasn't sure he did. This went against everything he'd learned about vampires. But . . . but now that Janet was saying it, and he was thinking about it, and Ashthorne had said much the same thing, there was some sense to it. If there were no vampires who were in control of themselves, they'd suck the world dry. Or they'd expose themselves and wind up at the pointy end of a stake.

It made sense. Goddess, he hated how much sense it made. "What do you want me to do about Dashfield?"

"We just need to kill this bastard, right?" Ava asked, a sharp grin curling up one side of her mouth. "What's one more bloodsucker? Eric's slay tally is through the roof."

"I'm afraid he's not going to make it that easy." Janet's posture had gone rigid, no longer the lax cat she'd been a moment ago. She was done playing games, it would seem, and was now ready to give them the bad news she'd come to deliver.

Anxiety twisted in Eric's gut, making him sick with it again. "Why not?"

"Well, for one, he's fucking ancient. He's not the oldest of the elders by a long shot, but he's certainly older than any vampire you've faced before." Janet scrubbed at her face, leaving behind a red mark, and it was so sickeningly familiar that for a second Eric forgot what she was. He just saw the girl he grew up with. "And for two, he's taken two of your baby Venator."

"No." Eric's stomach plummeted, his heart lurching in his chest. "Has anyone heard from Lu or Finn?"

CHAPTER 31

TONY WAS VAGUELY awake for about half the conversation with Mayor Chadwick. Not that he really needed to hear it; he knew it all already. Dash hadn't exactly kept his plans quiet, and Tony, once he was off the blood and the venom, was too good a Venator to let something like that slip by him. But then Janet said, "He's taken two of your baby Venator" and Eric muttered, only half coherent, "Has anyone heard from Lu or Finn?" and all of the sudden Tony was very much awake. Maybe more awake than he'd been in his whole life.

"What the fuck do you mean, *has anyone head from Lu or Finn?*" Tony asked, sitting up a little too fast and making his head spin with the motion. He didn't have time to regret it, or to lie there any longer while he waited for the wooziness of the werewolf venom to subside. He needed to be up. He needed to be out there, looking for his little sister and her weird little friend. He couldn't just sit there and do nothing. "You were supposed to be watching them, pretty boy."

Eric's head whipped around so fast, it looked like it might have hurt his neck, but he didn't so much as wince. "Oh, is that what I was supposed to be doing, huh? Funny. Lu's guardian didn't give me any fucking instructions when I went to see him *yesterday* to ask about him kicking her out. But maybe I missed it what with all the—"

"Eric," Hunter murmured softly, and it looked like he gave Eric's hand a tight squeeze. A warning, maybe. "Let's not say anything we'll regret."

"Oh, he won't regret it in the least bit. He's good at—"

"You either, Tony." Hunter shook his head. His tone had gone deep and authoritative. It sent a shiver down Tony's spine. "If we're going to get the girls back, you two need to shelve whatever relationship drama you've got going on, and focus on—"

"It's not relationship drama."

"—figuring out where the fuck Dash took them." Hunter glared at Tony, and Tony almost felt cowed by the look. Almost. Not quite. But Hunter was right: He needed to get his head out of his ass and go and get his sister. He could deal with the shitstorm that was Eric Marcelino at a later date. Preferably when his ears weren't ringing, and he didn't feel like he was about to vomit all over the ugly-ass plush rug Eric had replaced the old bloodstained one with. Tony wondered where he'd found it. Costco?

"Oh, I can tell you where he took them," Janet piped up, a pleased smile on her face. "For a price, of course."

"Of course," Eric grunted. He turned his narrowed brown eyes away from Tony and back to Janet. Tony ached all over to get Eric to look at him again, even if it was in disdain. Some attention was better than none. "What do you want?"

"Protection." It sounded simple when she said it that way, but Tony knew well enough it wasn't. If Dash wanted to get to her, he'd get to her. No number of people in the way would stop him.

Didn't mean Tony wasn't going to agree when it was his sister's life on the line. Fuck Janet Chadwick. "Deal."

"Now hold on a minute—" Eric protested, his gaze back on Tony. Goddess, it felt good to be at the center of his attention again. How had Tony gone without it for the last few months? He'd probably been fucking wilting and hadn't even known it. What the fuck was wrong with him? Fucking attention whore.

"No. You hold on a minute. Are you telling me that if someone came to you, Eric Marcelino—longest living Venator, head Venator of Ironport, the man with the highest slay average in not just North America, but in the world—and asked for help, that you would deny them?" All right, so he was laying it on thick. But Tony had learned a thing or two while he'd been fucking Eric's brains out all those months ago. The man had a praise kink. He liked to know he'd done a good job. That he was a good boy. Tony wasn't going to knock him for it—he was the exact same way—but you'd have to have lost your wits if you thought he wasn't going to use it to his advantage right then. He would use literally every tool in his arsenal to his advantage. Even if that meant getting on his knees and blowing every adult in the room. Which it wouldn't; Eric was too fucking pure for that.

"She's a vampire," Eric argued, but it was a token protest, Tony could tell. He'd heard enough of those from Eric in those weeks they'd been seeing each other to know exactly what they sounded like. Tony just needed to push. Just a little more.

"Yeah, she is. But like I said, she's asking for your help." He'd stake Janet fucking Chadwick later, after all of this was over. In the meantime, he needed to be on her side. "So what's it gonna be, head Venator? Are we gonna leave her to the wolves? Or are we gonna protect her?"

"You're just saying this because she knows where Lu and Finn are." Which was true.

But Tony could see how Eric had already made up his mind. Likely had before Tony had even said anything. Because if Eric and Tony had one thing in common, one thing that tied them together when all else was likely to rip them apart: it was that they would do literally anything for the people they loved. Including keep a bloodsucker safe. And

Eric loved his kids. Even Tony's bitchy little sister. Even after Tony had broken up with him in the worst way possible. He should have known he wasn't right in the head then—breaking up with someone at a funeral, what the fuck? That was worse than breaking up with someone via text! Even then, Eric had treated Lu like one of his own. Looked after her. Cared for her. Made sure she was fucking happy when Tony couldn't do it himself anymore.

"And what if I am? This is the best, quickest lead we've got." Tony shrugged, leaning forward to put his feet on the ground. He still felt like one wrong move would send him hurling his guts up, but by the Goddess, he was going to save his sister. Let Eric and Hunter try to exclude him from the rescue mission; it would only end in him following behind them. "You saying you don't want to save two of your brats?"

The other kids, who had been eerily silent throughout the whole debate, seemed to realize that Eric's mind was made up before he even said anything. All Eric had to do was nod, and they were already moving.

"I'll get the comms ready, they should still be charged," Bert said, heading for the stairs. "I'll load up the Ghost Tracer while I'm there."

"I'll fill the kit," Kate volunteered.

"Chase and I have got the med kit," Nik said, grabbing Chase's wrist and tugging him along behind him.

"I'm going to triple check the wards. If we're keeping a wanted woman here, we'll want to make sure nothing can get through them." Ava stood from her chair and made a beeline for the door.

That left Eric, Janet, Tony, and Hunter. And the silence that followed was fucking deafening.

"Janet," Eric said after a long moment, "why don't you go put the coffee pot on? I think we're gonna need it."

Janet took a moment, her eyes darting between the three of them as if she were taking in a particularly interesting show. But when Hunter shot her a look, she rose and headed for the kitchen without a word. Which left the three men behind.

Tension settled between them, making Tony antsy, but he refused to shift around in his seat. Refused to let whatever was between them make him appear weak, unsettled.

"When we get them back . . ." Eric said, breaking the standoff. Tony appreciated how he said *when*, not *if*. He appreciated that this was a foregone conclusion in Eric's mind. That there was no doubt they'd get the girls back safe and sound. "You can't go back to your place, it's not safe there."

"I know." Tony ran a hand through his hair, catching on the snarls and tangles left over from his fever-induced haze and the sweat it left behind. He'd kill for a fucking shower right that moment, but there wasn't time for it. In fact, the only thing keeping him from running off into the night to get his sister back by himself was the fact that he still wasn't exactly sure what the werewolf venom had done to him. "If you've got the room, I'd appreciate it if you let us move in here for a bit? Until we can get our feet back under us?"

Eric nodded. "I think that would be best." Then he lifted his head to look at Hunter, who was oddly still. "Any objections?"

"No," Hunter said through a clenched jaw. He didn't put voice to whatever misgivings he did have. Tony would have to steer clear of Hunter and Eric until he could get himself and Lu out of there. He didn't particularly want to become a home wrecker.

Eric turned his attention back to Tony. "I'll have Ava get a room ready for you once she's done with the wards."

Questions hung heavy in the air between them. *What are we? Where do we go from here? How the fuck are we all going to live together after what you did, you absolute asshole?* But none of them spoke at all. Tony glanced at Hunter, who was glaring at him, maybe out of jealousy, maybe out of protectiveness. A snide comment sat heavy on his tongue, threatening to loose itself and make this so much more awkward than it had to be.

"Well, now that that's settled," Eric said, drawing their attention back to him. He was still looking a little green about the gills from the dose of venom Dash had given him. Good thing he wouldn't be going into Dash's territory alone. "I think we need to talk about the elephant in the room."

Tony's gaze darted from Eric to Hunter and back. He couldn't mean *that* elephant, right? That elephant was going to take more than the few scant minutes they had before the kids returned with everything they'd need to raid yet another nest.

"Why the fuck did you inject yourself with werewolf venom?" Hunter asked, and Eric smiled, as if they were on the same wavelength. As if they shared some kind of psychic connection Tony wasn't privy to. It was fucking maddening.

But there was a promise. A "we'll talk about this, about *us,* later, when all of this is over" that seemed to go unsaid. Tony didn't have to be on their wavelength to feel it. They recognized this was a discussion that had to happen too. And like him, they seemed to realize there was no time for it just now. So they'd moved on to easier, safer topics.

Tony shrugged. "Seemed the thing to do at the time."

Eric snorted and rolled his eyes. "Man, be serious for like five minutes, would you? We need to assess how fucked up you are before we take you with us. Lu would have my head if you got killed in a raid I was at the lead on."

"Who says you'd be at the lead of it?"

"Are you going to explain, or am I going to bench you?" Hunter asked, moving closer, magic like electricity jumping from one finger to the next.

"All right. All right. Don't get your panties in a twist, sparky." Tony laughed, and shit, why did it have to be so fucking hot when Hunter raised his pierced eyebrow. Yeah, living with them was going to do Tony's head in, one-hundred percent, but what a way to go, right? "I have a friend down south who has a fair bit of magical knowledge. They're fae, I think. And when I told them that Dash was feeding me vampire blood, and it had created a physical thrall—I'm talking this-motherfucker-could-control-my-every-move kind of thing—they suggested that werewolf venom may counteract the effects of the blood. There were no guarantees, of course—"

"No guarantees that you'd fucking live through the process. What the fuck, McMahon?" Hunter sounded truly scandalized, if a little curious too. Tony could see his mind working behind those big dark eyes.

"I decided to take my chances." Tony shrugged. "Especially after he told me that if he died, any person under his thrall would die too."

"We don't have any evidence to support that." Eric's tone was professional, serious. He had gone into Venator mode, and that was likely for the best.

"We don't have any evidence to disprove it either," Hunter reasoned.

"Right," Tony agreed, "so I figured, either the werewolf venom killed me, or the vampire did. Either way, I wasn't leaving Lu open to further attack." He didn't add that he'd made the decision before Dash had taken his sister. It would lead to too many questions, expose too many of his own weaknesses, and seeing as Eric and Hunter were obviously a couple . . . well. It was better to play it close to the vest.

"Did it work?" Hunter moved to sit on the couch next to Tony, holding his hand out in question.

"I wasn't able to talk about what he was doing to me before, except in vague terms and hypotheticals, so I'd say it at least did the job of clearing the thrall out of my system. What else it did? I don't know." Tony offered Hunter his wrist, unclear on what he planned to do, but he trusted him.

He trusted both of them. And wasn't that just fucking weird? Trusting people. Who knew Tony could even fucking do that anymore? Not him.

Hunter hummed and pressed two fingers to the pulse in Tony's wrist, his magic reaching out for a moment to tingle along Tony's skin, through his veins. It wasn't scary like he'd always thought this kind of examination would be. Hunter's magic was gentle and warm, soothing all the aching places left behind by the blood and the venom.

"Anything?" Eric broke the silence with his nervous question after a moment.

"I can't tell. His magic isn't inherently Venator anymore, but it's not really werewolf either. I suppose we won't know until the next full moon." Hunter pulled back, taking that warmth and comfort with him, and Tony missed it instantly. "There aren't any signs of a thrall though, so your friend was right. The venom did burn that away."

"Great." Tony clapped his hands and leaned forward on his knees. "Where do we start?"

# Chapter 32

THROWING up wasn't going to expel the venom from his system, but it still made Eric feel better. Plus, he needed some time away from Tony's longing gaze, and Hunter's knowing one. He needed a minute to just breathe, to get himself back under control. A minute he apparently wasn't going to fucking *get* because almost as soon as the door was closed and the water was running in the sink, it opened again.

Hunter slipped through the crack, looking only a little sorry that he was intruding upon Eric's sanctuary. Which was more than Eric would probably get from Tony if it'd been him barging through the door.

"Can't a guy take a piss in peace?" Eric mumbled, annoyed, his elbows aching from where they dug into the hard top of the counter on either side of the sink. He'd been about to rinse his face, hoping it would settle the violent urge to vomit that the combination of vampire venom and the antidote left him with. Or at the very least wash away the traces of sweat lining his brow. It probably wouldn't do either, but it made him feel like he was doing something to help the sorry state of himself. Something to make himself appear more put together and ready for what was coming next. Fuck. He was tired. Tired, and sore, and the lights in the bathroom were leaving halos around everything, a migraine lingering at the edges of his vision. This was going to suck so hard.

"I think you already know the answer to that," Hunter said, his tone light, teasing, but when Eric met his gaze in the mirror, he saw no such expression on his face. No. Hunter's ebony-brown skin was pulled taut across his jaw, wrinkles forming around his eyes that Eric could only see clearly because Hunter had removed his glasses, perching them on the top of his head. He looked fucking exhausted. Eric wanted to wrap him up in his arms and hold him close until all of this was over. Which, confusingly, was also exactly how he felt about Tony as he watched him shift around on the couch a few minutes ago. They both looked so small in the face of everything coming for them. Eric wondered if he did too. If he looked like a child in the face of Goliath.

"Seriously, Hunter, say what you came to say and fuck off for a minute. I just need to breathe." It wasn't quite a whine, but it might as well have been one. Eric pinched the bridge of his nose in the hopes that the pressure would fend off the ensuing migraine a while longer. He just needed a couple of hours. Long enough to get the girls back safe without getting anyone else killed in the process. Goddess, if he was in top form, he'd probably make Hunter and Tony stay behind. Or at least try, anyway. He wasn't stupid enough to think he could actually *make* those two do anything.

"I saw how you were looking at him, Eric."

"Fucking hell. Please don't say this is a jealousy thing, Hunter. I don't have the energy for it." He really didn't. He was already tapped out as far as emotions went; if anyone else piled one more feeling on him, he'd probably cave under the weight.

"It's not," Hunter said, stepping forward to plaster himself to Eric's back, and crouching down a little to hook his chin over Eric's shoulder. It was easier to meet his eyes this way, to see the gentleness of his mouth in the mirror, half hidden by dark curly hair.

"Then what is it?" Eric whispered, almost afraid to break

the easy comfort he found in Hunter's arms. It was *too* easy, probably, considering everything that had happened the last couple of months, but what was that thing people said about trauma? It brought people together.

"I just wanted you to know that I saw it, and I don't mind, you know . . ." Hunter hummed, pressing his face into Eric's neck as if he could hide the word there, like he was embarrassed by it. "Sharing? If that's something he'd be open to."

Sharing. Eric turned the word over in his head. He'd never . . . well, that wasn't something he thought would ever be an option for him. Monogamy always seemed a given. But hadn't he had that beaten into his head all his life? If it wasn't a part of every television show or movie he'd ever watched, would it be what he chose for himself? Especially now. Especially faced with the full brunt of Tony and Hunter. He didn't know.

"You don't have to answer now," Hunter rushed to add. "And it's definitely something we'll have to discuss with him as well. I just thought . . ." Hunter shrugged. "I thought I'd take one thing off your mind before we go into this thing and possibly get ourselves killed. Let you know I'm not jealous or whatever, and I don't bear him any ill will."

"Oh? You thought this would make it easier?" Eric raised a brow in the mirror, a teasing note to his voice. It did ease his mind a little to know that Hunter wasn't going to fly off in a jealous rage at any given moment. That would make the raid go more smoothly, hopefully. Provided Hunter and Tony could get along long enough for them to get in, get out, and get back to the dorm. Eric sent up a quiet prayer to the Goddess that everyone would be able to keep their fucking egos in check long enough for that.

"Car's packed," Hunter said, not answering the question. "Tony is armed to the gills. We're ready to go whenever you are."

"I'll be out in a minute. I just need—"

"To breathe. I know. Take your time." Hunter patted Eric's hip lightly, as if he were soothing a nervous dog, then he turned and left Eric alone in the bathroom once more.

The address Janet gave them was in the warehouse district, which didn't surprise Eric. He'd known something was going on there with the vampires months ago, but hadn't had the time or the energy to go digging through all the businesses there. Plus, he'd have probably needed a warrant and Kalla's backup to start knocking on doors, and that was an added stressor that no one wanted. Absolutely no one.

Eric's car was quiet as they pulled up to the curb—he guessed all those tune-ups Tony insisted on a few weeks back had finally come in handy.

"We could park in the parking lot," Tony said, his leg jittering in the back seat hard enough it was practically shaking the car.

"Yes, and let them know we're here," Eric rolled his eyes. He glanced at Tony in the rearview mirror. Tony's eyes flicked around, his head twitching this way and that. There was a light behind the green, almost making them glow, but it might have been a trick of the eerie yellow streetlamp above. "That's a great idea."

"No need to be snippy, pretty boy." Tony turned to meet his eyes and glare.

"Down boys," Hunter called, holding up his hands before tapping the bud in his ear. "Mystery Machine, how's it looking?"

Bert released a long, aggrieved sigh that Eric knew was him restraining himself from telling Hunter that he needed to end all communications with the word *over*. "I've got two Venator heat signatures, and about ten, maybe twelve, vampire ones. Over."

"Maybe?" Eric asked.

"There are two creatures with low-level heat signatures, sir," Nik reported. "But they could be anything from a still-cooling corpse to a water sprite."

Tony jerked, jamming some part of his body into the door and wincing at the announcement. When Eric looked back at him again, he was rubbing his elbow.

"Or," Chase said, calm and collected, "they could be blood bank bags stored in a cooler. There's really no way to know for certain given the shape of them. Let's not assume the worst."

"Thanks, Mystery Machine, we'll be in touch." Eric shut off the car and reached for the duffle bag at Hunter's feet. It was the work of a minute to stuff his pockets full of stakes. "I'm getting that fucking sword Bert made for me out of the back."

"The twerp made you a sword?" Tony brightened a little, one corner of his mouth curling up in a smirk.

"He did. And maybe if you'd stop calling him names, he'd make you one too." Then Eric was out of the car, getting the sword and slinging it over his back. Hunter and Tony joined him a moment later. Tony looked bare without his signature hair pins, but otherwise Hunter had given him enough silver and pointy things to stock a steak house. Eric held out another silver dagger, needing to feel like he was protecting Tony in some small way. "Don't split up. Don't get separated. Am I clear?"

They nodded.

"All right. We're going in through the loading dock, and we're going to clear a path. Now's your chance if you don't feel up to this." Eric met Tony's eyes, a question raising his brows. He didn't want Tony to go in if he didn't feel ready. But he knew somehow that Tony wasn't going to give in that easily.

"Fuck off," Tony grunted, strapping the dagger to his thigh. "Let's put this fucker in the ground."

Chapter 33

"TECHNICALLY," Hunter said, making Tony's eyebrow twitch, "vampires don't go in the ground when they die. They just become—"

"I know what they become, smartass. I've been hunting vampires since I was old enough to hold a—"

"Enough," Eric cut in, seeming to trade places with Hunter as the voice of reason in their weird little trio. "Unless you want him to know we're coming."

"He probably already knows," Tony mumbled, but he fell silent, following behind Eric as they made their way around the side of the empty warehouse they'd parked beside. It wasn't the one where Dash was keeping Tony's little sister— that warehouse was two over—but it was close enough that if Dash was listening for their heartbeats, he'd probably hear them. All they could hope was that he was otherwise distracted.

Janet hadn't told them what the fuck Dash was doing with the warehouse spaces he had rented down in this part of town, but Tony supposed they'd find out shortly. He hoped it wasn't something that would turn his already unsettled stomach. He was keeping himself upright by sheer stubbornness, and he knew it showed by how Hunter hung close to him, his magic already sparking between his fingers. Jumping from one ring, to the next, to the next, like a static ball. It was lovely, really. Tony didn't remember seeing Hunter use his magic like this before, but it was a sight to behold. A modern wonder ranked right there next to Eric's neat and efficient strikes in a fight.

Tony shook himself. He didn't have time to daydream right now. There was shit to do. Leeches to stab, and the like. No time for horniness. Really, he shouldn't even *be* horny with how shitty he felt from the werewolf venom, but leave it to his overactive libido to look at a do-or-die situation and go "yes, now is the perfect time for sex." Stupid.

The door to the loading dock was open. Two vampires bustled about, moving cooler boxes sealed tight. Hopefully those were the weird heat signatures the kids had seen from the van a block over. Tony didn't think he could deal with a corpse right now. He'd never been particularly good at dealing with mortal dead bodies. Mortals were all . . . messy. With vampires, a person stabbed them with a sharpened piece of wood and they turned to dust, and that was the end of that. Mortals left behind . . . residue.

Eric motioned with his hand for Tony and Hunter to get the vampire to the right of the bay while he took the left. With a nod, Tony and Hunter moved as a unit. Hunter took the front, his magic latching on to the leech and yanking it down off the tall ledge where Tony could stake it through quickly, before it made a sound to alert the others.

Two down. Eight to go.

When Tony looked again, Eric was waiting for them on the ledge, his hands held out to help them up. There was no sound as he pulled them onto the cement floor that spanned the rest of the warehouse. Boxes lined the front of the bay, hiding them from whoever else remained inside—the perfect cover.

Another motion of Eric's hand, and the trio moved as one, pressing themselves in close to the boxes then peering over top to get a better view of what awaited them beyond.

The rest of the vampires were milling about. Moving crates and checking inventory, it looked like. Dash oversaw everything from the middle of the wide-open room. He had Lu and Finn tied to a set of chairs along the back wall. Their heads lolled forward as if they were asleep. Drugged on venom, probably. Hopefully not blood too; there would be no time to check, and Tony was out of werewolf venom besides.

There was no place to hide. Nowhere to keep the element of surprise. They would just have to go in, guns blazing. It wasn't the best way to do this, but they weren't being given much choice.

Eric's brow had creased, his bright honey-brown eyes flicking about the room as he did the mental math needed to plan their attack. But even as he tried to get a handle on the situation, Tony could see how he floundered. He was the most skilled out of them, tactically. Where Tony would run in without a second thought, Eric liked to plan, liked to be two moves ahead. But they hadn't been able to get their hands on plans of the warehouse, and there was no time to go back to the drawing board on this thing.

Plan Z it was.

Tony took a hold of Hunter's wrist and gave his fingers a tap when they sparked with surprise. Then he nodded toward the room as a whole.

Hunter frowned, but he seemed to get what Tony was saying. He snapped his fingers softly, and Tony's ears popped with the change in pressure as a sound barrier was put between them and the room at large. "I might zap the girls."

"They'll be okay," Eric whispered, catching on quick to what Tony was suggesting. "They're built for a little bit of a shock. Just don't turn the voltage up too high."

"They're out anyway, they'll be fine," Tony insisted. He'd never personally been on the receiving end of a stunner spell, and he was sure Lu would bitch and moan about it, but it was their best option. "Just wait until Eric and I are in position to pop out from behind the boxes."

"When your sister is pissed that—"

"Yeah, yeah. You can totally blame this on me." Tony flapped his wrist. "Now get into position. We don't have all fucking day."

Hunter gave him one more wary look, but with a nod from Eric, they shifted positions. Hunter moved more toward the center of the row of boxes where he could better aim his blast, while Eric and Tony moved off to either side. Eric held up three fingers, his eyes fixed on the room on the other side of the boxes.

Two.

One.

A flick of his wrist, and Hunter's magic shot along the floor, racing up the legs of any and all things touching it. The vampires cried out, registering the stunner, and Eric and Tony leapt into action.

The first vampire went down easy, Hunter's spell doing most of the work, but it didn't hold for long. It was difficult for Hunter to keep that many targets immobile at a time. Tony knew that would be an issue, and he probably couldn't do it a second time, not without hitting Tony and Eric. So they had to be quick.

The next vampire was a little more coherent. When Tony lunged for it, it staggered back, trying to get away, but tripped over the lid to one of the packing crates. It grabbed on to the front of Tony's shirt and pulled him down with it, and as he fell, he got a glimpse of Eric slicing his way through the crowd of vampires with his sword.

Hunter was at Tony's side, a stake in hand that he slammed through the vampire's chest before it could get its mouth any closer to Tony's neck in his distraction, then helped him to his feet. The two of them bobbed and weaved through what remained of the leeches. But the more they fought, the more it seemed the vampires decided they weren't as much of a threat as the wild man with the sword cutting his way toward their boss.

The leeches closed ranks, forming a barrier between Dash and Eric, leaving a clear path to the girls. They were still out, their heads hung low.

"We should wake them up." Hunter's hands slid off the ropes, losing their grip where they shook. The fighting was getting to him. He wasn't built for it the way Tony and Eric were.

"Let me do that, you keep an eye on Eric," Tony murmured, brushing his hands aside gently. He pulled the dagger from his thigh and started to saw through Finn's bindings. The battle raged on behind him, and he could hear Eric's grunts, his mumbled curses. He was flagging. Tony could tell. They didn't have long. He needed to get the girls loose and out with Hunter so he could help Eric.

Finn was free, her head leaning against Hunter's side so he could hold her up while keeping a look out. Tony started on Lu's ropes, doing his best to keep from looking her over for injuries when he needed to focus on the task at hand.

There was a yelp from behind him, then Hunter released a soft whine and Tony spun to find Eric hitting the ground, Dash looming over him, a dagger in his hand, fangs dripping.

"Hunter," Tony called.

Hunter didn't acknowledge him. Didn't take his eyes off where a patch of blood slowly seeped across Eric's chest.

"Hunter. Look at me." Tony grabbed his wrist, squeezed it tight enough that he could feel the bones grind together. Hunter looked down at him, the pupils of his dark eyes blown so wide, there was almost no brown left. "Cut Lu loose, get the girls out. I'll go for Eric."

"But—"

"Don't argue." Tony squeezed his wrist again, putting as much feeling as he could behind the words. "I'll keep him safe. But you need to get the girls out of the way so I can focus on him, all right?"

Hunter's eyes flicked over Tony's face, never landing on one feature, uncertainty and fear pinching his brows together. But after a moment he seemed to decide that Tony was good to his word. He nodded, leaned Finn back in her chair carefully, and took the dagger from Tony to finish cutting Lu loose. "I'm going to hold you to that."

"You do that." Tony gave his wrist one final squeeze, then spun around, using the momentum to throw himself across the room and straight for Dash, a stake tight in his grip. "Hey, Dash!"

Dash lifted his head, blood coating his lips, to smile at Tony, showing off red teeth. "My, my, my. You survived. What a surprise."

He was still holding on to Eric. His fingers curled in Eric's shirt, wrinkling and tearing the fabric beyond recognition. Tony approached slowly at first, but once he had Dash's attention, he picked up speed. Running across the room, ramming himself into Dash's chest to throw him off Eric, heedless of the dagger Dash still held in his hand. It nicked his side, sending searing pain through his nerves, but it wasn't going to stop him. *Nothing* was going to stop him.

Dash hit the ground with a grunt. The smile never left his face. If anything, it got wider. Turning snake-like and predatory. It looked like it made his jaw ache. Like it might swallow up his whole face just as it might swallow up Tony, all pointed teeth and bloody dominance. "Not under my thrall anymore, I see."

"Nope. Fixed that," Tony confirmed, adjusting his grip on the stake and positioning it over Dash's chest. Dash grabbed his wrist, his hand iron tight. He was stronger than Tony, especially in this state, but there was no way he was more determined, more angry. Tony had months of pent-up rage. Months of living under Dash's thumb. Of simpering and begging a creature who didn't care for him. Of being *used* and *violated*. Of being too high and too out of it to see that he'd lost something special, something important. And now, with Eric and Hunter so clearly an item, he'd likely never get it back. He'd never get it back, and that was all Dash's *fault*!

Dash murmured then leaned in to run his nose along the length of Tony's neck, heedless of the stake, the point pressed to his skin, leaving an indent. Just a little more pressure. If Tony could just press a little harder. He could drive it through Dash's fucking chest cavity and right into his heart. Then this would all be over.

Dash reared back once he'd gotten a big enough whiff, and hissed at Tony. But there was something in his eyes. Something that might have been real fear when Dash said, "Werewolf venom."

"You bet your boots, Chadwick." Tony smirked and pressed his weight onto his toes, pushing down hard enough with the stake that given Dash's sudden surprise, his inattention, it drove downward, right toward its target.

And Dash burst into . . .

Mist?

Not ash.

Not dust.

Mist.

Like a fucking cloud or something. Tony flopped down, having just enough time to jerk his head up so it didn't crack against the floor, but not enough to save his knees.

"Didn't know I could do that, did you, my darling?" Dash asked, his voice coming from everywhere and nowhere all at once. "The things you boys know about vampires couldn't even fill a kettle." The mist drifted forward, brushing cold and wet against Tony's cheek like a caress. "See you around, my darling."

Then it dissipated and Eric gasped, a rattling sound, and Tony didn't have time to wonder what Dash meant by that.

"All right, pretty boy, I got you," Tony said, scooting across the floor on his knees until he was right beside Eric. The wound on his chest was closer to the shoulder than the heart. Relief flooded through Tony so quickly, he nearly sagged. "Oh look, that's not so bad."

"Says you. He didn't fucking stab *you*," Eric grumbled and winced as Tony helped him up to sit. "Are the girls okay?"

"Yeah, Hunter got them out."

"Good." Eric nodded slowly. He allowed Tony to take much of his weight and apply pressure to his wound while they waited for help to come. "And you? Are you all right?"

"Jesus fuck, pretty boy, worry about yourself for a whole fucking minute, would you? He fucking *stabbed* you." Tony laughed a little, unable to help himself.

"Yes. I was just telling you that. And you didn't give me any sympathy at *all*! You're so mean to me, so unkind. Oh how ever will I survive?" Eric threw his weight about a little, trusting Tony to hold him up, letting the dramatics really take him. And all Tony could do was hold him, hold him *so* close, and laugh.

"You idiot," Lu growled, punching Tony with all the limited strength of a soaking wet kitten. The venom was still doing its thing, it seemed, but it didn't take much to knock Tony back toward the floor. Now that the adrenaline had worn off, the wooziness had set in. He was going to throw up, and it was going to suck. But he'd wait till Eric was taken care of by the Huntsmen medics first.

Eric snickered from where his torso rested on Tony's lap, but he didn't interfere. Smart man.

"What the fuck were you *thinking*, sending me away like

that?" She snarled, her lip curling up to show off an impressive number of teeth. Tony wondered idly where she'd learned that. From him, probably.

"I was thinking that maybe I should get my kid sister—"

"I'm not a *kid*!"

"—out of a bad situation before the big bad vampire decided to use her as a fucking snack!"

"I'm not a kid! And I can take care of myself when it comes to vampires. I'm a Venator too. Or did you forget with your head so far up your—"

Tony leaned toward her and pulled her into a tight hug, cutting off anything else Lu might have bitched about. He pressed his face into the wild red curls on top of her head, careful that they didn't crush Eric, and murmured, "I missed you."

"Yeah, well . . ." Lu blew out a long breath, tickling the skin on his neck. "I didn't think about you at all."

Warmth settled into his chest at the tone of her voice. She was still annoyed with him, but she had mostly forgiven him too. They were back to normal. Mostly.

"Brat." Tony laughed but didn't push her away.

"Asshole," she fired back.

"If this is you two making up, I'd hate to see you fighting," Eric cut in. When Tony pulled back from Lu to look down at him, he was smiling, a little dazed but happy. Which was . . . Tony couldn't deal with that right now.

"Medics are on the way," Hunter said as he joined them. "Do you want the kids to start processing the scene?"

Tony snorted. "Yeah, because they'll definitely come in here and do their job rather than fawn over pretty boy while he's bleeding."

"Tony's right." Eric shook his head, his hair more mussed where it brushed against Tony's jeans. "Leave them in the van until the medics have at least sewn me up."

"They're going to complain that's unfair, since Lu is here."

Hunter raised his eyebrow, but Tony thought he saw a bit of a smile tugging at the corners of his lips.

"They'll get over it." Eric flapped his hand, begging for Hunter to come closer, and Hunter complied, kneeling near their small huddle until Eric could take his hand and give it a squeeze. They shared a look that left Tony feeling wholly on the outside, but he couldn't move, not with Eric sprawled across his legs. So he just had to sit there and watch as these two idiots made moon eyes at each other.

Thankfully, Lu gagged, breaking the tension.

Chapter 34

WITH BOTH ERIC and Tony out of commission, that left only Hunter to spearhead the processing of the warehouse where they'd found Dash and his cohorts. A task he wasn't wholly sure he was qualified for. Sure, he knew more about evidence than any of them. But he didn't know fuck all about the field. He was more content to look at the evidence after it'd been removed from the scene. In a sterile environment. Safe.

This environment was not sterile. Nor was it safe.

And the pressure of getting this right for all of them increased every second he stood among the shipping crates. The stacks seemed to grow taller, boxing him in. Trapping him there among the dead. At least someone had swept up the dust and fangs left behind. The weight of the little pouch of teeth wasn't much in his pocket, but it was something solid, something he understood. He knew what to do with vampire teeth. Knew how to examine them and find answers.

"This place is disgusting. I'm glad I was high off my ass when they dragged me through here the first time." Lu clicked her tongue in a move that she'd clearly learned from her older brother. Hunter did his best not to roll his eyes. He could do without the attitude right now. He just wanted to get this done so he could go back and check on Eric and Tony. Leaving them with Ava to watch over them was the next best thing, but that didn't mean he had to like it. And after seeing Eric covered in his own blood from a stab wound, the image viciously similar to that mission with Britt, Hunter had struggled against every instinct to let Eric go home with the others.

But the medics made it in time, he reminded himself. *Eric is fine.* Or as fine as someone could be with a hole in their shoulder. Plus Eric was a Venator, he would bounce back in no time. He just needed rest. And the best way for him to get that rest was for Hunter to take charge of the brat pack and get some answers.

"Stop complaining. That's what the gloves are for." Kate threw a pair of black latex gloves at Lu, her tone prim.

Lu snatched them out of the air and looked like maybe she was going to snipe back at Kate, but Finn got in the middle, literally. Put herself bodily between them and nodded to Lu before she turned to cut Kate with a harsh glare that Kate only snorted at. Still, it was enough to halt the bickering for the moment.

Which Hunter was grateful for. He was already getting a bit of a headache, and magic burnout rang like exhaustion in his ears. Gods, it had been so long since he'd had to push himself like that. He really needed to train more if he was going to follow those two idiots into battle again. Or maybe revisit the idea of joining a coven and tying himself to the land. It wasn't ideal; he'd never wanted to be tied down. But if it meant protecting Eric, and the kids, and Tony? He supposed he'd make that sacrifice. Even if it meant he'd never be able to live anywhere else long term.

"Let's just get this done. So we can go home," Bert called, silencing everyone from where he was crouched beside one of the shipping crates, trying to get it open. He wasn't quite strong enough, and after he struggled for a moment, Nik joined to help him. The lid came off with a clatter, and both stumbled back under the force. Hunter was on his way to join them when the smell hit him. Rancid and metallic.

"Blood," Nik said, covering his nose with the neck of his shirt. "It's turned rotten." He leaned further in the crate to inspect and pulled out what seemed to be a bit of spell paper. "Whatever magic he was using to keep it cold must have worn off."

"Because he left? Or because the witch who helped him let it lapse?" Bert asked, peering over Nik's shoulder at the paper.

"No way to tell." Nik pulled a plastic baggie from his pocket and slid the paper inside carefully before sealing it up. He set it aside on the top of one of the other crates. "Help me check the labels. If they're all the same, we can just take one."

Bert blanched but set to work.

"Do you think they're all blood?" Chase asked, shifting his weight from foot to foot. He'd been nervous since they walked in, not that Hunter could blame him. It was daylight out now, but as they'd recently learned, that didn't mean they were safe, not necessarily. And with the only official protectors in the group currently up the mountain wounded . . . well.

"I've set up a ward. We're good here," Hunter murmured softly to Chase, pressing his shoulder into his brother's. Chase looked up at him through bright green eyes. They didn't look anything alike, being stepbrothers as they were, but Hunter could see how the reminder that Hunter was there for him eased something inside Chase.

"Okay," Chase whispered back.

With a nod, Hunter turned and grabbed a crowbar. "Only one way to find out." He grunted as he started on the next crate. They were harder to open than the kids had made it look. No wonder Bert had had so much trouble. "We'll have to call in a disposal team for this. Kate."

"Already on it." When he turned to look at her over his shoulder, Kate had a phone pressed to her ear while her other hand brushed her long brown locs out of her face. "Yeah,

Kalla? We need a disposal team for the warehouse." There was a brief pause, and she grumbled, clearly annoyed by something her sister had said on the other end. "Yes, it is a biohazard, Kalla." Another pause. "I am aware of that."

Hunter shook his head and returned his attention to the work ahead. They opened several more crates. Some of them were full of rancid blood, but others had medical supplies, housewares, anything someone would need if they were—

"What? Is he moving house?" Lu frowned down at a crate full of what looked like linens. Her fingers curled around the lip of the crate.

"Wouldn't we be so lucky," Nik muttered sullenly.

"He's got enough blood here to hold him over for a couple of months." Bert poked at one of the bags and it made a disgusting congealed sound.

"Maybe he was going into hiding?" Finn asked. She hadn't spoken much during all this, and Hunter had to wonder if she was uncomfortable or if she still wasn't feeling well after being drugged by Dash.

Should he have sent her and Lu back to the dorm to recuperate with Tony and Eric? They had both said they wanted to help with the warehouse clean up. But maybe he should have been the adult in the situation and told them to rest instead. Eric would have known better what to do. Tony would have been able to make them do it. Hunter was floundering. He was not adult enough to be left in charge of these children.

"Or he was preparing for something," Chase offered, a note of fear in his voice.

"Or *someone*." Nik leaned back on his heels.

"Someone like who?" Lu shifted her weight from one leg to the other, her fingers tapping against the mouth of the crate.

"I suppose we'll find out," Hunter said, hoping to make everyone calm down, but all it seemed to do was rachet the tension in the air up another notch. Fuck, he was bad at this. It didn't help that he was scared too. That he could see what the others saw.

"They all have intake slips for Ironport," Chase offered. He'd found a clipboard somewhere and was looking down at the manifest for the most recent shipment.

"That doesn't mean this was their final destination." Lu frowned, her nose wrinkling in a way that made her freckles look like a blur. "It just means he hadn't gotten the chance to send them along yet."

Hunter shook himself. Speculating was getting them nowhere fast. All it was doing was scaring everyone, and they didn't have time for fear, not right now. They needed to get everything collected so he could take it back to the lab and examine it. Maybe then he'd have some answers for them. "Come on, let's finish this up. Kate, how far out is the disposal team?"

Kate checked her phone. "Ten."

"Okay, Bert and Chase, go dig through the office, see if there's anything there to tell us who all this is for. Maybe he's got a log or something. Everyone else, let's separate everything into things the disposal team needs to take care of, and stuff we can donate. No sense in all these blankets going to waste. I'll go over everything back at the lab and send it along to the appropriate places." Hunter clapped his hands once, the way he'd seen Eric do countless times to get the attention of his class, but it didn't seem to have the desired effect. They all just blinked at him. He cleared his throat. "Get to work."

It took them a moment, but eventually they turned to their tasks, and once everyone was working together instead of speculating, it didn't take long at all for things to be organized, evidence to be collected, and Bert and Chase to return from the office.

"Find anything?" Kate asked hopefully.

"We've got some paperwork, but nothing to tell us what

all this is for. Just more manifests." Chase's shoulders sank as if he'd failed them all.

"That's all right." Hunter moved over to take the box where the two boys had stacked all the papers they'd found in the office as well as a heavy laptop. "Maybe I'll find something when I comb through it all. That's what I'm good at, right? You guys did a good job gathering everything. Leave the analysis to me."

Even as he said it, Hunter recognized that it was going to take fucking months to analyze everything they'd found by himself. But that was all right. He couldn't fight, but he could do this. He could always do this.

Chapter 35

IT WAS A BEAUTIFUL DAY. The thunder was rumbling. The lightning was striking. And a delightful pitter patter of rain on the roof threatened to lull Hunter to sleep . . .

"I swear to Diana, if you don't stop itching, I'm going to super glue oven mitts to your fucking hands," Eric hissed.

"I'd like to see you try, pretty boy," Tony snarled back.

There was a soft *thwap*, followed by a yelp and a growl.

You know, if the two grown men he'd set up in the living room would keep their mouths shut long enough for him to relax. Seriously, who knew Venator could be such fucking babies? Hunter would have thought two highly skilled warriors would be able to sit on the couch without wiggling and annoying each other non-fucking-stop for more than a couple of minutes.

"If you two don't stop it, I'm putting you back in your rooms," Hunter called.

"He started it," Tony grumbled.

"Fuck off!" Eric shouted, then winced when he must have pulled his stitches doing something stupid, like trying to hit Tony back.

Fucking toddlers, both of them. And yet, Hunter didn't think he'd have it any other way. He still wasn't close to Tony —didn't think he ever would be—but he could see how Eric cared for him. Could see how they fit together. They hadn't talked about it yet; there hadn't been time or energy in the week since Dash escaped, what with moving Lu and Tony into the dorm, and treating the weird aftereffects of Tony's decision to take werewolf venom. Because of course it would cause him to break out in fucking hives like an allergic reaction. Ridiculous.

Hunter came back to the living room, a tray of snacks and drinks balanced carefully across his palms. "If you two can't play nice, I'm going back to the kitchen, and you both can just fucking starve."

"Fine," Tony grunted.

Eric shot Hunter his best puppy-dog eyes, big and light brown and bottomless. Like tipping into a pool of honey. Hunter would have been helpless against them a few years ago. When he was younger and more besotted with everything Eric was. He was still besotted, but he was older now, more in control of his urges. For the most part.

"Eric," Hunter chided, waiting. He wasn't going to move from that spot until they'd both agreed to act like adults for at least the duration of the movie they'd picked out. Which wasn't too much to ask, surely. He just wanted them to sit still and not bitch at each other for all of an hour and a half. Grumpy little fucks.

To be fair, if he was dealing with what they were, he'd probably be grumpy too. Being itchy all over or having a hole in his shoulder would definitely turn him into ten different shades of bitch. He couldn't really blame them for that. But it didn't mean he had to put up with it either.

"I'm just asking for an hour and a half of peace. Then you can go right back to annoying the piss out of each other." Hunter looked Eric dead in the eyes and widened his own gaze, returning the puppy-dog eyes tenfold, and Eric crumpled like a cheap suit.

"Fine." Eric shifted around, getting himself comfortable so he could focus on the TV screen.

Hunter set down the tray on the coffee table, adjusted Eric's pillows, gave Tony another dose of antihistamine, and settled in himself for at least a half an hour of peace.

Before Tony started itching again.

Before Eric needed more pain killers.

Before the kids got back from classes.

Before they had to face the threat of Dashfield B.M. Whatever-the-fuck-his-real-surname-was the vampire all over again. It wouldn't be long. But Hunter would take it, and treasure it, for as long as he could.

ABOUT LOU WILHAM

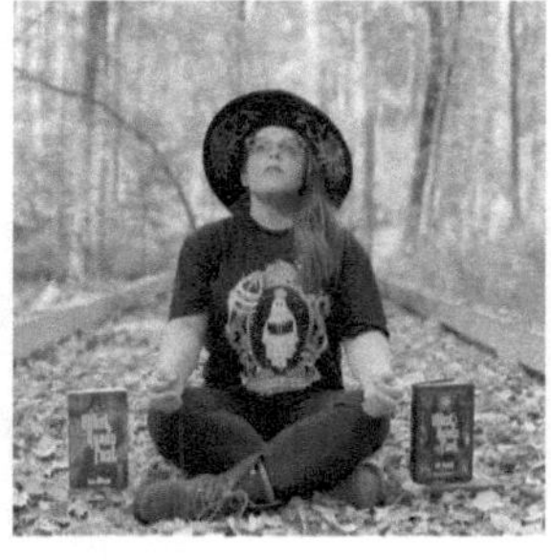

Born and raised in a small town near the Chesapeake Bay, Lou Wilham grew up on a steady diet of fiction, arts and crafts, and Old Bay. After years of absorbing everything, there was to absorb of fiction, fantasy, and sci-fi she's left with a serious writing/drawing habit that just won't quit. These days, she spends much of her time writing, drawing, and chasing a very short Basset Hound named Sherlock.

When not, daydreaming up new characters to write and draw she can be found crocheting, making cute bookmarks, and binge-watching whatever happens to catch her eye.

Learn more about Lou and her future projects on her website: http://louinprogress.com/ or join her mailing list at: http://subscribepage.com/mailermailer

facebook.com/LouWilham

instagram.com/lou.wilham

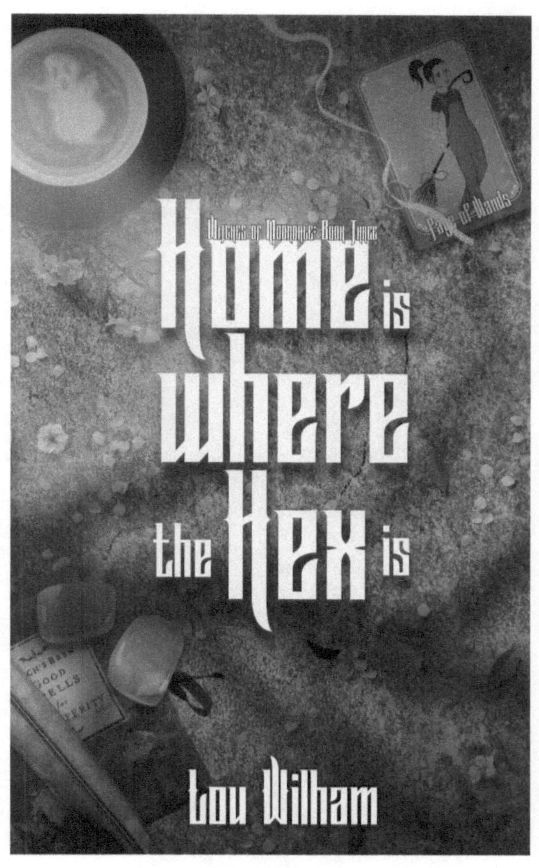

Sneak Peek!

continue reading for a sneak peek of Witches of Moondale
book #3: Home is Where the Hex is

Please note: This is an unedited sneak peek.

Available: Oct 9, 2024
Pre-order your copy now!

HOME IS WHERE THE HEX IS

RUS JERKED AWAKE.

Her left foot was *freezing* where it hung over the edge of the bed, the blanket not covering it. She must have kicked the covers off in the middle of the night. But that isn't what woke her. No. There was something holding onto her, the grip cold, but insubstantial, wrapped tight around her ankle.

Something not alive.

A spirit.

When reaching across the bed for Az turned up cool, empty sheets, Rus shimmied herself closer to the nightstand, careful not to dislodge the shade's grip as she bent her head over the edge of the bed to peak down beneath it. The face peering back at her was young, with wide eyes staring unblinking, and glassy. Likely a little older than Aihuan when they died, but not by much.

"Hel—" Rus croaked, stopped, cleared her throat, and tried again, "Hello there, little one. Would you mind letting go of my foot?"

They looked at her for a moment, head titled, then released her ankle with a muffled, "sorry."

"It's all right." Rus shot them a little smile, and slid from the bed to kneel on the floor next to it. "Why don't you come out here, and we'll have a chat?"

They frowned, their upturned nose crinkling in thought. "Why?"

"I just want to know why you're here." Rus scooted back to give them room as they slid out from underneath the bed, joints popping and jerking in a way that was no at all human. Objectively terrifying, if Rus didn't know exactly how spirits tended to forget how living things moved. "Can you tell me your name?"

"Isabel."

"That's a nice name." Where had Aihuan found this one? The school? The graveyard? The coffee shop? They were going to have to have a discussion—*again*—about bringing spirits home. Thankfully this one wasn't some nastier being masquerading as a child, but it was only a matter of time before Aihuan came across one of those. It was a miracle she hadn't thus far. "Do you know what happened to you Isabel?"

"I was sick." Isabel shrugged, not meeting Rus' eyes. They looked around her attic bedroom instead. Taking in the pile of clothes in the corner that Az was consistently on her about, the mess that was her workspace, and the wilting plant Az was trying to revive on the windowsill. Az hadn't moved in, but she'd made herself at home there just the same. Mixed her dirty laundry in with Rus'. Piled her books on one nightstand. Added one of Indigo's crocheted blankets to the end of the bed. It made the space homier. And Rus had hardly noticed until that very moment, seeing it through someone else's eyes. "I waited."

"You waited for what?"

"For my mama to come," Isabel said, meeting Rus' gaze finally. "But she never did. And then I laid down."

Tears lodged in Rus' throat making it hard to find her voice again, but find it she did. Because someone needed to help Isabel move on. To see their mama again. "How long have you been stuck here?"

Isabel shrugged again. Rus didn't know why she'd bothered asking. Time moved differently for spirits. But it was a point of pride to gather as much information as she reasonably could before she helped a spirit move on. To document it at least for herself so that she could find patterns in the kinds of spirits that stayed and the ones that didn't. So far not much had come of the data, but one day, maybe it would. "Huaner said you could help me find my mama. That's why she brought me."

Of course she did. It would be annoying if it weren't so painfully sweet. Aihuan believed her auntie Rus could help every spirit, and didn't see any reason why she shouldn't. It wasn't like it hurt Rus to do it, she just didn't want Aihuan bringing every stray shade into the safety of their home.

"You can, can't you?"

"I'll do my best." Already Rus' magic flittered around her fingers like mist, putrid, and green, reaching out to answer its witch's call. But even if she didn't say it, she knew that Isabel's mama might already be gone. She may have reincarnated hoping to find her child again somehow. Rus couldn't leave Isabel to languish though. They needed to be given the opportunity to find peace, whatever that looked like for them. And they couldn't do that on this plain.

"What do I need to do?" Isabel asked, their voice small as they shrank back into themselves, away from Rus' extended hand and the magic that had settled into the scars on her bare arm.

"Just take my hand, and the magic will do the rest."

"Will it hurt?"

"No. It won't hurt at all." She didn't know that, not for certain. But many a spirit had returned from the After to aid her when she needed it, and not one of them had ever complained. Add that to the fact that they never screamed when she sent them over. She'd have to ask next time a spirit visited her to help out. It'd be good to have an answer once and for all. Then she'd have something to tell the spirits who asked. She hoped it made them feel warm when they crossed. Safe. Loved.

Isabel stared at Rus' hand for a long moment, their fingers twitching where they rested against their thigh, warring with their indecision. Unsure. Rus couldn't blame them for that. She didn't have any answers about the After. She didn't know what it was like there. She didn't know how it felt to get there. She didn't know how spirits adjusted. Nothing. All she knew was that's where the dead belonged, not on the plain of the living where they would either fade, or slowly lose their grip on themselves and what was real making them destructive.

"This is what Huaner meant when she said I could help you," Rus pressed. She didn't know what time it was, but she could hear Fernando and the kids downstairs eating break-fast. She needed to get down there and help get the girls ready for school or she'd never hear the end of it.

When Isabel didn't move, Rus let out a soft sigh. "Would you like to say goodbye to Huaner first?"

Isabel nodded, the bob of their head making their hair fall into their face. They looked like that scary little girl from *The Ring* like that.

"I'll go get her. But then we need to get you moving along, all right?"

Another nod, and Rus stood, her knees creaking as she went. The back stairs groaned to announce her presence in the kitchen as she came into view of the round table where her little family sat. Well. Most of her little family. Az was in class already. "Huaner?"

"Hmm?" Aihuan asked, raising her head from where she'd been shoveling waffles into her mouth.

"Can you come upstairs with me for a minute?" Rus asked, careful not to let on that there was a spirit in the house.

Meiling was still afraid of them, and had grown comfortable in the knowledge that they couldn't cross the threshold of 157 Mourning Moore unless invited in.

Aihuan looked at Rus for a moment, then her eyes widened, and she nodded, wiggling down from her chair. When they'd made it to the landing on the second floor she looked up at Rus and asked, "Are you mad?"

"I'm not mad." Rus' shoulders drooped on a deep exhale. It was hard to be mad at Aihuan when she was technically doing the right thing, and when she looked adorable doing it. Big brown eyes, and curly hair wild around her face. She probably hadn't brushed it. Another task to add to Rus' ever lengthening list for the morning. "But I do recall asking you to please not bring them into the house. Remember?"

"But it was cold out last night." Aihuan's bottom lip poked out, her eyes going even bigger somehow. Goddess above and below, Rus was a fucking sap for the puppy eyes, and everyone seemed to know it.

"Huaner, we agreed they could wait on the back porch, but not in the house," Rus let her tone dip into something more authoritative. This was a rule, firm, and set in stone. She could not budge on this. Lest Aihuan bring something dangerous into their home on accident. "Understood?"

"Yes, Auntie Rus." Aihuan huffed.

"That's my little monster." Rus smiled, and pushed the door open to her bedroom where Isabel waited. The spirit lit up when they saw Aihuan, their face forming a bright smile the likes of which Rus had never seen on a ghost before, and they moved forward to hug Aihuan tightly.

"You're going then?" Aihuan asked, but she sounded happy about it. No sadness or regret tainted her voice. No hint that she'd miss her new friend. "Auntie Rus is going to help you cross over?"

"She is. I just. . ." Isabel looked at Rus for a moment, then ducked their head shyly. "I wanted to say goodbye."

"This isn't goodbye," Aihuan said with a smile full of wisdom far beyond her years. Rus wondered where the fuck she'd learned that. Az probably. Elwoods were like that, chock full of wisdom bursting at the seams with their goodness. Az especially. "It's just see you later."

"How much later?"

"Who knows! But if you want to come back and visit you just have to call out to Auntie Rus." Aihuan turned to look up at Rus, her expression earnest. "Right, Auntie Rus?"

"Right." Rus nodded, offering what she hoped was a confident smile. "Just call for Icarus Ashthorne, and you can come back to visit."

"But even if not." Aihuan shrugged. "I'll see you again someday."

And wow, okay, Aihuan being that all right talking about her own future death was just weird. Rus needed to cut this short before these two sent her into an existential crisis, she didn't have time in her schedule for one of those today.

"All righty, let's get this show on the road. You've got school." Rus swiped at her face hoping neither child would notice how the corners of her eyes burned with tears, but if the looks on their faces were anything to go by, they had. She reached out her hand, her bright green magic reaching with her, and took hold of Isabel's shoulder.

There was a moment, where Isabel looked up at her, and smiled, then the spirit was gone. Sent to the After, to hopefully be with their mother. Maybe she'd been right, maybe it didn't hurt them after all. Quiet settled around Rus and Aihuan, and they both breathed a little deeper before Aihuan looked up at Rus and asked, "Can I have some chocolate chips on my waffles?"

"Uncle Nando said no, didn't he?" Rus laughed softly, brushing her fingers through her hair and getting caught in the tangles.

"Yes." Aihuan huffed.

"I'll make you a deal, you let me brush your hair, and you can have exactly ten mini chocolate chips on your waffles. How's that sound?"

"Mm!" Aihuan dipped her head in agreement, and they headed back down to the kitchen where Fernando and Meiling waited.

"Az was gone early this morning," Rus said, hoping to head off any conversation about what had just happened upstairs as she made her way to the pantry to grab Aihuan her chocolate chips. When Fernando raised an eyebrow in question as she dumped exactly ten onto Aihuan's plate Rus just shook her head.

That seemed to be enough of an answer for him, but the little white mouse on his shoulder—his familiar, her name was Calida, Cal for short—moved onto her back paws, pressing her little face in toward his ear to murmur to him. When she was done, Fernando smiled a little, and nodded before returning his attention to Rus. "I thought you said Az wasn't moving in?"

"She's not. She just spent the night last night." Heat crawled up Rus' neck at the mention of Az spending the night. It wasn't like they had *done* anything. Not yet, anyway. There was time. And still lots to talk about and sort out between them. But she hadn't thought about *that* being where the conversation would head when she'd brought it up. In retrospect, maybe she should have. Still it was a good way to head off the discussion about the spirit who'd been hiding under her bed when she woke up.

"Last night. And the night before that."

"And the night before that," Meiling added unhelpfully.

"And the night before that!" Aihuan agreed, shoving a big bite of waffle into her mouth.

"Are you three going to get to a point anytime soon?" Rus groused. She'd poured herself a cup of coffee, unable to force down the little smile that came from seeing Az's mint green mug on the drying rack next the sink. Damn it.

"Why don't you just ask her to move in already? Make it official." Fernando pressed, hiding his own coy smile behind a mug that looked more milk than coffee. He was being a jerk, and he knew it, bringing this up in front of the girls. Thankfully, they didn't seem to mind one way or the other. They liked having Az around, but they weren't going to try forcing her hand.

"It's a process." Rus turned to look out the window, the dreary late spring mist creating a fog that she could only just see the house next door from. The last owners had moved out a couple weeks ago. Nesta was the realtor on the sign, but they'd asked Rus to take a look at it before they really put their effort into selling it. They needed to know if the last owners left anything behind, like unsettled spirits. She'd have to check on that this afternoon, after the rush at Necromancer's had calmed down. It would be easy money, as far as Rus could tell. She almost felt guilty accepting the commission. But, well, Aihuan was growing like a cemetery weed, and she and Meiling would need summer clothes soon. "I don't want to rush things."

The not rushing things had been entirely her idea, not Az's, because Rus knew they couldn't go back to how things were, and she wasn't sure how they'd work now. Nor if they'd work at all. Maybe they wouldn't. Maybe once all the drama and the danger had died down, Az would see what a fuckup Rus still was, and leave her like she should have all those years ago.

Meiling snorted loud enough that it sounded like it might have hurt. When Rus turned to look at her, she was smiling, sarcastic and cutting. Fucking teenagers man. "You'll be married by next year."

"Next year? I'm calling November," Fernando joined in. "We've got a pool running."

"Oh a Samhain wedding!" Meiling brightened. "Auntie Rus a Samhain wedding!"

"What pool?" Aihuan, who was the only one *not* a traitor in this fucking house, asked. "Can we go swimming in it?"

"It's not that kind of pool, JieJie." Meiling rolled her eyes. "It means they're betting."

"You know telling one of the people the pool is about that you've got one going kind of skews the results, doesn't it?" Rus sneered at Fernando, who held up a hand and rocked it back and forth. She scoffed, clicking her tongue, and pushed it from her mind. Because giving it too much thought, looking at it too closely, would only intensify the ache in her chest. The reminder that maybe that was a thing she wanted. A thing she shouldn't want. A thing she shouldn't let herself want. She wasn't right for Az. Never would be. It—

"It doesn't matter." Rus sniped, her sour thoughts turning her tone to something less playful. "A'ling, the bus is here!"

Meiling grunted, dropped her dishes in the sink, and headed for the door. "Bye Huaner!"

"Bye MeiMei!" Aihuan stuffed another bite into her mouth that was more chocolate chip than waffle, and the door creaked open to let Meiling run down the walk for the bus.

"And you, little monster, agreed to let me brush your hair, remember?"

"Fiiiiiine."

"What about me?" Fernando asked, his eyes dancing with good humor. Little shit.

"I'm not talking to you until I've finished my coffee." Rus held her mug up as if she were cheers-ing Fernando and took a big gulp from it. "Till then, nothing out of you."

Fernando held up his hands in surrender, but there was a grin on his face that said this conversation was far from over. Because nothing about returning to Moondale was ever going to be easy.

ACKNOWLEDGMENTS

I always start these things but thanking the reader, and this one is no different. I want to thank you—whether you're a returning reader or Lou is new to you—for picking up my little indie published book, supporting my dream, and following along with Tony, Eric, and Hunter on their journey. Without readers, I can't do what I do, so I greatly appreciate the support.

If you loved every moment of Eric, Tony, and Hunter's story (as I hope you did) please leave a review, follow me on social media, or give me a shout out. I love hearing from you guys, it's really the best part of writing.

Next I'd like to thank my family who supports me in this weird journey I'm on to become an established author. They show up to my signings, they listen to my rants about my characters, they look at my covers and tell me when they're complete shit (I design my covers FYI), and they're the best people to have in my corner, no joke.

Then there is the small hoard of beta, and sensitivity readers I had look at this bugger to tell me if any of it actually made sense, and if I'm as funny as I think I am (turns out I am). You guys provided so much helpful feedback you don't even know.

And of course my editor, Brenna. Who loves these idiots as much as I do, and it shows!

And last but certainly not least, thank you to my small writing family. Tiss, Elle, Whitney, and Nancy—without you there would be no Lou.

MORE BOOKS YOU'LL LOVE

If you enjoyed this story, please consider leaving a review.

Then check out more books from Midnight Tide Publishing!

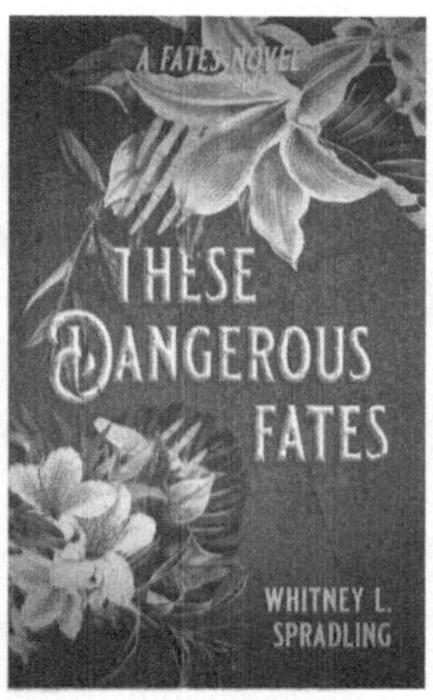

These Dangerous Fates by Whitney L. Spradling

I live in a magical world. A world filled with vampires, shifters, and mages.
Mysteriously, I was born without powers.

After living the past two years in a personal hell, enduring abuse from a fiance I didn't choose, I finally snapped. An act of self-defense against my fiance angers my father, and in retaliation for my actions, he creates the ultimate contest. One that only the most powerful magicals can compete in to win my hand in marriage.

It sounds bleak, but anything has to be better than my current situation. At least, I thought so, until *they* appeared in the middle of the night to whisk me away.

A vampire prince.
A wolf without a pack.
A powerful mage.

My three captors do everything they can to win the contest, and as the attraction between the four of us grows, so does their desire to keep me safe.

When the mystery of my birth comes into play, we begin

to question everything I thought I knew about my life. Am I just a human with no magical powers? Or am I something else entirely? One thing is certain, if my captors cannot keep me safe, more than my heart is at stake: my life is on the line.

Available Now

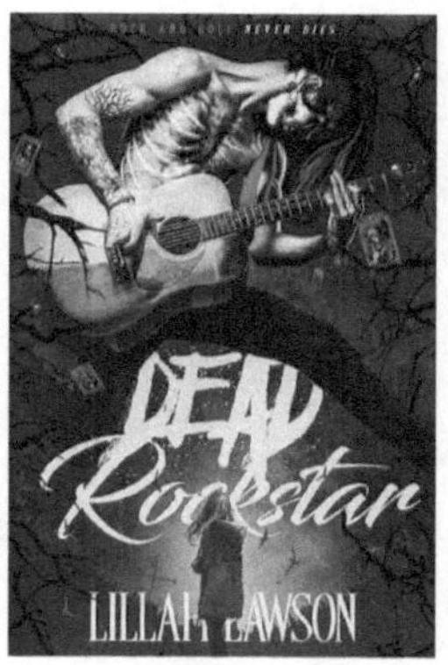

Dead Rockstar by Lillah Lawson

Stormy Spooner is at her wits' end. Careening towards bitter after a nasty divorce, she sometimes wonders what her life is becoming.

After unearthing a cryptic set of lines from a dusty album cover, Stormy tries the impossible: to resurrect Phillip Deville, enigmatic former frontman of the Bloomer Demons. Stormy's love for her favorite dead rockstar knows no bounds...but it was all supposed to be a joke.

When she answers a knock on her door the next day and finds herself face to face with the dark-haired rock god of her every teenage fantasy, her entire world is turned upside down.

Turns out, she's awakened more than just Philip, and Stormy will have to do battle against a cast of strange characters to keep herself and her new undead boyfriend safe.

Available May 15, 2024